“Thank yo

“You gave me quite a scare.” Would she no
the tremble in his voice that he couldn’t hide?

“Me, too.”

To keep from touching her, Wyatt pressed his hands to the new boards. If only he had the freedom to pull her close and comfort her. But he didn’t, and never would, because he would never be free from the sting of his past.

Cora sucked in air. “I owe you for saving my life.”

He tried to snort but it sounded more like a groan. “Let’s hope you wouldn’t have died.”

She faced him, but he kept his gaze riveted to the spot where she almost fell. “Wyatt, if you need or want anything, feel free to ask. If I can, I’ll give it to you.”

Slowly his gaze sought hers and he fell into the darkness of her eyes and the sweetness of her invitation. He had needs and wants. Acceptance despite his past, someone who trusted him, believed in him, loved him. His throat tightened. His heart ached with longing. If only she could give him what he needed.

Books by Linda Ford

Love Inspired Historical

The Road to Love
The Journey Home
The Path to Her Heart
Dakota Child
The Cowboy's Baby
Dakota Cowboy
Christmas Under Western Skies
"A Cowboy's Christmas"
Dakota Father
Prairie Cowboy
Klondike Medicine Woman
**The Cowboy Tutor*
**The Cowboy Father*
**The Cowboy Comes Home*
The Gift of Family
"Merry Christmas, Cowboy"
†*The Cowboy's Surprise Bride*
†*The Cowboy's Unexpected Family*
†*The Cowboy's Convenient Proposal*
The Baby Compromise
†*Claiming the Cowboy's Heart*
†*Winning Over the Wrangler*
†*Falling for the Rancher Father*
***Big Sky Cowboy*

*Three Brides for Three Cowboys
†Cowboys of Eden Valley
**Montana Marriages

LINDA FORD

lives on a ranch in Alberta, Canada. Growing up on the prairie and learning to notice the small details it hides gave her an appreciation for watching God at work in His creation. Her upbringing also included being taught to trust God in everything and through everything—a theme that resonates in her stories. Threads of another part of her life are found in her stories—her concern for children and their future. She and her husband raised fourteen children—four homemade, ten adopted. She currently shares her home and life with her husband, a grown son, a live-in paraplegic client and a continual (and welcome) stream of kids, kids-in-law, grandkids and assorted friends and relatives.

Big Sky Cowboy

LINDA FORD

HARLEQUIN® LOVE INSPIRED® HISTORICAL

Recycling programs for this product may not exist in your area.

ISBN-13: 978-0-373-28282-1

BIG SKY COWBOY

This edition published by arrangement with Love Inspired Books.

www.Harlequin.com

Printed in U.S.A.

For I know the thoughts that I think toward you,
saith the Lord, thoughts of peace, and not of evil,
to give you an expected end.

—*Jeremiah* 29:11

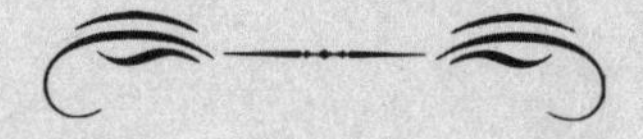

To adoptive parents who, like the Bells,
welcome into their family children not born to them.
May love and joy shine forever on your family.

Chapter One

A farm near Bar Crossing, Montana
Summer, 1889

Squee.

What was that awful noise?

Wyatt Williams eased back on his reins and glanced over his shoulder to his brother, Lonnie. The sixteen-year-old shrank back as if he wished to disappear into the saddle.

Squee. Squee.

The sound came again, rending the air and filling it with tension.

Wyatt stared at the farm ahead. From where he sat he had a good view of the place. A pretty little house with a bay window and a little veranda faced the road. A tumble of flowers in every hue of the rainbow surrounded the house. A garden as precise as a ruler ran from the river to the trees at the back of the lot. There were several tidy buildings, some pens and the naked skeleton of a barn.

Wyatt considered his brother and the mare he led.

Fanny was heavy with foal. The weeks of moving had taxed her strength. He couldn't push her farther.

His gaze went past Lonnie and the horse. He couldn't see the other mares that he hoped to start a new ranch with, but he knew they were tied securely down by the water. He only wanted permission from the farmer to camp by the river until Fanny foaled, and she and the newborn grew strong enough to resume their journey. Plus their supplies were running low and he hoped to restock here. He could ride to the nearby town for what he needed, but it seemed unnecessary. Wyatt studied the sign nailed to the gatepost.

For Sale—Eggs, Milk, Cheese, Garden Stuff.

His mouth watered. Fresh food had never sounded so good.

"Wait here," he told Lonnie, and rode forward.

From around one of the outbuildings came a squealing pig with a floppy-eared, big-footed dog barking at its tail.

A young woman skidded around the corner, blond braids flying. "You get back here, you little troublemaker." She dived for it, catching the animal for about ten seconds before it slipped away, squealing righteous indignation and leaving the gal in the dirt.

Wyatt drew to a halt and grinned.

The woman picked herself up and shook a finger at the dog. "Grub, enough. I'll never catch the crazy pig with you barking and chasing after it."

Wyatt took *Grub* to be the dog's name, for it stopped and yapped and then turned back to pig chasing, which seemed to be the sport of the day. The young woman took off after them. The pig veered from side to side.

She pounced on it again, but it wasn't about to be captured. It wriggled free and headed in Wyatt's direction.

His horse snorted.

"Rooster, you never mind. He's just a wee oinker." Wyatt reached for his lariat, swung a lazy loop and dropped it over the pig's head.

The little pig yanked on the rope, trying to get free. The squeals that erupted about deafened Wyatt and, he guessed, anyone within a hundred yards.

The gal blinked at Wyatt. "I just about had him." Her brown eyes challenged him. Seemed she didn't care to have someone interfere in her work.

Her attitude tickled Wyatt clear to the pit of his stomach. He grinned. "You're welcome."

She planted her hands on her hips. The flash in her eyes told him how hard it was for her to maintain her annoyed look.

He tipped his head toward the pig, who continued to fight the rope and put up an awful fuss. "Ma'am, if you don't mind me suggesting it, why not let me lead the pig to his pen." Though he guessed "lead" was only a wish.

She nodded decisively. "No doubt that would be wise. Come along, then." She moved toward an enclosure while Wyatt dragged and tugged and generally fought his way after her, Rooster snorting his protest at the indignity.

She held the pen gate open. Wyatt dismounted and pushed the pig through the space she gave him, then slipped off the rope. Five other little pigs rushed forward, joining in the melee. An old, fat sow huffed over to them.

The young woman sighed and wiped her hand across

her brow, leaving a streak of dirt to match the three on her dress.

The dog sat on his haunches watching the pig.

Wyatt gave the dog further study. "Does he always wear a grin?"

"A grinning dog and a crying pig. Who'd believe it?" The girl hooted with laughter.

Wyatt couldn't remember when he'd last heard such a freeing sound. His grin widened, went deep into his heart.

She calmed her chuckles, though her quivering lips warned him it might resume at any moment.

From behind him came a strange sound. He jerked around to see the source. Lonnie had moved close enough to see and hear, and he laughed, too. A sound almost foreign to Wyatt's ears.

Lonnie noticed Wyatt watching and immediately sobered.

Oh, how Wyatt wished his brother would stop being so tense around him. Lonnie was even more jumpy around strangers, and yet…

Wyatt looked at the woman before him. Had her laughter drawn Lonnie forward? He shifted his gaze toward the pigs. Was it the animals that attracted Lonnie?

Whatever it was, Wyatt was grateful.

"I don't believe I've seen you around before." The pretty young woman drew his attention back to her.

"Nope. Name's Wyatt Williams. This is my brother, Lonnie."

"Pleased to meet you both. I'm Cora Bell. What can I do for you?"

"My mare needs to rest." He indicated Fanny. "The rest of my animals are down at the river. We want permission to stay there until she's ready to travel again. We could use some supplies, as well. I saw your sign on the gate and thought…"

"I can certainly sell you anything we have. You'll need to talk to Pa about your animals, though. Come along."

He dismounted, handed Rooster's reins to Lonnie and strode after her.

She led him to a small outbuilding and stepped inside. He followed into the dim interior.

"Pa, I brought you company."

A man emerged from behind a stack of wood pieces, old barrel hoops and broken wagon wheels. He wiped his greasy hands on a stained rag.

Cora introduced the pair.

Mr. Bell held out a soiled hand. "Pleased to meet you. What brings you to our part of the country?"

Wyatt repeated his request. "I'll only stay until my mare and her foal are ready to travel, then I'll be on my way."

"Got someplace to be, do you?"

Mr. Bell likely only meant to make conversation, but the question made Wyatt face the fact that he didn't know where they were going. How far would they have to in order to get away from their past? How far before Lonnie could forget their abusive father? How far before people would forget Wyatt had gone to jail for beating up the old man?

Not that he'd done it. Lonnie, sensitive and quiet, had snapped one day and turned on their father. Knowing his brother would never survive in jail, Wyatt had confessed to the crime. Now, a year later, he was out. Of course, no one would let that be in the past. Pa had died while Wyatt was in prison. Perhaps the beating had done irreparable damage. Or maybe Pa's hard life had caught up with him. Ma, God rest her soul, had lived long enough to see Wyatt free again. Then she'd wearily given up as if life was just too much effort.

Wyatt had sold their farm in Kansas and was headed as far away from there as possible. He planned to buy a bit of land someday and start over. He'd be a rancher. Raise horses. Find peace. He'd brought along a half-dozen mares to start a herd with. He and Lonnie—wanting to forget their past and hoping for a happy future. Somewhere. Sometime. He rubbed at the tightness in his neck. Maybe in Canada they could start over without him constantly looking over his shoulder.

He shuddered, then sucked in a lungful of air and forced his thoughts under control. He would not think of those who might recognize him from the trial. Or even those who might have their own reasons for tracking him down. For instance, a certain jailbird who hated Wyatt and vowed to make him pay for Wyatt's interference when the man tried to bully his way into power in jail. Not that he figured Jimmy Stone had enough get-up-and-go to ride after them. But the man had gotten out of prison a few weeks after Wyatt, and Wyatt hadn't been able to forget the man's threats.

"Headed north," he said, answering Mr. Bell's question.

"You've about run out of north." The old man scratched his whiskered chin. "Unless you're headed for Canada."

"Might be." Even if he had particulars about his destination, he wouldn't be sharing them.

Mr. Bell studied him a moment. "You sound like a man running from something."

"Could be I'm running to something."

Mr. Bell didn't blink. "So long as your running poses no threat to me or my family."

Wyatt didn't answer. He couldn't give that kind of assurance. "My mare's about to foal."

Mr. Bell limped toward the door. "Let's have a look."

They made their slow way toward Lonnie and the mare. Lonnie tossed the mare's rope toward Wyatt and backed away at their approach. No one but Wyatt seemed to notice Lonnie's odd behavior. The others were too busy eyeing Fanny. He introduced his brother to Mr. Bell, who greeted him, then returned his attention to the horse.

Mr. Bell ran his hand along Fanny's sides and walked around the horse then tsked. "She needs to rest. Where did you say you come from?"

"Didn't say."

Mr. Bell straightened and fixed Wyatt with a look that caused him to hastily add, "Been on the road awhile."

"That's no excuse for exhausting a mare this heavy in foal." The look Mr. Bell gave him would have made many a man stammer some kind of apology, but Wyatt had faced harsher looks and far bigger men without revealing a hint of weakness.

"Been looking for a decent place to stop for a few days now."

"Huh."

Apparently that wasn't a good enough excuse. And Wyatt wasn't about to tell anyone that every time he mentioned stopping Lonnie had begged him not to.

Until now, he hadn't been able to ignore his brother's request.

Cora grinned at Wyatt. "Best you know Pa can't abide any carelessness with God's creatures or His creation."

"I gathered."

"Cora, run and get some of Ma's tonic. Be sure to tell her it's for a mare in foal."

"Yes, Pa." She trotted away.

Wyatt watched her go, then realized Mr. Bell was studying him, and shifted his gaze back to the mare. "Do I have your permission for me and my brother to camp down by the river with my stock?"

Mr. Bell rocked his eyes from Wyatt to Lonnie to the mare and out to the river a couple of times as if measuring…considering.

If he knew the facts he would no doubt be asking them to move on.

Mr. Bell nodded. "Can't hardly ask you to take this mare any farther. You're welcome to pen them here and throw your bedrolls in the shed."

Wyatt didn't have to look at Lonnie to know his face would be pinched. "Thanks, but we'll be comfortable camping down by the water."

"Fine. Before you take the mare there, I'll give her some tonic to strengthen her. Do you have oats?"

Wyatt shook his head. "I'm out. Would you have some I could purchase?"

"I'll see to it." Mr. Bell faced Wyatt. The man looked almost old enough to be Cora's grandfather. He had a strong face, lined from years of both good times and worry. His hair was thick and gray. "I'll be keeping an eye on you." The look he gave Wyatt said a whole lot more than his words.

Wyatt understood the man's warning. Wyatt's vague answers had given him reason to be suspicious. If Mr. Bell knew the truth—a history of family violence and time in prison—he'd chase Wyatt and Lonnie away in spite of Fanny's condition.

Wyatt kept his gaze on Fanny.

Would he ever escape the shame and regret of his past?

With a smile on her lips, Cora made her way to the garden shed. How quickly and easily Wyatt had dropped a loop over that silly piglet's head. But, oh, the fuss the pig had made. Better entertainment than a circus.

Wyatt had laughed easily, but she'd seen so many secrets behind his dark eyes. She'd also noticed how his brother had pulled away from them all. It wasn't simply shyness. No, there was something unusual about his reaction.

Her amusement fled. She suspected he hid something. Secrets, in her opinion, made people forget things they'd promised to those they pretended to care about. She might be considered innocent, but despite being only twenty years old, she knew that much for certain. Like her supposed beau, Evan Price. Pretending to really care about her while all the time planning to leave for the goldfields. Goodbye came far too easy for him. She drew in a deep breath and forced her thoughts to things she needed to do yet today.

Between the wandering pig and the visiting cowboy she was way behind in her chores, and she picked up her pace. She had butter to churn and cheese to start. The sale of these products, plus whatever people offered in return for the healing powders that Ma made from medicinal plants, brought in the cash to pay for what they couldn't raise themselves.

A quick glance at the garden informed her that Lilly had not pulled weeds as she'd agree to. Heaven alone knew where she'd wandered off to. Likely she was searching for the mama cat and her newborn kittens. Ma and Rose were in the garden shed, and she turned her steps in that direction.

Rose stepped from the garden shed, saw her and waved. "We're making progress." Rose wanted Ma to write down all medicinal remedies. That meant Rose was writing as Ma recited them.

"Good," Cora said. She stepped into the shed. "Ma, can I have some tonic for a horse?"

"Horse tonic?" Rose asked.

Cora jabbed her finger over her shoulder. "Company."

"Really?"

"Yup." It wasn't as if they never had company. Lots of people dropped by to purchase eggs or butter or cheese or garden produce or something for an ailment.

She explained to Ma and Rose about the mare.

Ma shook dust from her ample apron. She ran her hands over her gray hair and patted her skirts smooth. "Let's have a look."

The trio walked to where Pa and Wyatt stood talking next to the mare. Lonnie and the other two horses were gone. As she expected, Pa had allowed them to rest down by the river. "Ma, this is Wyatt Williams. Wyatt, my mother, Mrs. Gertie Bell. And this is my sister Rose."

As the others studied Wyatt, Cora also took a good look at him. Dark hair showed around his black cowboy hat. His brown eyes were fringed with long lashes. And despite the shadows in his eyes, he looked as though he smiled often.

Eighteen-year-old Rose's red hair drew Wyatt's gaze like a moth to flames, but he shifted his gaze past her and said hello to her mother.

Ma nodded to Wyatt, then turned her attention to the horse. "Poor thing looks exhausted. This tonic ought to make her feel better."

Lilly drifted by, saw the crowd and shifted direction. "What's everyone doing here?"

Rose and Lilly were twins, although as different as the flowers they'd been named for.

Lilly cradled one of last year's kittens.

Cora moved to Lilly's side as she introduced Wyatt yet again. "That's our family."

"Pleased to meet you all," he said. "I don't plan to be a nuisance. We'll be down by the river until Fanny here and her new baby are ready to move."

Another wanderer. Here today, maybe tomorrow or even the next day, then gone as fast as he could pull his boots on…or, in this case, as soon as he deemed his horse fit to move on.

Cora'd had her fill of wandering men. First her birth father had abandoned her and the twins when she was five and the twins just three. The day was burned into her memory.

Papa in a wagon, riding away with a promise to return. "Wait for me. I'll be back," he'd said. But he'd never returned and she'd never known why.

And then Evan. Cora wondered how she could have

let herself care for him in the first place. Once bitten, twice shy. She'd not be so willing to trust a man again.

"You're fortunate you ended up here," Rose said. "Our ma is known for her healing powders and ointments."

"I'm grateful, though it was the sign on your gate that caught my attention. Then I saw your sister chasing after a pig and had to ride closer."

Cora groaned. Now Lilly would get all concerned.

"What pig?" Lilly looked about ready to cry. How many times had Cora told her sister that, at eighteen, tears shouldn't be so close to the surface?

"One of the little pigs," Cora said.

"But which one?"

"I couldn't say. They all look the same to me." Fat, pink or otherwise, and noisy. She darted a glance at Wyatt. He flashed a grin as if recalling the chase they'd had.

She almost laughed and choked the sound back so she wouldn't be called upon to explain herself. She drew curious looks from both sisters. She patted her chest as if she had a tickle.

But Lilly had not lost sight of her concern over the pigs. "Was the pig all pink or did it have spots?"

Cora honestly could not say. She'd been entirely focused on getting the creature back into the pen before it had decided to root in the garden the way one had done last week. She'd managed to salvage some of the bean plants, but half a dozen were beyond help. After all her hard work planting and weeding.

"There was a black spot on its rump," Wyatt said.

Cora stared at him. How had he noticed when she hadn't?

"That was Mini," Lilly said. "I hope you didn't hurt him. He's the littlest one, you know."

"He looked fine to me," Cora said.

"I'll check on him." Lilly dashed off with Rose after her.

Pa gave the horse the tonic, then he and Ma wandered away, leaving Cora alone with Wyatt.

She wasn't sure what to say. Was she supposed to escort him down to the river? She blurted out the first thing that came to mind. "My sister worries so much about those pigs." She realized she might not appear to be sympathetic and she truly was. "Don't get me wrong. I adore my sister. Both of them. They mean the world to me."

He studied her a moment, his eyes filled with those dark secrets she'd noticed before. "I guess your family is your life."

She'd never thought of it that way, but it was true. "Yes, they are." She wanted to ask about his family, but before she could, he spoke again.

"Your pa said I could buy some oats for my horses. Could you tell me where I can find them?"

She went to the shed and pointed to the bins in the corner. "I'd better get back to my work." She returned to the workroom off the kitchen to churn butter. Even with all the windows open, the room was far too warm. She needed to get a springhouse built so there'd be a cool place to store the butter and cheese during the summer. But she never had enough time, and Pa, bless his heart, tried to help, but he was getting far too old and sore for heavy work.

As she pumped the handle of the churn, her thoughts returned to the cowboy.

When she'd first seen him, she'd hoped he'd come in answer to the notice she'd nailed up in the store several days ago, offering a job to someone who would help her build a new barn. It seemed Mr. Frank, the store owner, was right. No one was going to risk displeasure from the Caldwells by helping the Bells.

The Caldwells objected to the Bells farming in the midst of their ranch land. It was only a mistake, they insisted, that the Bells had been able to file on that particular piece of land. They'd made it clear the Bells should pack up and leave. Pa was equally convinced that the little bit of land they owned next to the river shouldn't matter to the Caldwells. The cowboys and cows could access the river for miles on either side. So he refused every effort the Caldwells made to convince him to relocate.

But Wyatt had only stopped to take care of his horses, not to help with the barn.

A thought grew. Maybe he'd be interested in helping with the construction work in exchange for oats for the animals and supplies for himself and Lonnie. He certainly looked strong enough to handle the work.

The man hid secrets, but did it matter? He meant to move on. All she cared about was getting the barn finished this summer.

But first she'd make sure he posed no threat to her family.

How was she to find out?

Chapter Two

Wyatt led Fanny to the river. Lonnie scrambled to his feet and backed away at their approach. Wyatt hoped to see the fear and tension disappear when Lonnie saw who it was, but neither did.

He sighed. "Lonnie, why do you act like I'm going to hurt you? You know I won't."

Lonnie nodded and mumbled. "I guess."

Guess? Was that the best the boy could do? Wyatt let it go. He could only hope that time would heal Lonnie's wounds. "Mr. Bell said we could stay here. Help me make camp." He tossed the end of a rope toward Lonnie. "Stretch it between those trees." They'd make a rope corral to hold the mares.

Lonnie jumped to do as Wyatt said. Jumped too fast, Wyatt figured. As if he thought that if he dillydallied, Wyatt would boot him. How long would it be before Lonnie stopped expecting to be treated the way their pa had treated him?

Wyatt had set his mind to being patient and soft-spoken with the boy, even when his fearful attitude made him want to shake him.

"That ought to hold them for now. I bought oats from the Bells. How about you give the mares a ration?"

Lonnie eagerly did so. The only time he truly relaxed was around animals. Not that Wyatt could blame him. He, too, had plenty of reason not to trust people. Jail had been a harsh teacher in that regard.

"Now let's get a camp set up for us."

"How long are we going to stay?" Lonnie rocked back and forth on the balls of his feet.

It was his usual worry stance. Wyatt remembered him doing it from the time he started to walk. Wyatt secretly smiled as he recalled those good memories before their family had been affect by their pa's moods. Pa hadn't always been violent. Wyatt could say exactly when it happened. Seemed it was sometime after Lonnie was born.

"We'll have to stay until Fanny foals and the baby is strong enough to travel."

Lonnie held one corner of the tarpaulin they were securing between trees for shelter. "But didn't she have some kind of tonic? Won't that make her able to go farther?"

"No, it won't." As Mr. Bell said, they had pushed the poor animal too much already.

Lonnie let his corner of the canvas droop.

"We can't run forever." Wyatt kept his voice calm and soothing. "Can you hold your corner tight?"

Lonnie jerked the canvas taut. "Why not?"

"We'd run out of money, for one thing." Besides, he ached to settle down. Had from his first day in jail. One thing he'd promised himself while behind bars—once he got out he'd find a place where he could belong and find peace. He still clung to that dream, though he didn't know the when or where of it.

"We could go into the bush, and hunt and fish."

"I suppose we could. We'd be hermits. You think you'd like that?"

"Maybe."

He tied Lonnie's corner of the tarpaulin and stepped back. "There. Looks like a nice home for us." He reached out to drape an arm across Lonnie's shoulders.

Lonnie shrank away.

Wyatt closed his eyes. It hurt like crazy to be treated this way by Lonnie. "We'll move on after Fanny's foal is born and it's strong enough to travel."

"How long will that be?" Lonnie asked.

"I expect a month or so."

"A month!" Lonnie stalked away to the bank of the river, mumbling under his breath. "What if they find out?"

"We'll make sure they don't."

He wanted so much for Lonnie to feel safe with him. To feel safe around other people.

During his days in prison, Wyatt's only consolation had been reading his Bible and praying. Prayer was unhindered by bars. He'd promised himself to trust God every day and in every way. If he meant to keep his vow, he had to believe they'd been led to this place. Seemed the Bells were the kind of people to extend hospitality for the sake of his animals.

Could it be they would also accept a jailbird? But he wasn't ready to cast aside his doubts and caution. Not until he'd had a chance to see what sort of folk they were. Even then, parts of his past must remain a secret. But he wanted Lonnie to feel at ease with them. Lonnie's constant nervousness would surely make people suspicious that something wasn't right.

"The Bells seem like nice people." The thought of Cora laughing brought a smile to Wyatt's face. "You didn't meet the twins."

Lonnie turned, an eager expression on his face. "Boys? Are they my age?"

"Girls. And they're about as big as Cora."

"Oh, well." Lonnie moseyed over to Wyatt's side and sank down beside him. "How old you figure Cora is?"

"I don't know."

"You could ask me." At the sound of a lilting voice, Wyatt jerked about to see Cora standing nearby. "You said you were out of supplies so I brought you some things." She held up a sack.

Lonnie jerked to his feet and hurried over to the horses.

Wyatt did his best to hide his disappointment at Lonnie's retreat and turned back to Cora with a smile that didn't chase the throb from behind his eyes.

At the way her gaze followed Lonnie, he knew she wondered at the boy's sudden withdrawal.

"He's shy," he said by way of explanation.

"Lilly is much the same way."

"So how old are you?" He hoped it was the kind of question that would divert her from following any suspicions she had about Lonnie's behavior.

"Twenty," she answered, her gaze still on the boy. "And you?"

"Twenty-one." He felt a lot older. Old enough to be weary, though that was as much the result of a year in prison as from being on the road for weeks. "Lonnie's sixteen."

She took a good look around. "You've got a pretty good setup here."

"It suits us."

She nodded. Her gaze came to him and she gave him serious consideration.

What did she see? He banked every thought but survival. She must never guess his secret. "Care to sit a spell?"

She sat on a log to his right.

"I'd offer you cookies and coffee, but I have no cookies and haven't built a fire yet, so I don't have any coffee."

She smiled, sending golden light through her eyes. "Maybe I can help."

She opened the sack she carried and pulled out new potatoes and carrots so fresh he could smell them. She held up a jar of milk, then set it by him. She unwrapped a generous piece of cheese and set down a half-dozen eggs.

Despite his practice of hiding his feelings, he felt his eyes widen with pleasure at such delights. He swallowed a rush of saliva. He hadn't seen food such as this in so long it was but a hungry memory.

Then she removed another packet from the sack and unfolded the paper. "Cookies. Ma said you looked hungry." She grinned with such innocent happiness that his heart twisted into a knot.

Her smile would not be so warm and welcoming if she knew the truth about him.

She would never know.

His gaze clung to the cookies. They'd had nothing but hard biscuits and jerky for three days. "Lonnie, she brought milk and cookies," he called. "Come have some."

"What kind?"

Wyatt almost laughed. As if it made any difference. Lonnie was every bit as hungry as Wyatt. "Cow's milk."

Lonnie snorted. "I mean the cookies."

"Oh." He knew what Lonnie meant but he went out of his way to force his brother to talk to him.

"Oatmeal and raisin," Cora said. "Ma made them, and she's a very good cook."

"Your favorite, if I remember correctly," Wyatt added.

Lonnie still hesitated.

Wyatt pulled three tin cups from the supplies and held them out to Cora. She unscrewed the lid from the jar and poured milk into each cup. He handed her one cup and took a long drink from another.

"This is so good. I haven't had fresh milk since—" He smiled as Lonnie moved closer and sat down as far away from Cora as possible and took the cup of milk Wyatt offered.

Cora passed around the cookies. "Have two." They needed no urging.

For a moment they enjoyed the snack without need for words.

Cora, who only ate one cookie, finished before Wyatt and Lonnie. "Where do you plan on going?"

He'd answered the question when her pa had asked and she knew it. And her quiet tone didn't make him believe she only made conversation. She wanted to know more about him. And he couldn't blame her. Two strangers camped so close to their home posed a risk. But not the sort she probably imagined.

"We'll know when we get there."

"I suppose. When did you leave your home? Where did you say it was?"

"Didn't say. We've been on the road a couple weeks." Give or take. He didn't intend to offer any more information. Out of the corner of his eyes he saw Lonnie's leg bouncing and shot him a look of assurance.

"You have any other family?"

Wyatt choked back the mouthful of cookie, suddenly as dry as dust. He took a sip of milk to wet his mouth.

Lonnie grew as still as the log on which he sat. Wyatt wondered if he even breathed.

"No other family," Wyatt said softly.

"No ma and pa?" She sounded shocked.

"Ma died a couple months back." Wyatt figured she'd hung around just long enough for Wyatt's return. Long enough to make Wyatt promise to take care of Lonnie. Even without Ma's admonition, he'd have made sure Lonnie was okay. He'd been Lonnie's guardian and protector since Ma had put the tiny baby, only one day old, in Wyatt's arms. She'd hugged them both. Wyatt had put his finger in Lonnie's palm and the baby's tiny fingers had curled around it.

It probably wasn't manly to say it, but it had been love at first touch.

He loved his troubled little brother even more now.

"I'm so sorry." Cora's voice thickened as if she held back tears. "I can't imagine not having a ma."

The river rumbled by, on its way to the ocean, where it would become part of something so much bigger it would disappear. Was that how death was? Or maybe it was only how it felt to those left behind, because he knew Ma had gone to something better where her pain and fear disappeared and she became whole and happy again.

"What about your pa?" Cora asked.

Her words vibrated through the air. Wyatt kept a firm look on Lonnie, silently begging him not to overreact.

Lonnie met his eyes, correctly read Wyatt's message, and didn't speak or move.

Relieved, Wyatt smiled and nodded reassurance. He didn't break eye contact with Lonnie as he answered Cora.

"Our pa's been dead several months now." He'd survived the beating but from what Ma and Lonnie said, it seemed something inside him had been broken. He never regained his strength but slowly faded away to a shadow before he died, which was a mercy for Lonnie. It had freed the boy from the fear of more abuse. But from what Wyatt had put together about the year he'd been missing, he figured the boy was made to feel ashamed because he had a brother in prison, and he remained afraid even after Pa was dead and gone.

Cora touched the back of his hand, bringing his attention to her. "I'm so sorry. You're both far too young to be orphans." She pulled her hand back to her lap.

His skin where she'd touched him burned as if he'd had too much sun in that one spot. He'd not been touched in a compassionate way in so long he didn't know how to respond.

"At least we have each other." He managed to squeeze out the words. He gripped Lonnie's shoulder, felt the tension and held on until the boy began to relax. "We will always have each other."

Cora stared at her empty cup. She tipped it as if she could dredge up another drop of milk and that would somehow give her the words to express her sorrow at their state. No wonder Lonnie acted as though the world was ready to beat him up. Likely that was how it felt.

It was enough to make her want to offer Wyatt and Lonnie a home with the Bells, where they'd find the welcome and warmth she and her sisters had found.

Mrs. Bell had found five-year-old Cora and the twins two days after their real father had ridden away.

Cora remembered how she'd been ready to defend them. "My papa's coming back," she'd told Ma Bell. She'd looked down the trail as if he might suddenly appear. "He'll be here any second now." They were the same words she'd spoken to the twins throughout the lonely, fear-filled days and night. But the twins had gone readily into Ma Bell's open arms and been comforted.

Cora had needed a little more persuasion.

"Your sisters are tired and dirty and hungry," Ma had said. "Why not come with us? I'll help you take care of them."

It was the only argument she would have listened to. Their mother had died a few weeks previously, but not before she'd made Cora promise to take care of the twins.

Their father had never returned, though Cora had watched for him for several years. She'd given up looking for him, but she would never forget the promise she'd made to her mother, which meant she must be very careful about every decision she made. On the other hand, Ma and Pa Bell made the promise easy to keep.

The Bells had loved the girls from the first. She wished everyone could have people like them—loving and true. They'd never once given her any reason to doubt them or their word.

"I'm sorry you don't have parents," she said as she handed Wyatt the empty cup.

Wyatt nodded as he took it from her. "How much do I owe you for the oats and the food? They're very much appreciated. Thank you, in case I forgot to say that earlier."

Normally she would name the price and take the money, but his question gave her a way to see more of him, assess how honest he was. "You can settle up with Pa later."

"I'll do that."

She rolled up the sack she'd brought the supplies in and rose. "If there's anything else you need, don't hesitate to ask."

Wyatt rose, too, and smiled at her. "Much obliged."

She studied him. He had a nice smile, but it didn't erase the dark shadows that lingered in his eyes. It was those shadows, and his reluctance to say where he and Lonnie had come from and where they were going, that made her wary of him. "Bye for now."

He nodded. "Goodbye."

She glanced past him to Lonnie. "Bye, Lonnie."

The boy's head jerked up, his lips parted, his eyes wide. "Bye." The word squeaked from him.

Was he afraid of her? But why?

His eyes went to Wyatt, who stood with his back to his brother.

Was Lonnie afraid of his brother? That gave her cause for concern. One thing was certain. There was something not quite right with this pair, and until she knew it wasn't anything that threatened anyone in her family—including herself—she would not be encouraging any contact. She silently prayed as she returned to the farm. *God, make the truth known, clear and plain. Protect my family. May we serve You in sincerity and truth.*

Rose and Lilly watched for her return. "Did you find out anything?" they asked in unison.

"Their parents are dead." Her voice trembled. "I can't help feeling sorry for anyone whose parents are dead."

The girls nodded.

Cora said, "Makes us all the more grateful for being adopted by the Bells."

"We need to tell them again," Rose said.

The girls agreed they would be more faithful at telling their parents how much they appreciated their love.

Cora knew the twins wondered about their birth parents, but she was the only one with any recollection of them. Not that it mattered. They were now the Bell sisters.

"Did you find out where they're going?" Rose asked.

"How did the mares look?" Lilly added.

Cora chuckled. "I could tell which one asked each question without seeing either of you. Lilly's first concern is the animals. Rose's is to have all the questions answered."

The girls faced her as a pair. "Well?"

She grinned and teased them. "Well, what?"

"The mares?" Lilly prodded.

"They looked all right to me, but I honestly didn't look very closely at them. Wyatt and his brother built a rope corral that looked fine."

Lilly sighed long. "The mare he had here was foot weary and about ready to foal. I'm wondering how the others are."

Cora gave a little shrug. "I'm sorry, but I can't say."

"Did they say where they were going? Or where they were from?" Rose demanded.

"No more than they told Pa."

"Hmm." Rose's brows furrowed. "Why do you suppose they don't say?"

Lilly shrugged. "Could be any number of reasons. No need to imagine some deep, dark secret."

Rose huffed. "I'm not imagining anything. I just don't like unanswered questions. Or unfinished business. Seems to me if a person has nothing to hide they can answer civil questions."

Lilly gave her twin a fierce look. "Or maybe they just want to be left to themselves."

"Girls," Cora soothed before the pair got really involved in their differing opinions. "I've decided we should give the two of them a wide berth until we're certain they pose no risk."

"Risk to who?" Rose demanded.

"Their poor animals." Lilly shook her head.

"A risk to us," Cora corrected. "To you two. To Ma and Pa. They seem harmless enough, but I don't intend to believe first impressions. Now let's get the chores done and help Ma with supper."

She brought in the two milk cows and milked them while Lilly fed the pigs and chickens. Rose gathered the eggs and went to help Ma.

That evening they kept busy with shelling the peas they'd picked earlier. It gave them plenty of time to talk and even more time to think.

Even without the conversation circling back to the two newcomers and their horses, Cora's thoughts went unbidden to Wyatt sitting down by the river in his crude little camp. Hungry, orphaned and caring for a younger brother who seemed troubled, to say the least.

Or was she being like Rose and, in her search for answers, making up things that had no basis in fact?

One thing was certain. She would not let down her guard until she had some assurance that it was safe to do so.

Wyatt didn't come to pay Pa that evening. Perhaps he'd taken the feed and victuals and moved on. In the morning, Cora slipped close enough to see that they were still there. Lonnie was brushing Fanny until her coat shone. Where was Wyatt? She looked around. Then she spotted him, headed up the hill toward the house.

She bolted to her feet and scampered back before he got there. Slightly breathless, she hurried to meet him.

"Good morning. I came to pay your pa," he said, snatching his hat from his head. His face was slightly reddened, as if he'd scrubbed it hard in cold water. He was freshly shaven. She hadn't noticed his well-shaped chin yesterday. His damp hair looked black.

"He's in his work shed. I'll take you to him." She led the way to the weather-stained building where Pa spent many happy hours.

"Pa," she called. "Mr. Williams has come to pay for the oats and the food I took him last night."

Pa's head poked around a cupboard. "Can't you take care of it?"

"Not this time, Pa."

He considered her a moment, seemed to understand she had her reasons and emerged. "So what did you take him?"

She told him. "I'll leave you to it." She backed away

and ducked around the corner of the building to listen. Perhaps she'd see his true character in how he treated Pa. To many, her pa appeared a crippled old man. But he had his wits about him and saw far more than most realized.

Pa named a sum and coins rattled as Wyatt paid the amount.

But Wyatt didn't move away.

"What do you think of this?" Pa asked and Cora knew he wanted Wyatt to look at his latest invention.

"Interesting. What is it?" Wyatt sounded sincere.

"I'm trying to figure out how to hoe four rows at once."

Cora smiled. Pa was always experimenting and inventing. Some things turned out well, others not so well, but like Pa said, you had to try and fail before you could succeed.

"I'm not sure I've got the angle of the hoes just right. Could you hold it so I can check?"

Wyatt's boots clumped on the wooden floor as he moved to help Pa. "It's a mite heavy," Wyatt said.

"Do you think it's too heavy for the girls? Bear in mind they're good strong girls."

Wyatt grunted a time or two. "Seems as if it would be a big load, especially if they're supposed to pull it through the soil."

"You could be right. Maybe if I shape the hoes to a point?"

"Might work."

A thump, rattle and several grunts came from the shed.

Cora edged around the corner so she could see what they were doing.

They'd turned the hoe over on its back and Wyatt squatted next to Pa. "Maybe like this?" He indicated with his finger.

"That might do it."

"You maybe should get some metal ones. They'd cut through the soil better."

Pa gave Wyatt an approving smile. "Yup. Figured to do that once I get the working model figured out." He rubbed his crippled leg. "Sure can't move about the way I used to."

Cora saw Pa's considering look. She didn't want him to get it in his head that he'd return to work on the barn. He was getting too old and had already had one fall. No, she'd do it by herself before she'd let that happen. She sprang forward.

"Pa—oh, hi, Wyatt. Did you two sort out the payment?"

"Sure did."

Pa turned back to his hoe. "I'm going to try that."

Wyatt patted Pa's back. "Don't hesitate to ask if you need help with it. Or anything."

"Maybe you'd like a tour of the place." Now, why had she offered that? She didn't have time for a social visit. Not with beans to pick and potatoes to hill and hay to cut and stack. She could be three people, and the twins could be doubled, and the work would never end. Which, she supposed, about described the lot of most farmers. But having offered, she had little choice but to show the stranger around and learn more about him.

One way or another.

Chapter Three

Wyatt would enjoy seeing more of this tidy little farm. He didn't mind the company, either. The young woman's chatter was a pleasant change from Lonnie's dour complaints about having to stay in one place. No amount of explaining about the necessity of stopping for Fanny's sake satisfied him. Wyatt had been grateful to leave the boy cleaning up the campsite after breakfast.

He and Cora fell in, side by side. The lop-eared dog trotted alongside them. He tripped over himself and skidded into the ground.

Wyatt chuckled. "What kind of dog do you call that?"

"He doesn't mind what we call him, so long as we don't call him late for supper."

Wyatt laughed. She sure did have a way of easing his mind.

As they walked beside the garden, Cora explained that they grew enough to supply their own needs and sell to others. But she stopped when they reached an overgrown patch of wild plants.

"We don't ever touch that," Cora said. "It's Ma's healing plants. She is the only one who can tell which ones are good and which are weeds. To me, they all look like weeds. She lets them grow wild and untamed. I've suggested she should tidy them to rows so we can clean up the patch." Cora sighed. "By her reaction, you'd think I'd told her I planned to plow it under. So it stays that way."

Wyatt studied the unruly growth, and compared it to the rest of the neat garden. He understood the need for order, allowing the plants to be better tended, but something about the untamed patch pulled at his thoughts. Wild and free. He shifted back to study of the tidy garden. Order and control. He'd had enough of the latter while in prison, but the former didn't satisfy him, either. Was it possible to have something in the middle?

Cora cleared her throat to get his attention. He must have been staring at the plants long enough to make her wonder why they interested him so much.

"Maybe it could do with just a little taming," he said, as if that had been his only thought.

"That's what I said to Ma."

They proceeded down a pathway between the two gardens. Grub, seeing the direction they headed, loped ahead of them.

"Ma and Pa have planted berry bushes of all sorts—raspberries, gooseberries, currants, chokecherries—and fruit trees. We get lots of berries, but not much fruit. Seems we always get frost too soon and the winters are too severe. Pa's been grafting fruit trees to wild trees to see if that will work."

The idea intrigued Wyatt. Was this a way of combining wild and free with tame? Would it work for a tree? How about a man? "Has it?"

"There is a lot of winterkill, but a couple of trees

have given us sour little apples. Pa is determined to produce a decent apple. Says he'll call it a Montana."

They passed the bushes and reached a fence. Three cows grazed in a little pasture.

"I'm currently milking two of them."

A flock of sheep nibbled in another fenced area of grass, and a field of green oats lay beyond.

"The sheep are Lilly's project."

A trail led toward the river and they followed it. When they reached the water's edge, she stood in the shadow of the trees. They were downstream and out of sight from where Lonnie waited at the camp Wyatt had set up. He stood at her side with the sound of the water rumbling through his thoughts.

"This is one of my favorite spots." She sighed. "I can see so far. Look." She pointed. "The prairies roll away like giant waves."

He followed her direction. Indeed, the prairies were like a golden ocean. They went on and on. No walls. No bars. A man could fill his lungs to capacity here.

She shifted, brushing his arm as she pointed to his right, sending a jolt through his nerves. Even an accidental touch startled him. He wondered if she noticed, and if so, what did she think? Would she put it down to unexpectedness? Of course she would. She had no way of knowing that any contact in jail had signaled violence, and before that, Pa's touch had taught him to jerk away.

No wonder Lonnie was so anxious about even gentle touches. But Wyatt would teach him…teach them both to welcome such.

Cora spoke softly. "In that direction you see the hills with their hollows full of trees." She turned still farther.

"And the mountains in the west. 'Tis truly a beautiful land, and like Pa says, we are to be good stewards of it."

"I never thought of being a steward of the land."

"I take it you're planning to have a ranch and raise horses."

It was an obvious conclusion. "Kind of hope to."

"Are you opposed to farmers?

He shrugged. "Not opposed to much of anything."

She shifted and pinned him with a look. "Don't you believe in seeking good and avoiding evil?"

Her look reached into his chest to squeeze his heart. He stiffened as pain and regret oozed out. "I hate evil." She'd never know how much of it he'd seen.

She nodded silent approval and his heart beat smoothly again.

He heard the sound of horses' hooves and turned to see two riders approach. Beside him, Cora stiffened, alert and cautious.

Wyatt gave his full attention to the pair. Nothing out of the ordinary as far as he could tell. Medium build, lean as cowboys usually were. Dusty, work-soiled cowboy hats pulled low to shade their eyes. They rode slowly, as if studying the surroundings, or perhaps looking for a wayward horse. But he'd seen no sign of a wandering animal.

They rode closer, seemed to be aiming at the river. One spoke to the other. He couldn't hear their words, but mocking laughter carried across the distance. They were fifty yards away when they reined up and stared at Cora and Wyatt. He realized they were in the shadows and the pair hadn't noticed them until then.

The bigger of the men pushed his hat back, allowing Wyatt to see a swarthy man with a deep scowl. There was something about him that sent sharp prickles up Wyatt's spine. He'd seen the same expression many times in prison, usually on the face of a bully. Someone who used intimidation to make people obey him.

He guessed Cora felt the same because she tensed even more. Her fists curled so tight her knuckles were white.

The man turned his horse and the pair rode away. Not until they were out of sight did Cora's shoulders sag.

"You know those two?" he asked.

She sucked in air with such force he figured she hadn't breathed for several minutes. She coughed as her lungs filled.

Wyatt patted her back gently, as if calming a frightened animal. "Are you okay?"

She nodded. "I'm fine. The big cowboy is Ebner. He works for the Caldwell Ranch." Her lip curled. "I believe he is responsible for almost all of the harm we've suffered."

He nodded. Just as he thought. He'd dealt with men of that sort before and ended up with an enemy or two. Not that it bothered him. He refused to back down from any bully.

"What kind of things?" he asked her.

"He's cut our fences, chased the milk cows until he might have killed them. He's turned Caldwell cows into our garden and let the pigs loose." She waved her hands as she described the events. Her voice rang with the injustice of it.

He caught her hands and stilled them. Realizing the liberty he'd taken, he dropped his arms to his sides. But not before a longing as wide as the prairie swept into his heart, making him aware of how empty and barren his life was. He wanted so much more than the right to hold her and comfort her. He longed for a home and love. He hoped to gain the first for Lonnie's sake as well as his own. Winning Lonnie's trust would have to satisfy his desire for love. He'd never ask or expect a woman to share the shame of being associated with a jailbird.

"Why do these men bother you? Doesn't their boss know?"

"Mr. Caldwell likely orders them to do it. From the time we settled here, he's been trying to drive us off."

"Why would he care about your farm?"

She shrugged, her eyes full of anger. "I've asked that question many times. He told Pa it breaks up the perimeter of his ranch and blocks access to the river." She snorted. "As if a few acres of farm are any hindrance to his animals watering at the river. But sodbusters are not welcome."

"Isn't there a marshal in the area? Surely he can protect your rights."

"The Caldwells manage to stay within the law. They claim they can't help it if the cows don't understand fences. Only once has the sheriff been convinced the wires were purposely cut, and of course no one confessed to it, so there wasn't anything the sheriff could do."

"Well, you'd think the man would realize how unimportant a few acres are." Even as he said it, he guessed it wasn't about the acres but about the man's pride. A rich man, likely used to getting what he wanted, and for whatever reason, he wanted the Bell farm. Or to be rid of the settlers in his midst.

"It's mostly that he's a Caldwell and wants to own everything on this side of the river," Cora commented.

She turned her gaze from the trail of dust kicked up by the cowboys' retreating horses and looked at him. Her dark eyes flashed with anger. "Maybe they saw you and thought we'd hired a guard."

His plans did not include being a bodyguard to anyone. Except wasn't that what he'd been for Lonnie? And continued to be?

But neither would he stand by and watch a bunch of cowboys bully the Bells. Not just because they had been kind to him, though that was reason enough, but because he would never stand by while people were pushed around for no reason. People could be pushed too far. He'd seen that with Lonnie and vowed to never again stand by and not take action. It had been the reason he'd stood up to Jimmy Stone. While he was here waiting for Fanny to foal, he'd keep his eyes open to any sort of trouble.

Cora turned and stepped away from the river. "I need to get at my chores."

He followed her. They reached the edge of the garden and she stopped.

"Is there anything you need?" she asked.

"No, thanks. I enjoyed the tour of your farm."

She met his eyes and smiled, and he was struck by the friendliness of her look. Her brown eyes were bottomless, as if she had nothing to hide.

Of course she didn't. She'd been open with him.

He jerked his gaze past her lest she see the vast ocean of secrets he hid, and must always hide, if he and Lonnie hoped to have any chance of starting over.

"I need to get back to Lonnie," he mumbled, and trotted away. His mind whirled with so many things—the beauty of the well-developed little farm and the endless land and the look on the face of that Caldwell cowboy, but mostly Cora's pride in who she was and her fear at the approach of those riders.

It wasn't right that this idyllic home should be marred by bullying cowboys. Cora had been kind to him from the start and he wanted to do something to show his gratitude.

He passed the partially constructed barn. Did they have neighbors or friends who were going to help finish it?

Seeing the building gave him an idea. A way he could repay the Bell's kindness and watch the Caldwell cowboys. He'd offer to work on the barn.

He'd talk to Mr. Bell about it as soon as he'd checked on Lonnie.

"Cora, our prayers have been answered," Pa said to her later that morning.

She straightened from hilling the potato plants and tried to think which prayer he meant.

The one for good weather? Well, seemed they had that to be grateful for.

Enough rain and sunshine to promise a bountiful crop? Again, it seemed that prayer had been generously answered. *Thank You, God.*

Or did he mean the one about protecting them from the mischief of the Caldwell cowboys?

Or perhaps the one he and Ma made no attempt to hide—to provide good, Christian husbands for the three girls and to give them many grandchildren while they were young enough to enjoy them. She grinned as she thought of that prayer. Then her amusement fled. They'd actually thanked God when Evan had ridden off.

"He wasn't the man for you," Pa had said.

Ma had hugged Cora. "You'll see it's true, once you get over being hurt."

Cora knew they were right. It was her pride that was hurt more than her heart.

"Which prayer is that, Pa?"

"The one asking for someone to help finish the barn."

She jerked to full attention and glanced around. "Someone came in answer to my advertisement? Guess Mr. Frank was wrong." She wondered who was prepared to ignore the Caldwells' displeasure, but saw no one and returned her attention to Pa.

"In answer to our prayers, not your notice."

"What do you mean?"

"He didn't see the notice."

Cora shook her head as if doing so would make her understand what Pa was talking about. "Who?"

"Wyatt, of course."

"Wyatt?" She'd been thinking about it all morning—weighing the pros and cons, mentally listing what she knew about him against what she didn't know—and she still wasn't ready to take a chance on him, lest he be hiding something that would bring danger into their lives. "But, Pa, what do we know about him?"

"What do we need to know except he's big and strong and willing to help?"

"Indeed." Except maybe where he was from and where he was going and what was in between the past and the future. Wyatt Williams made her want to know all his secrets.

"When's he planning to start?"

"I said you'd tell him what to do."

She was glad Pa didn't want to climb up the ladder

and show Wyatt what to do, but she glanced at the potatoes yet to hill, then over to the barn. She couldn't be in two places at the same time. Rose and Lilly were helping Ma can peas and make rhubarb preserves. She sighed and took the hoe to the shed.

Grub stirred himself from the cool garden soil and ambled after her. Despite her frustration, she smiled as she looked at his grin. Something she'd not really noticed until Wyatt pointed it out.

Maybe working with the newcomer wouldn't be so bad.

She patted Grub's head. "Are you coming with me to find him?"

Grub wriggled so hard his hind legs got ahead of him and he almost tumbled into a tangle.

Cora laughed and patted his head again, then turned toward the river and the place where Wyatt and Lonnie camped.

"You looking for me?"

She cranked her head around, feeling about as awkward as Grub.

Wyatt leaned against the corner of the bare barn walls, so relaxed and at ease it made her want to suggest they forget work and go for a walk. But he wasn't here to waste time and neither was she.

"Pa said you offered to help build the barn."

"Yes, in exchange for feed for my horses and some supplies for Lonnie and me, and he agreed."

"I'm glad to have some help." She stopped a few feet from the building and studied it. "We got this far—" The external walls were up, holes in place for windows and doors. "But Pa fell and hurt his leg." She shook her head. "He's getting too old to be running up and down the ladder." She had to admit, though, his movements were more of a crawl than a run.

She closed her eyes against the fear that claimed her every time she thought of Pa falling.

"Is he hurt bad?" Wyatt's quiet voice made it possible to talk again.

"He says it's nothing, but I see the pain in his face when he moves too fast or turns too suddenly. It could have been so much worse." Her voice broke and she paused to take in two calming breaths. "I saw him fall and thought—" Her throat clogged with tears and she couldn't go on.

Wyatt unwound from his casual position and closed the distance between them. "God protected him."

She nodded, grateful for his kind words. "And gifted us with more time with him." She shook the depressing thoughts from her mind. "Do you have experience with construction?"

"I've helped put up a few buildings. Guess I know enough to put the right board in the right place and nail it solid." His face wreathed in a grin. "If not, I hope you'll correct me."

She chuckled. "All I know is what I've learned from Pa. But I was only twelve when he built these other buildings, and mostly I handed him nails." Her amusement grew as she thought of those days. "He let me hammer in a few nails and praised my efforts, but I believe he pulled out the bent nails and hammered them in straight when I wasn't looking."

"Sounds like he's a good father."

"The best." A movement caught her eye and she saw Lonnie hiding in the shadows. "Are you going to help, too?" she asked him.

Lonnie ducked his head, as if he didn't plan to answer, then lifted it and faced her squarely. "I mean to do my share."

"That's all anyone can expect, isn't it?"

Even though he remained in the shadows, she saw a flicker of acknowledgment in his eyes. The boy seemed hungry for approval. Too bad Pa wasn't going to be supervising. He was the expert on giving encouragement and approval but she'd be second best if she could.

"The tools are in the shed."

"I already got them," Wyatt said, pointing toward the saws and hammers next to the stack of lumber.

"Then let's get at it." She headed for the lumber pile. "Stu Maples, who owns the lumber yard, said we'd never be able to build the barn on our own—a bunch of women and a man getting up in years." She chuckled. "But he didn't mind selling us the lumber."

Wyatt grabbed a board, laid it across the sawhorses, measured and cut it. "Lonnie, help me put it in place."

Lonnie raced forward and grabbed an end.

Cora followed them. As soon as the board was in place, she started nailing.

Wyatt left her and Lonnie to do that while he cut another piece. They soon worked in a smooth rhythm.

"How long have you been here?" Wyatt asked.

"Eight years. Before that we lived in town. But Pa wanted us to be able to grow and produce more so we'd be self-sufficient."

"Seems you got a little bit of everything."

"Chickens, sheep, pigs, milk cows, the garden. I guess we have most everything. We make cheese, spin the wool and can the produce." She knew her voice rang with pride.

Wyatt chuckled. “And you’re very proud of all your family has achieved.”

She straightened and grinned at him. “Guess I make it pretty obvious.”

Wyatt handed her the next board. “I’d say you have good reason to feel that way.”

“It’s my family I’m most proud of. We’re strong and…survivors, I guess you’d say.”

“Huh?” He paused from sawing a board to look at her. “Survivors? Oh, I suppose you mean the Caldwells.”

“That and other things.” Their gazes connected across the distance as he seemed to contemplate asking her for further explanation.

She didn’t mind providing the answer, whether or not he asked the question. “Not all fathers are like my pa.”

Lonnie dropped a board and jerked back, a look of such abject fear on his face that she automatically reached for him. She meant to comfort him, but he threw up his arms as if he expected her to—

Hit him?

She looked to Wyatt for explanation.

He focused on Lonnie. “It’s okay, Lon. No harm done. Just pick up your end again.”

Lonnie shuddered. His wide dark eyes slowly returned to normal and he bent to retrieve the board.

Cora continued to stare at him, then shifted her study to Wyatt. There was something seriously wrong with Lonnie, and if Wyatt planned to stay on the place, she needed an explanation.

Wyatt met her look and shook his head.

She nodded. Now was not the time or the place, but she would be sure to find an opportunity very soon. If whatever caused Lonnie’s fear threatened the safety and security of her family in any way, she would insist they move on.

But would he tell her the truth?

Her experience with men didn't give her much confidence that he would.

Chapter Four

Cora returned to the task of building the barn for another half hour, then straightened. "I'm thirsty. Let's get a drink."

Wyatt dropped everything and followed her toward the pump. Even Lonnie didn't hesitate.

She pumped and Wyatt filled the dipper.

"Thanks. I'm about parched." He drank three full dippers, then took off his hat and poured some over his head. He shook the water from his face and planted his hat back on his wet head. "That's better. Thanks."

Her eyes followed the trails streaking from his wavy, dark brown hair down his sun-bronzed face and dripping off his chiseled chin. Chiseled chin! She snorted. What kind of observation was that? Right up there with her mental description of his chocolate-colored eyes with flashes of evening shadows in them and a certain sadness that she'd noticed before and put down to something in his past that he hid.

She drank from the dipper and considered pouring the rest of the water over her head. It might cool her face, but it would do nothing to cool her thoughts.

She splashed cold water on her face and handed the dipper to Lonnie, who drank his fill. Then, with a grin teasing his lips, he lifted his hat and poured water over his head.

Wyatt stared at him.

Cora laughed, which brought two pairs of eyes toward her. She couldn't tell which of the two was more surprised, but Wyatt recovered first and tipped his head back and laughed. Then, his eyes sparkling, he squeezed Lonnie's shoulder.

Cora could see the boy start to shrug away and then stop himself, and the pleasure in Wyatt's eyes went so deep that it made her eyes sting.

She could hardly wait to hear Wyatt's explanation for his brother's odd behavior.

Rose trotted toward the garden, likely to get potatoes for supper.

Lilly sang as she went to feed the pigs.

"I need to do chores," Cora said.

Wyatt nodded. "We'll work a bit longer." He and Lonnie returned to the barn while Cora made her way to the pasture to get the cows. First, she did her usual check on the pasture fence. It had a habit of mysteriously breaking down and letting the cows wander away. Not that there was any mystery about the cause of the frequent breaks. The cowboys from the Caldwell ranch broke the wires and generally made life as miserable as possible for the Bells.

She found no breaks in the fence. The cowboys must be too busy to harass them at the moment. The sun headed toward the mountaintops, signaling the end of the afternoon as she finished inspecting the fence and took Bossy and Maude home, lowing for feed and milking.

She gave them each a few oats, grabbed the milk buckets and milked the cows. As she rose to turn the cows into the pen, she almost ran into Wyatt as he rounded the corner at the same time.

He clamped his hands on her shoulders to steady her. "Whoa there, girl."

His warm and firm hands held her like an anchor. His fingers pressed into her shoulders, easing an ache she'd developed while hoeing in the garden and then hammering nails. A scent of warm soil, hard work and strength filled her nostrils and tugged at something deep inside. She fought to right herself—not physically but mentally. When had she ever reacted so strongly to a simple touch? Or the nearness of a man? She certainly hadn't had these unexpected feelings around Evan.

Evan! Remembering him made her pull back.

Wyatt's hands dropped to his sides.

She sucked in air to keep from swaying. "Sorry," she murmured. "Wasn't paying attention. Truth is, I don't usually see anyone around when I'm milking." It was one of the times she could count on solitude.

"Let me guess. No one else wants to share the task."

She couldn't decide if he teased or not and wouldn't look directly at him to gauge. She was finding it much too difficult to think clearly already. "Did you want something?" Of course he did. What other reason would he come to the shed?

"I think you and I need to talk."

"Yes, we do."

"Would you like to go for a walk after supper?"

Her thoughts hammered against the inside of her head. It sounded like a courting request, but of course it was only a way for them to talk.

No reason for her to be on edge.

"That will be fine." She took the buckets of milk and headed for the house. She could walk with a man without her heart racing ahead with possibilities.

Wyatt knew Cora would demand to know about Lonnie's reaction. He thought of what he'd say while he and Lonnie tended the horses and built a small fire to fry up the potatoes and the last of the eggs. He hated to always be asking, but he needed more eggs and meat if the Bells could spare some. Lonnie needed to eat better. The boy was as scrawny as a poplar sapling.

"Did you like working on the barn?" Lonnie asked.

Wyatt wasn't sure what the boy wanted with his unexpected question. "I like building things. Always have."

"Huh. What have you built?"

"Have you forgotten I built that rocker Ma had?"

"Pa broke it after you went to jail."

Wyatt glanced both ways out of habit.

Lonnie jerked around and studied the surroundings. "Sooner or later they're gonna find out."

"Maybe so, but I don't intend to tell them." He turned the conversation back to building.

Lonnie looked interested for about thirty seconds, then his expression soured. "Suppose that's why Pa broke it? 'Cause you built it?"

"Likely. But I still had the fun of making it and seeing her rock in it."

Lonnie stared at the fire.

Wyatt waited, hoping he would say something more. When he didn't, Wyatt returned to Lonnie's original question. "The Bells have been hospitable to us. Mr.

Bell is finding it hard to get around, and the womenfolk shouldn't be trying to build a barn on their own. So maybe God brought us here to help them."

"God don't care where we go or what we do." Those few words carried a whole world of misery that Wyatt would erase if it was possible, but he knew it wasn't. He could only pray Lonnie would find his way to trust. Not only trust God but trust people.

"I guess I have to believe otherwise or life looks mighty uninviting."

Lonnie's only reply was to sag over his knees.

"Supper's ready. Hold out your plate."

Lonnie did so and ate in a distracted way.

Wyatt waited, hoping his brother would open up and say what he was thinking.

Lonnie finally spoke. "Did you see the pigs?"

"Uh-huh."

"They sure are cute, aren't they?" Lonnie's eyes lit with joy in a way Wyatt hadn't seen in a long time.

"How about we have pigs on our new farm?"

Lonnie nodded, a genuine smile on his face. "I'd like that."

"Me, too." If it made his brother smile like that he'd raise a hundred pigs. "I asked Cora to go for a walk with me this evening."

Lonnie bolted to his feet. "You're going to court her? What's gonna happen to me? Nobody will want a young brother tagging along. You ever think of that?"

"You don't need to worry. In the first place, I don't think anyone is going to want a jailbird. But even if that wasn't the case, you and I are brothers. We stick together no matter what." As an afterthought, he added,

"This isn't courting. Just need to straighten up a few things with her."

"Like what?"

Wyatt wasn't about to tell him the whole reason—that Cora had grown curious about Lonnie's odd behavior. Instead, he said, "What all she needs done so we can earn our keep."

"Oh." Lonnie sat down again and nodded, but the fearful look did not leave.

Wyatt squeezed the boy's shoulder. "If it ever comes to choosing between you and someone else, I promise I'll choose you."

Lonnie nodded, but kept his eyes on the dying flames of the fire. "Want me to wash the dishes?"

"We'll do them together." He filled the basin with hot water from the fire and Lonnie grabbed a towel. The few dishes were soon done.

"What are you going to do while I see Cora?" Wyatt asked. He must talk to her but didn't care for leaving Lonnie alone.

"Guess I'll watch Fanny. Maybe she'll have her foal tonight." Worry lined his forehead. "What if she foals while you're gone? Something might go wrong."

"I expect she'll be fine, so don't worry."

"But what if—"

"You go up and find Mr. Bell. He'll know what to do."

Lonnie rocked his head back and forth.

Wyatt grabbed his chin to stop the movement. "Would you let your choices hurt Fanny and her baby?" He waited as Lonnie considered the question.

"Guess I wouldn't."

He released Lonnie's chin. "I knew you wouldn't, but kind of figured you needed to know it, too."

Lonnie snorted but a smile tugged at his lips and Wyatt knew he'd gained a small victory. He almost wished Fanny would foal while he was out walking with Cora so Lonnie would go to Mr. Bell for help. Wouldn't that be a giant step forward for his brother?

"I'll see you later."

Wyatt climbed the hill and leaned against the corner post of the garden fence to wait for Cora. The scent of flowers wafted through the air on a gentle breeze. Birds sang and scolded from the trees and fence lines. Grub wandered over and flopped down at Wyatt's feet. He scratched behind the dog's ears and earned a moist lick of Grub's tongue.

The dog equivalent of thanks.

Wyatt filled his lungs to capacity with the warm, sweet air. If only life could be like this always.

The screen door squawked open and Cora stepped out. She glanced around until she found him. The air between them shimmered with tension. She would demand answers. He must say only enough to satisfy her questions. At all costs, he must protect their secret.

She smiled, and the tightness in his chest eased.

He continued to lounge back as she crossed the yard toward him. All day, as they'd worked on the barn, she had worn a floppy straw hat. Now her head was bare. The sun shone on her hair, making it shine like gold. Each stride she took said she knew who she was. Moreover, she liked who she was and was confident of her place in the world.

He wished he could share that feeling.

As she approached, her smile never faltered. Her eyes said she had purpose.

He knew all too well what that purpose was. And he meant to delay the moment as long as he could. He pushed away from the fence post that had been his support for the past fifteen minutes and smiled at her. He was glad of her company despite the reason for it.

"Let's walk," she said.

His smile deepened. Maybe she wasn't any more anxious for the moment of truth than he.

He fell in at her side and they made their way to the river and turned to the left to walk along the bank.

"The wildflowers are so bountiful this time of year. I love the summer flowers." She pointed out a patch of brown-eyed Susans and bluebonnets. "There's some balsamroot. Ma uses the root to make a tonic and cough medicine."

Content to let her talk and simply enjoy the evening, he turned toward some flowers. "Does your ma use these for anything?"

She squatted by the patch of flowers, touching the blossoms gently. As she lifted her face to him, a smile filled her eyes. "Yes, she does." Cora straightened. "Every year, when the brown-eyed Susans—or, as she prefers to call them, black-eyed Susans—are at their best, she fills a jug with the blossoms and puts it in the middle of the table." She looked into the distance, the soft smile still on her lips. "And she repeats a poem about the black-eyed Susan who was a woman. Her sweet William was sailing away and she feared he would forget her. He said she would be present wherever he went. Her eyes would be seen in the diamonds they found, her breath would be sweeter than any spices and her skin prettier than any ivory. Every beautiful object he saw would remind him of his pretty Susan."

She drew in a slow breath. "It's a lovely poem." She shrugged. "Now you'll think me a romantic, and I'm not."

"What would be wrong if you were?" She'd certainly sent his mind on a lovely romantic journey. Oh, that he could promise some sweet Susan such fidelity. His heart hurt at the knowledge that the best he could offer any Susan was to protect her from sharing the shame of his past. For, although he'd done nothing wrong, he'd learned people only saw the fact that he'd spent time in jail.

She laughed, a merry little sound. "I'm Cora, the practical sister." She turned her steps back to the riverbank. "I take care of business."

"Because you have to or because you want to?"

She stopped dead and turned to face him squarely. "Why, both, of course."

"You mean your sisters or your ma or pa couldn't look after business if you didn't?" He didn't know why it mattered one way or the other to him, but for some reason it did. Perhaps because he felt as if she was creating a prison for herself—one with no walls or bars or guards except of her own making. And jails, real or otherwise, were not pleasant places.

She shrugged. "I suppose they could, but they don't have to. Come this way. Shh." She pressed her finger to her lips as she tiptoed toward a swampy area. "I like watching the baby ducklings." She plopped down as if prepared to stay awhile.

He sank to the ground beside her. He'd been dreading this walk and the talk that was to accompany it.

But sitting by the slough and watching birds was fine with him.

The mother duck had flapped the ducklings into hiding in the reeds at their approach, but as they sat quietly, the little family soon emerged and resumed looking for food.

He realized Cora had shifted her attention from the birds to him and studied him intently. Slowly he brought his gaze to hers. The moment had come, and he drew in a deep, steadying breath.

"I want to know why Lonnie is so afraid," she said, her voice soft, as if she thought he might react the way Lonnie had.

He'd considered how to answer, had even rehearsed what he'd say, but now it didn't feel right, so he stared at the water before them and tried to shepherd his thoughts into order.

"The reason he acted like that was because you said not all fathers are like your pa. He knows too well the truth of those words." Wyatt slowly returned his eyes to her, wanting to see her reaction, assess her response.

Her brown eyes softened and he drew in courage at the thought that she was sympathetic.

"My father beat us regularly." He recalled so many times being kicked or hit with something—whatever his pa could lay his hands on. One time, the old man had come after him with an ax. It had been one of the few times Wyatt had defended himself.

She touched the back of his hand. "That's awful. I'm so sorry. Poor Lonnie. No wonder he shrinks back when someone gets too close."

Wyatt nodded. The pressure of her fingers on his skin unwound a tightness behind his heart. "The worst part was not knowing what Lonnie endured the last year of Pa's life."

The movement of her fingers stilled. Slowly she withdrew her hand.

He tried to think what he'd said to make her pull away and look at him as if he'd admitted to some terrible behavior.

"Where were you that you didn't know?"

He resisted an urge to thump his forehead. He'd opened the door a crack and she meant to walk right through.

"I had to be away."

"You left him?" Her shock echoed through his head. Every day he'd prayed that Lonnie would be safe. In fact, it was in prison that he'd learned to pray and been forced to trust God, simply because there was nothing else he could do.

"I had no choice," he murmured.

She shook her head and turned to stare ahead. "I would never abandon my sisters."

"Sometimes you don't have any alternative." Misery edged each word, but she didn't seem to notice. Or perhaps she didn't care.

"I can't imagine any reason strong enough except death." The look she gave him seemed to point out that he was very much alive, so he couldn't claim that excuse.

His eyebrows went up. She had laid down a challenge—*give me a good reason or face my censure.*

He could not give her a good reason. That secret remained locked up for Lonnie's protection as well as his own.

She jumped to her feet. "I'd better get back before Pa comes looking for me."

He rose more slowly, aching with disappointment, though why it should be so he would have to reason out at a later date. He only knew he wished their time together could have ended differently. He touched the spot on the back of his hand where her fingers had rubbed.

Then he flung his hands apart. Bad enough to be condemned for supposedly abandoning his brother. Think how much worse it would be if she learned he'd been in jail.

No woman would ever touch him in a gentle, accepting way once the truth was discovered. It hadn't taken many days of freedom to learn this truth. People crossed the street to avoid him. Fathers and mothers dragged their daughters away as if a mere glance at him would ruin them for life. And discovery was always a possibility no matter how far he and Lonnie went. Nor had he forgotten the threat of one Jimmy Stone. Jimmy knew where they lived. He'd made a point of reminding Wyatt of the fact when Wyatt had got out of prison. Wyatt didn't doubt the man's intention to get revenge. He wasn't even that surprised when he heard a man fitting Jimmy's description had been asking about him. If Jimmy meant to find him, he would, unless they could outrun him. They had to move on as soon as possible to escape their past.

Wyatt had even considered changing their names but drew a line there. He was Wyatt Williams and he'd live and die with that name.

Cora steamed away. How could Wyatt have left Lonnie, knowing full well the abuse he would suffer? Had he done it to escape his father's wrath? He claimed he'd had no choice. She snorted. A person always had a choice. Some chose to fulfill their responsibilities. Some chose to abandon them.

All her life she'd lived with not knowing why their papa, as she always referred to the man who had been their father, had walked away from them. She couldn't even remember their last name. Not that it mattered at all.

What mattered to Cora was that a man had shirked his role as a father. For whatever reason. No doubt he would also say he didn't have a choice, but she couldn't believe there was any good reason to abandon three little girls in the middle of the prairie. They would surely have perished if Ma hadn't been out looking for her medicinal plants and found them.

The twins had quickly responded to her hugs and kisses and the food she'd shared with them from her satchel. Cora had been more guarded. Her papa's promise to return had sustained her the two days and a night of fear.

Ma had asked a few questions—enough to know Cora's papa wasn't coming back.

Agitated by the memories, Cora spun to confront Wyatt, who had followed her. "There is no good reason for abandoning family. Ever."

"You certainly have very strong opinions about it. But how can you possibly understand? You enjoy your parents' love and have two sisters to share it with. You simply couldn't begin to understand."

"Oh, I understand far better than you think." She stomped three more paces. She would not blurt out the words on the tip of her tongue, but she knew exactly how it felt to be left behind, and no excuse in this world or the next would be enough. She might just tell him that. She turned again. A hornet flew in her face and she brushed it away. It didn't leave but stung her on the cheek.

"Ouch."

Others buzzed around her, a swarm of angry hornets bent on attack. She swatted at them, shook her skirts to discourage them and stepped backward. Her heel caught on a clod of dirt and she fell down hard, smacking her head on the ground.

The hornets buzzed about her, stinging her hands and face.

Wyatt scooped her up and raced for the river. "What are you doing?" She hung on as he jostled her.

They reached the edge of the water and he set her down. "You were standing on their underground nest." He pushed aside her hair to examine her stings, pulled up her hands to look at the exposed skin. "You were fortunate. Only six stings. Sit here." He scooped up some river mud and returned to her side. "This is the best way to stop the pain. Close your eyes."

She did so. There was no denying the stings hurt. He held her chin as he plastered mud on the three on her face.

Her face grew warm. Surely he would put it down to the aftereffects of the stings, not to the sharp awareness of how gently he spread the mud, how firm his cool fingers were on her chin. Yet she felt no fear. He would not hurt her. How could she possibly know that? Hadn't she learned not to trust so easily? But none of her lessons applied to Wyatt. Or was she blindly ignoring what her head told her?

He released her chin and picked up her hand.

She quietly drew in a calming breath and watched him apply mud to the backs of her hands. "You must have had a good mother." The words came out of their own accord.

She waited, wondering how he'd respond.

He shook the rest of the mud from his hands and wiped them on the grass, then he raised his gaze to hers.

"I did. But how do you know?" His eyes were almost black as she looked at him, silhouetted against the bright sky behind his head.

"Because you have a gentle touch." Again, she spoke the truth from her heart without any thought to how he would react.

His gaze held hers, unblinking and as dark as a starless midnight.

She held her breath, waiting for him to speak or shrug or somehow indicate he'd heard and maybe even show what he thought about her words.

He laughed.

She stared. Of all the reactions he might have had, this was the most unexpected. "Why is that funny?"

He stood to his full height and grinned down at her. "Here I was thinking you would find me rough. After all, you have a mother and sisters who would normally tend your needs. I kept expecting you to tell me I was a big oaf." He laughed again. "A gentle touch, you say. I will never forget that."

He squatted in front of her. "How is your head? You took quite a fall."

Her head buzzed from the swirling confusion of her thoughts. Not from hitting the ground.

"I'm fine." She pushed to her feet. "What about you? Didn't you get stung?"

He shifted his gaze to a spot over her shoulder. "Nothing to be concerned about."

"Really? And yet you drag me over here and plaster mud on each bite?" She tried to sound teasing, but her voice caught with an overwhelming sense of tenderness. "Let me see." She grabbed his chin just as he'd done with her and felt him stiffen. He wasn't a lot different from his brother. Afraid of touches. Expecting them to be cruel. If he stayed here long he'd learn otherwise. Ma and Pa were the gentlest pair ever.

She saw no sign of stings on his face but detected three on his neck below his ear. "You have been stung. I'll get some mud." But when she tried to stand, he shook his head.

"There's some here." He pointed toward a clump that had fallen from his hands.

She loaded her finger with some and applied it to his bites. Beneath her fingertip his muscles knotted. She ignored his tension. Being this close gave her plenty of chance to study him more closely. Tiny white lines, from squinting in the sunshine, fanned out from the corners of his eyes. His black whiskers roughened sun-tanned skin.

When the stings were well bathed in mud, she wiped her fingers in the grass.

She turned her eyes toward him. His gaze jerked away as if uncomfortable with all the touching of the past few minutes, even though it had been impersonal for both them. Hadn't it?

Swallowing hard, she put eight more inches between them.

"Are you feeling up to walking home?" he asked.

His tender look caused her throat to tighten. Then some little imp made her press the back of her arm to her forehead dramatically and wobble slightly.

His arm came around her shoulders and steadied her.

"Do you think you could carry me all the way?" She managed to make her voice quaver.

"I think I'll go get my horse."

She laughed. "I'll walk. I'm fine."

He nodded, a wide grin on his face. "I figured you were."

They gave the area of the hornet's nest a wide berth.

"I'll be sure to tell the others its location." She surely didn't want anyone else to be attacked. Though, on second thought, if Ebner or some other troublemaking Caldwell cowboy got a sting or two, it sounded like justice to her.

As they neared home, she slowed her steps. "Wyatt, why would you leave Lonnie with your pa, knowing what he was like? I need to understand. I want to understand."

He stopped, faced her squarely. "I'm afraid I can't tell you anything more. I had to, and that's all I can say."

She sighed. It wasn't enough and yet she couldn't believe his reasons had been selfish. Or was she letting his taking care of her for a few minutes erase her sense of caution?

Chapter Five

Wyatt kept his gaze straight forward as they returned to the farm. His fingers tingled from touching her tender skin. His neck muscles twitched at the memory of her ministrations.

When he'd seen the hornets attack her and then heard her head smack the ground, his heart had raced. He'd had to force himself to release her when he got her to the river. Something almost primitive had urged him to hold her and protect her.

He swallowed a snort. If Mr. Bell learned the truth about Wyatt, he would reveal his wrath. How would the man do that? In Wyatt's experience the only way was with fists and boots.

Rose was in the garden when Wyatt and Cora tramped by. She looked up, saw the mud on her sister's face and her mouth fell open.

Wyatt would have slipped away to avoid being questioned, but since Cora had banged her head hard he couldn't leave until he'd informed her ma.

Rose trotted over to join them. "Looks like you fell into some mud."

"I stepped on a hornet's nest," she said. "The mud takes out the pain."

Rose turned to Wyatt. "You got stung, too?"

He nodded. "It's nothing."

"Ma will want to check on you both." Rose hustled them toward the house. "Ma," she called.

Wyatt glanced over his shoulder. "Lonnie will wonder where I am." But before he could escape, the Bells crowded around them, all asking questions at the same time. Cora explained about the hornet attack and where the nest was.

"Wyatt rescued me."

Mr. Bell eyed Wyatt closely.

Wyatt couldn't tell if the man was grateful for the rescue or wondering if Wyatt had been too forward. He didn't intend to hang around waiting to find out, and edged past Lilly.

"Did Ma look at your bites?" she asked.

"I've got to get back to Lonnie," he mumbled.

"I'll let him know you've been detained." Before he could utter a single word in protest, Lilly trotted away.

He groaned. Lonnie would not welcome a visitor.

Mrs. Bell caught his attention. "You did the right thing in applying mud, but I have an ointment that will help even more. You wait here while I get it." She hurried over to the shed near the garden.

Wyatt shifted from foot to foot and looked longingly toward escape.

Cora patted his arm. "Relax. Ma's remedies are the best."

He nodded. How could he hope for her or anyone to overlook the fact he'd been in jail? If the Bells ever learned the truth, Wyatt would be run off the place. And yet…yet…what was the harm in enjoying the ministrations of a loving family until they learned the truth? Perhaps they never would. The depth of his longing frightened him, and his mouth puckered with the anguish of such futile hope.

Mrs. Bell returned. "You two come in the house and let me take care of those stings."

Cora smiled at his helpless shrug. "It won't hurt a bit, I promise."

He nodded. It might not hurt now, but it would eventually. There was no point in hoping for any other outcome. But he allowed himself to be shepherded inside, where Rose washed Cora's stings. Mrs. Bell cleaned away the mud on his neck and applied the ointment while he stared at the floor. Every touch of the older woman's cool fingers reminded him of Cora's gentle touch and tightened the tender strands of hope about his heart.

Lilly burst into the house. "I brought Lonnie back with me."

Wyatt jerked to his feet and stared at his little brother hovering at the open door.

Lonnie's eyes were wide, his fists curled into white-knuckled balls.

"Come right in and join us," Mr. Bell called from the end of the table where he watched the proceedings.

Lonnie slid in and plopped on a chair next to Wyatt. "Heard you got stung. You okay?"

So worry over Wyatt's well-being had spurred him into joining them. It certainly made a few hornet stings worthwhile. "I'm fine. Nothing that requires all this fuss."

Mrs. Bell tsked. "The girls will tell you fussing is what I do best."

"That's right," her daughters chorused, and Mr. Bell added a deep chuckle.

Mrs. Bell moved away toward the stove. "Let's have some tea and cookies."

"There's more." Wyatt remembered what had brought him here in the first place. And it wasn't to share tea and cookies with Cora's family, as appealing as that sounded. "Cora fell on her back trying to get away from the hornets. She banged her head pretty hard."

Mrs. Bell shifted direction toward Cora and the twins rushed to her side.

"Let me have a look." Mrs. Bell took Cora's chin in her hands.

Wyatt squeezed his hand into a ball. He'd done the same thing, and despite his genuine concern about her injuries, longing had risen within him. A need to hold and comfort her. A desire to let her see into his heart, to confess his secrets and receive her understanding. Fortunately, he'd been too busy to give in to such foolish thoughts.

"Where did you hit?" Cora's ma asked her.

"Back of my head."

Mrs. Bell's fingers explored through Cora's hair, loosening wisps from the braid to feather around her head.

Wyatt ducked his head to keep from staring at the shiny strands.

"I feel quite a knot," Mrs. Bell said. "How does your head feel?"

Cora laughed. "Like someone messed my hair."

The twins laughed and Mrs. Bell made a dismissive sound.

"You be sure and let me know if you feel sick or have a headache."

"Yes, Ma." She grinned at Wyatt then turned back to her mother. "Didn't you say something about tea and cookies?"

Mrs. Bell hustled away with Rose at her side, and soon the goodies were placed on the table.

"I saw the rest of your horses," Lilly said.

Cora groaned. "Lilly, he's been on the road. They won't look like horses kept in a pasture and fed oats every day."

Wyatt leaned back. "Did you think I neglected my horses?" Did Cora think the same? After he'd stopped his journey to care for Fanny? After he'd personally taken care of Cora's bites?

But when he saw Lonnie perched on the edge of his chair, his fists on his knees, Wyatt sat back. He knew it would only take one loud word for his brother to jump to his feet and race out the door.

Cora's hands grew still.

He guessed his question had caught her off guard.

"I guess I didn't know what to expect." Her voice was low as if she meant the words as a warning.

He took them as such. She wasn't prepared to trust him until all her questions were answered. And he couldn't answer most of them. That left a vast, uncrossable chasm between them.

"I saw them for myself and they look well cared for," Lilly said.

Mr. Bell murmured approval. "How is Fanny?"

"No foal yet," Lilly and Lonnie answered at the same time.

Mrs. Bell poured the tea and passed the cookies.

It was nice. Like a family ought to be. But Wyatt had to work to keep from jiggling his legs. Families talked about everything. Asked all sorts of questions. At least, that was what he'd seen with his friends' families when he was a youngster. He had to get out of there before the questions started. He ate his cookie in three bites and drank his tea in four swallows with little regard for the way it burned on the way down. Then he pushed to his feet.

"We need to get back to the animals." It seemed an excuse that the Bells would approve of. "Thank you for the tea and cookies and ointment. Come on, Lonnie."

The boy was already on his feet, headed for the door.

"Wait." Mrs. Bell pushed her chair back.

Lonnie reached the door and made his escape.

Wyatt's breath stalled halfway up his throat. Was she about to demand to know more about them? After all, they'd sat around her table. Didn't that require a certain amount of honesty and openness? He considered bolting after Lonnie.

"I'll send some ointment with you. Put it on if your stings hurt and for sure in the morning." She handed him a small jar.

"Thank you again." He strode toward the door, grabbing his hat on the way out. Not until he reached back to shut the door did he realize Cora had followed him.

"I'm sorry for sounding as though I thought badly of you," she said.

He twisted his hat round and round. "No need to apologize."

"I believe there is. You rescued me from the hornets and knew enough to plaster on mud, and I repaid you by being doubtful of you. I'm sorry." She planted herself in front of him so he couldn't escape.

He met her look for look, banking his surprise and the thrill of her fledgling trust. But despite his best intentions, her look probed deeper than he wanted. He feared she would see into the depths of his heart. See his secret. Perhaps even see the shame and sorrow he carried as a daily burden. With a great deal of effort, he shifted his gaze away.

He meant to say again that there was no need for apologies, but the words that came out of mouth were "Glad I could be there to get you out of trouble." Where had that come from? Certainly not from any spot in his brain that he was familiar with.

She laughed, bringing his gaze back to her. The bite below her eye had swelled a bit, making her smile somewhat crooked, and he laughed in spite of himself. She stepped aside. "See you tomorrow?"

"Yup. Got a barn to build." His words were filled with amusement, anticipation and a dozen other things he should be better at resisting. Things like enjoyment of a young lady's company.

"Good night, then," she murmured.

"Good night." He had to force his feet to move, but once started they hurried after Lonnie as though he couldn't wait to get away.

Which, to his dismay, couldn't have been further from the truth.

Ma and Pa waited at the table for Cora to return. Rose and Lilly had already gone to the bedroom the three girls shared.

"Good night, Ma and Pa," Cora said, crossing the room to give them both a hug. "Have I told you lately how grateful I am that you found us and adopted us?"

Ma kissed her cheek and Pa squeezed her to his side.

"We love you like our own," Ma said.

"I know it." Perhaps God in His mercy had saved them from a father like Wyatt's.

She kissed both their cheeks, then went to her bedroom.

"Is he as nice as he seems?" From where she sat on the side of her bed came Rose's voice, filled with longing. Cora knew Rose hoped for a beautiful future. Of course, if any of the three could hope for such, it would be Rose. She was as beautiful as her name. Her red hair attracted lots of attention, some good, some not so good. But most of all, Rose had a loving heart.

Cora studied her sisters.

Rose, intent on fixing things. Lilly, clinging to the present, sure it alone provided happiness. They couldn't have been more different in their outlooks.

"Wyatt seems like a decent man. He told me his father beat them. That's why Lonnie is so nervous."

Both of her sisters gasped.

Rose spoke first. "It always amazes me how cruelly people can treat their own flesh and blood."

Lilly shifted to her twin's side and hugged her.

They all understood Rose meant more than a man like Mr. Williams. Their birth father had been so cruel as to leave the girls, never to return.

After a moment, the girls sighed and crawled into their separate beds.

"Cora, Lilly, do you dream of getting married and having your own family?" The silence lengthened as

Rose's question hung in the air, quivering with hope, yet so full of risk and danger.

Lilly sighed heavily. "People always want to know who our real parents are. I can't remember them. Ma and Pa are the only parents I want." She paused, a moment full of heaviness. "Or need."

Rose persisted. "Are you afraid to fall in love?"

"Maybe." The word from Lilly beat against Cora's thoughts.

"I thought I loved Evan," she said. "But he left. Just like our birth father."

Cora's reminder silenced them. She had to say something to lift the pall. "Wyatt says Grub looks as if he's grinning all the time."

Her two sisters chuckled at the idea. For a few minutes they laughed about their silly, useless—but well-loved—dog. Then silence settled about them, filled with contentment. Here they knew they were loved, and Ma and Pa would never hurt them.

Cora shifted, trying to get settled. Her thoughts drifted to Wyatt. Despite his confession that his father beat them, she saw something more hidden in his gaze.

As she lay there waiting for sleep, her thoughts flooded with the memory of Wyatt's touch. She touched her cheek where the hornet had stung her and where Wyatt had so tenderly applied mud.

A smile curved her lips. She tried to inform her wayward thoughts that it meant nothing. She'd only been surprised by the warmth of his hands and amazed that he could be so gentle, given his confession about a cruel father.

But she failed so badly to make her brain settle down that she curled her hands into fists and insisted she knew better than to let such things affect her. It was only because it was late at night and they had talked about their papa that she ached for such touches. Only she wanted them to be meaningful, given from a heart of love and faithfulness, not casual, given out of necessity of dealing with stings.

Tomorrow, in the light of day, her common sense would exert its hold on her and her thoughts would return to normal.

Despite her mental warnings, a smile clung to her lips as she fell asleep.

The next morning, after breakfast and chores, she made her way to the barn. Wyatt and Lonnie had already arrived, and the sound of sawing and hammering had begun.

As she crossed the yard, she reminded herself that she was the practical Miss Cora Bell.

She grabbed a hammer and went to join them.

Wyatt climbed down from the ladder and stood studying her with such intensity she almost shied away from his look. "What?" she demanded when it seemed he would never stop staring.

"Are you winking at me?"

Lonnie, standing at Wyatt's back, smothered a giggle.

"I am not. Why would you say such a thing?" Then she remembered her eye had swollen almost shut from the hornet bite. She made a sound of exasperation. "You know it's a bite. And one would think you'd be polite enough not to mention it."

"Oh, sorry." His unrepentant grin said quite the opposite. "Guess I've forgotten how to be polite." He drawled the words. "With just me and Lonnie and some horses we got kind of sloppy, I guess." He turned and winked at Lonnie. "Isn't that right, boy?"

Lonnie laughed again. "I have to say, Miss Cora, you do look a little—" He seemed to search for a word.

"Funny?" she asked. "Strange? Odd?" She planted her fists on her hips and silently waited to see if they would push the matter further.

Wyatt crossed his arms over his chest and did his best to make her think he wasn't still amused. "He means no insult. Do you, Lonnie?"

Lonnie crossed his arms over his chest and rocked back in a perfect imitation of Wyatt. Only Lonnie looked worried, as if he thought one of them would object to his teasing. "No insult meant, ma'am."

"Now it's ma'am? From odd to ma'am? What did I do to deserve that?"

Wyatt understood she was teasing and laughed. "It's awfully hard to take you serious when you keep winking."

"Oh, you." She bent down, yanked out a handful of grass and tossed it at him. "Now, are we going to get to work or not?"

Wyatt studied her again. Then shook his head. "I don't think *we* are. We are working up above our heads, using a ladder. With your eye swollen like that, I'm afraid your balance might be off. Not to mention you fell on your head."

"I am fine." She ground the words out. Since when did he tell her what she could do?

"Not for climbing up a ladder."

"Says who?"

"Me."

Lonnie tapped Wyatt's shoulder. "Don't argue."

Cora immediately repented. "It's okay, Lonnie. I'm not angry."

"Neither am I," Wyatt assured him.

"But," Cora continued, "I haven't changed my mind. I need to help."

Wyatt sighed. "Why? Don't you think I'm capable?"

She stared at him. "Do you have to turn everything into some kind of personal attack?"

His mouth grew into a tight line and his eyes narrowed. He looked at her without blinking.

So he meant to be stubborn about this, did he?

"Do you have to always be in control of everything?" He spat each word out as if it tasted bad.

"I do not." They glowered at each other.

Lonnie shifted from foot to foot and watched them nervously.

Cora knew she was overreacting. In fact, she was being as stubborn as he. How ludicrous. "We're acting like little banty roosters." She burst out laughing.

He stared and then a grin slowly grew until his whole face relaxed. He tipped his head back and roared with laughter.

She sobered as she watched him. Goodness, but the man had a nice laugh. His merriment rippled through her insides.

He stopped chuckling but continued to grin at her in such a way that she felt blessed.

She must have hit her head harder than she thought to be so silly.

He nodded toward the garden. "Weren't you in the midst of hilling potatoes?"

"That's not very subtle." Yet she couldn't help but be amused by his attempt to divert her from the barn.

He took off his hat and rubbed his hair, mussing it into a riot of waves, making her want to smooth it back into place. "I'll tell you what. Lonnie and I will help in the garden today."

Cora considered the idea. "I haven't had such a good offer in a long time." She let a beat of silence follow her words, then added, "Maybe forever. Usually I have to beg people to help hoe."

He nodded. Did she detect a look of regret? But what better way to see what the man was made of? Would he find excuses not to work or would he put his back to the task and dig in?

"Like I said, we'll work in the garden this morning."

Lonnie groaned. "Do I have to help?"

Wyatt considered his younger brother for a full twenty seconds then shrugged. "Do you have another way of paying for your food?"

"I could snare a rabbit and roast it."

"Fine. You do that."

The boy scampered off.

Cora stared after him. "I thought you'd insist on him helping." It disappointed her that he hadn't.

"Unwilling help isn't much help most times, wouldn't you say?"

She nodded. But still she wondered if Wyatt shouldn't ask a little more of his brother.

"Besides, I want him to learn he can disagree with me without me getting angry."

Her disappointment gave way to respect. Wyatt had made a noble choice, not a lazy one. He really cared about his brother.

Which made it all the more confusing to know he'd left Lonnie to face their pa's beatings alone. Why would he do that? What could have constituted an "unavoidable" reason?

There were too many unanswered questions about Wyatt Williams to let herself be influenced by gentle touches and noble choices.

Chapter Six

Cora led the way to the garden, retrieved a pair of hoes from the shed and handed him one. "There's weeding to be done." She pointed toward a row of carrots, moved to the next row and set up a steady rhythm of chopping down weeds.

Wyatt hadn't used a hoe since he was a boy at home, and within half an hour remembered how much he hated it. Hoeing was hard work. Where was Mr. Bell with his four-in-one invention?

Cora didn't pause for anything but worked steadily up and down the rows.

He wiped his brow. The sun was way too hot. His mouth grew dry but he would not stop to get a drink. His admiration grew for the tough young woman working at his side. Seemed she didn't let challenges slow her down. He let his thoughts go in a direction he knew he should not allow. What would she do if she learned the truth about him? Would she turn her back on him, or would she fearlessly face the dishonor of his past? Not that he'd ever make her choose.

He bent his back to the task and started down another row. In a short while, Cora appeared before him with a bucket of water and a dipper.

"Thought you might be getting thirsty by now."

He leaned against the hoe. "I'm about parched."

"You're welcome to stop and get a drink or pour water over your head anytime. I don't expect you to work nonstop. After all, I'm not a slave driver."

"Good to know."

"Did you think I was?"

He shrugged. "I didn't know what to think." He'd learned to work without complaining or expecting a break long before his prison days. He drank his fill of cold water and returned to hoeing.

Cora set the bucket at the end of the garden and picked up her hoe again.

A few minutes later, Rose and Lilly joined them.

"With all this help we'll have the garden clean in no time," Cora said, sounding as relieved at the thought as he was.

Again he wondered if Mr. Bell had finished adjusting the four-in-one hoe.

Then, as if Wyatt's thoughts had called him, Mr. Bell crossed the yard dragging the massive hoe behind him. He reached the edge of the garden and turned the blades over into the soil. Each of the four matched the spaces between the rows.

"Let's see if it works. Who wants to try it first?"

To Wyatt's surprise, none of the girls volunteered. "I'll give it a try. Anything that makes this work easier would be a great invention." Did the three girls smile behind their hands?

He grabbed the sturdy handle and tugged the hoe. He grunted and leaned into it with all his might. His muscles strained and then the inertia gave way to motion. Slow, torturous forward movement. The hoe stalled. His neck spasmed in protest. He looked behind to see what caused the problem. Nothing but a lump of dirt. He pulled and pulled and pulled.

The hoe refused to move, and he bent over his knees gasping for breath. As soon as he could breathe halfway normally he faced Mr. Bell. "Sir, it would take a small horse to pull that thing."

Mr. Bell nodded as he studied the useless tool. "You might have something there." He turned the hoe over so he could drag it and trotted back to the workshop.

Cora groaned loudly, making no attempt to hide her frustration.

Cora looked at Wyatt, her eyes narrowed and accusing. "Next we'll have a herd of small horses dragging clunky hoes in the garden, ripping up everything in sight. I can see it already."

Rose and Lilly came to her side.

"You have to understand something about Pa." Cora explained to Wyatt. "He's always coming up with these really good ideas, but usually they end up causing more work for us. But we love him, so we generally laugh and carry on."

Rose continued the story. "Like the time Pa bought turkeys."

Lilly said, "He figured he could get them to eat the weeds from around his fruit trees."

Rose took over from her sister. "Pa soon discovered he couldn't teach turkeys anything. They raided our garden so often it became a full-time job to keep them out."

"So Pa thought he'd get a dog to herd them," Cora added.

Beside her, her sisters chuckled and she nodded. "Wait until you hear what he brought home to herd the turkeys." Unable to stop laughing, she pointed to Grub sitting at the end of the garden, his head cocked as he listened to them.

"Grub? He got Grub as a herding dog?" A chuckle began in the pit of his stomach. "Did he keep them out of the garden?"

Three heads shook in unison. Cora waited, her eyes filled with expectancy.

She didn't have to wait long. Wyatt tried to picture the flop-eared dog trying to control turkeys. He wondered if Grub would end up tripping on his ears or falling over his feet or barking after the turkeys had all disappeared into a safe hiding place. No wonder the girls laughed. Chuckling, he returned to his work.

His smile lifted his lips throughout the morning and seemed to lighten the work, as well.

Lilly started to sing and the others joined her, the twins singing soprano and Cora a throaty alto.

"She'll be coming round the mountain when she comes…."

They paused and looked at Wyatt.

He continued to hoe as if he wasn't aware of three pairs of eyes on him.

"Sing with us," Cora said.

He continued to attack the weeds.

"Wyatt?"

"You wouldn't want me to."

"Why not?"

He stopped hoeing and looked at her. "I don't sing. I growl." Fellow inmates had jeered at him, so he knew it to be true. Not that he hadn't been aware of the fact long before then.

Cora glanced at the others, who both listened intently. "Surely it can't be that bad."

"Or it could be worse."

"Oh, come on. Join us. Singing is fun."

"Yeah," the twins echoed, and taking his silence for agreement they began again.

"She'll be coming round the mountain when she comes...."

Aware of three sets of eyes on him, he growled, "Yee-haw."

Cora nodded soberly. "We accept your yee-haw." And she started the song again.

He good-humoredly contributed his part.

The sun rose overhead. Shouldn't Lonnie be back by now? Wyatt looked toward the spot where he'd appear if he came from the campsite. No sign of him. He glanced around but didn't see Lonnie in any direction. He bent back to the hoeing but every few seconds looked about for him.

"Are you worried about Lonnie?" Cora asked.

"He's a big boy." Still, Lonnie had spent so much time hiding from people, Wyatt wasn't sure he could handle himself in the open.

"You're plainly worried. Why don't you check on him?"

"I think I will." He returned the hoe to the shed and jogged toward the camp. "Lonnie."

No answer. No boy stretched out sleeping in the shade.

Wyatt shaded his eyes and searched the prairie for signs of his brother. Nothing. He scanned the trees along the river, straining for movement in the shadows. A crow stirred the treetops, but nothing else.

Should he be concerned? Should he start looking?

"He's not back?" Cora called from up the embankment.

"No." Wyatt told himself Lonnie was old enough to look after himself, but he wasn't convinced.

"Do you want help looking for him?"

He wanted to say no. Because he wanted to believe Lonnie was okay. But if the boy had stumbled into trouble…

"I'd feel better if I knew he wasn't lying injured somewhere."

She trotted down the incline to his side. "Do you want us to search together or split up?"

"You know the country better than I do, so maybe we should stay together." Besides, he rather preferred to have her company.

They made their way downriver, calling Lonnie's name often and stopping every few feet to look around them.

He was the one who spotted a bit of twine and snagged it up. "He's been this way." He would have used the twine for snaring a rabbit.

"Then we'll keep heading in this direction." She marched past him.

Wyatt stared at the bit of twine he held and was hit by a memory, strong and vibrant.

"Wyatt?" Cora came back. "What is it?"

He couldn't stop staring at the bit of rope and remembering. "It was the summer I was sixteen and Lonnie eleven. I'd gotten a job working in the hardware store, hoping to use the money I earned to buy myself a horse. Pa raised fine riding stock but refused to give me my own horse. Said it didn't hurt a boy none to walk. 'Shank's mare will take you any place you need to go,' he used to tell me. So every day I walked the five miles to town to work at the Kansas Hardware and Supplies." He'd liked the job just fine. "Mr. McIver was a fair man to work for and seemed to like what I did. Every day I thought about what sort of horse I'd get. Maybe a mare so I could start my own herd. Or a fast gelding so I could win money racing at the local fairs." He stopped as bitterness surged up his throat.

Cora brushed his upper arm. "What happened?" she asked in a quiet, caring way, as if she guessed it was an unhappy story.

Her gentle touch and sweet concern neutralized the bitterness and he sighed. "My father happened." A moment passed and then he continued.

"To this day I don't know what he was mad about, but he was in a rage when he rode up to the store and bellowed my name. Mr. McIver went outside to suggest he calm down, which only made Pa worse. He jumped from the horse, pushed Mr. McIver aside and stormed into the store." He held up the bit of twine. "I'd been cutting some store string when my pa came in. Still held it in my hands when we got home. He grabbed me by the scruff of the neck, cuffed my ears until they rang and dragged me from the store."

He couldn't go on as he thought of his humiliation.

"Wyatt." Her hand smoothed up and down his arm. Soothed his shame and sorrow at the memory of that day.

"Several upright citizens stood on the sidewalk watching. One man had his daughter at his side. A pretty young thing I thought was my friend. Her father hurried her away and informed her she was to have nothing more to do with me. Ever."

"Oh, Wyatt. As if it was your fault."

"Well, you know how it is. The sins of the fathers will be visited on their children." His rejection by decent folk had started long before he'd gone to jail. His jail time had only provided more reason to look at him with disfavor.

"Or maybe man judges by outward appearance but God looks on the heart."

He took a moment to digest her comment. "It would be nice if man also judged by the heart."

"How do you know that some don't?"

"I suppose I haven't seen much evidence of it."

She looked thoughtful a moment, then asked, "Did you buy yourself a horse that summer?"

"Never went back. My pa made sure of it." He had ridden his horse home while Wyatt had walked. He'd been tempted to dawdle but Pa would have known if he did, and Wyatt hadn't intended to provide him with any reason to strap him. Though Pa hadn't much cared whether or not he'd had a reason. His own bad mood was motive enough.

Wyatt didn't wait for Cora to say anything about his lost job. Or his lost dream of buying a horse. He'd eventually purchased his own just before he'd gone to jail. Pa had gladly taken over the horse. But now Wyatt and Lonnie owned all that was left of Pa's once fine breeding stock.

"I need to find Lonnie," he said. Perhaps he, too, had been overwhelmed by bitter memories. Wyatt couldn't guess what Lonnie would do if he took a mind to run.

Cora fell in step with him as they continued to follow the river. They reached the rocky ford that led to town and Wyatt halted. "He wouldn't go into town."

"Okay. Then where would he go?"

Wyatt turned full circle to study his surroundings. Trees along the river. Hills undulating to the west. Open prairie to the east. For some reason, the open spaces called to him, speaking freedom. "What's over there?" He pointed east.

"It looks flat, doesn't it?"

She waited for him to nod. "But there are hollows where a horse can disappear."

If Lonnie had discovered he could hide from view, wouldn't he think that a good thing? "Let's go see."

They crossed the river on rocks and tramped over the grassy land. If he wasn't concerned about Lonnie he might have enjoyed the sun on his shoulders, the scent of wild grass wafting up to him and the swing of Cora's sure stride at his side.

"Look around you," she said, and he did. "See how the ground rises up around us."

"I see what you mean." They had gone down enough of an incline to be in a wide hollow. "Lonnie could be hurt in a place like this and we'd never find him."

"God sees him. He will lead us to him."

She spoke with such confidence he stared at her. "You believe that completely, don't you?"

"God sees everything. His eyes wander to and fro across the land."

Wyatt didn't doubt that for a moment. "I mean, how can you be so sure He'll show us where Lonnie is?"

"Because I asked Him to. Doesn't the Word promise

if we ask, we will receive?" She stopped in front of him. "Don't you believe in God and His love?"

"I do, but I sometimes have trouble trusting Him when things aren't going the way I think they should." Her faith put him to shame.

"Oh, you mean you think you know better than God what is best."

Said that way, it sounded presumptuous. "No. I don't think so."

"If God asks you to trust, do you decide you can't? Or won't?"

"Lady, you sure are blunt."

"I believe in speaking the truth. Kindly, of course."

"Of course." They had climbed to a spot that gave them a wide-open view. And he saw nothing but miles of grass. "For all we know, he is twenty miles away."

"'You have not because you ask not.' So ask God to show us where Lonnie is."

He wanted to point out that she'd asked and believed, but she'd no doubt have forty-five arguments as to why he had to do the asking.

"That is, if you believe God can show you."

Believing God *could* had never been a problem. Wondering if He *would* was an entirely different matter. But with Cora watching him, silently challenging him, he knew it was time to put his faith to the test. "Do you expect me to pray aloud?"

"Do you object to doing so?"

Surprisingly enough, he didn't. Somehow her faith reinforced his and he felt an invisible link between them. He bowed his head and closed his eyes. "God in heaven, You see everything. You know everything.

Could You please show us where Lonnie is? And please keep him safe. He's all I've got left. Amen."

"Amen," she said. "Now let's find him."

She headed off.

"How do you know that's the right direction?"

"Does it feel wrong to you?"

He shrugged. "Can't say one way or the other."

"Then it will do."

"I can't argue with that." He caught up to her and they walked on. They approached a small rise.

"Let's go there," he said. "We'll be able to see farther."

They climbed to the top and looked about. In the distance, he spied a small animal and pointed it out to Cora. The animal moved. "It's not an animal. It's Lonnie." He shouted his brother's name but Lonnie couldn't hear.

Cora picked up her skirts and raced toward the boy but Wyatt outdistanced her and reached him first by seconds. They both crouched by Lonnie's side.

Lonnie sat with a frightened rabbit in his hands. He looked up at Wyatt. Dried tears streaked his cheeks. "I couldn't kill it."

Wyatt eased the rabbit from Lonnie's grip and set it free. It sat huddled and afraid for a moment, then hopped away in a crazy zigzag.

Wyatt watched Lonnie. He didn't know how to deal with this situation. The boy had gone out to snare a rabbit for their meal. How did he expect to do that without killing the animal?

"I never killed an animal before." Lonnie shivered. "I couldn't do it."

Wyatt nodded.

Cora sat cross-legged in front of Lonnie, her elbow brushing Wyatt's arm. Wyatt took comfort in her presence.

"Lonnie, I don't know what to say," Wyatt said.

Lonnie rubbed his leg, brushed away a bit of fur. "I'd sooner go hungry."

"That's fine." Though he doubted Lonnie would enjoy being hungry.

"I don't understand how someone could hurt an animal."

Wyatt waited, hearing the agony in Lonnie's voice and knowing the boy had sat there, maybe for hours, trying to sort out his feelings.

"If I can't hurt an animal, how could I hurt a person? Especially someone I knew and was supposed to love? How could anyone do that?" He groaned as if feeling real physical pain.

Wyatt knew the pain was in his memory. As was the reality of being treated cruelly by a father who was supposed to love him.

Cora took Lonnie's hands.

Lonnie ducked his head, likely not wanting her to see his dried tears or the depths of his pain.

"Lonnie, you ask a very good question. How can people hurt each other? How can love hurt?"

He raised his head and nodded.

"It isn't supposed to. But sometimes things get broken and don't mend. Like this man in town who broke his leg and it never healed properly. He has to use a crutch, and Ma says he endures a lot of pain."

"Does it make him mean?"

"Not that I know of. But what if his heart had been

hurt and it didn't get tended to, so it never healed? Maybe that person wouldn't be able to love."

"And he'd be mean?"

Cora nodded. "I guess so."

Lonnie shook his head. "Can someone fix him?"

"I think God could, but I also think there are people who were hurt when they were so young they don't know they're broken. It's all they've ever known."

Wyatt sat back on his heels. Was he broken inside? Was Lonnie? About all they'd ever known was hate and anger. Was that to be normal for them?

Not if he could help it. God had led them to Lonnie. Perhaps He'd also led them to the Bells so he and Lonnie could learn how to be different from their father. If that was so, he needed to spend as much time as possible with Cora and her family, learning everything they could and maybe getting fixed inside.

Cora got to her feet. "Let's go home." She held out a hand to both Lonnie and Wyatt.

Wyatt took her hand and held it even after he was on his feet. She didn't pull away or he would have put some distance between them. Perhaps she sensed that he felt the need of healing and she didn't mind doing what she could to help. A smile started deep inside and claimed his entire being before it settled on his lips.

Cora knew God had provided the words she'd offered Lonnie. But as she spoke them, she realized they were for herself, as well. Her papa had left them. There had to be something broken inside him that he did such a vile thing. Thinking of it that way made it less hurtful.

She clung to Wyatt's hand as they tramped across the prairie, needing the strength his presence provided.

He was so patient and gentle with Lonnie. Whatever secrets he hid that had forced him to leave Lonnie with an abusive father, she grew more and more convinced he was a good man.

They crossed the river and returned to the farm. When she saw Pa waiting at the end of the lane, Cora slipped her hand from Wyatt's and eased away from his side.

Pa sheltered his eyes with his hand and waited until they drew closer to speak. "I was beginning to get worried."

"Everyone is fine," Cora said. "Lonnie lost track of the time."

"Ma saved some dinner for you. You'd best hurry in and eat it so she can clean up."

"Yes, Pa." It was on the tip of her tongue to suggest Wyatt and Lonnie might like to eat, too, but at Pa's look she hurried away. Just before she stepped inside, she glanced back. Pa and Wyatt were talking, while Lonnie made his way toward their camp.

She'd check this afternoon and make sure they had plenty of food. After all, they were working in exchange for supplies.

The kitchen was empty when she stepped inside. Ma would be napping and the twins were out doing something. Maybe they'd finish hoeing the garden and hilling the potatoes so she could go back to working on the barn.

She quickly ate the cheese sandwiches Ma had left for her, then cleaned the kitchen.

Ma came out as she finished. "You were gone a long time."

Cora explained how she'd gone with Wyatt to find

Lonnie and discovered him upset about hurting the rabbit. "Can people broken inside be fixed?" she asked.

Ma sat across from her and took her hands. "It's a shame that people get their hearts and souls hurt. Usually it's at the hands of another person. That is so wrong." She shook her head. Her thumbs rubbed the back of Cora's hands in a comforting way.

Again, Cora's heart welled with gratitude that she and the twins had been adopted by such loving parents.

"I'm sure God can heal such a person," Ma continued. "But often He uses other people to do it." She thought a moment. "I expect God brought Wyatt and Lonnie here so we could be part of their healing. Especially Lonnie. That poor boy." She'd told her parents how violent Wyatt's father had been.

Cora smiled. If God wanted her to be part of healing for Lonnie and Wyatt, she'd gladly do what she could.

That afternoon she persuaded Wyatt she was fit as a fiddle and able to return to helping build the barn.

"We're doing the joists next." His voice revealed a hefty dose of doubt.

"I can help with that." She eyed the timbers that would support the floor of the loft. No way would she shirk from helping with them. She pulled on her leather gloves. "I'm ready."

He quirked his eyebrows and signaled for Lonnie to bring a rope. Wyatt fashioned a pulley, then they carried a beam to the ladder and Wyatt climbed to the top of the walls. "Lonnie, you guide it." Wyatt pulled the wood steadily upward.

"What am I going to do?" Cora demanded.

"Help Lonnie steady the beam."

Was he trying to appease her? But she stood with

Lonnie and did as directed. One by one the beams were lifted up and nailed in place. And the afternoon slipped away.

Wyatt climbed down and wiped his brow. He downed three dippers full of water and poured two more over his head.

Cora watched the water wash over his skin and tried not to be distracted. How was she to be part of their healing if all they did was grunt and lift all day long? She turned to the ladder. "I want to see how it looks." She climbed to the floor of the loft—or what would be the loft when the barn was completed. All it was now was open beams.

She nodded her approval and began to back down but only got partway before Wyatt's hands clamped around her waist and he lifted her to the ground. Her heart caught in her throat at the unexpected touch. She calmed her jittery nerves and turned to face him, determined to show him the kindness she experienced every day. "Thank you," she murmured, and at the way he looked at her she could manage no more.

At that moment, Ma crossed the yard toward them and Cora stepped back two feet, not wanting Ma to think she'd been acting inappropriately with their guest.

"Would you please join us for supper?" Ma asked.

Lonnie stiffened as if he feared to sit around the table with them, even though he'd been persuaded to join them for tea and cookies. Come to think of it, that day he'd perched on the edge of his chair the whole time, expecting danger and ready to flee.

She shifted her gaze to Wyatt. He gave Lonnie a reassuring smile, then turned to Ma. "It's most generous of you and we accept."

Cora wondered how it was that Wyatt wasn't as fearful as Lonnie. Did it have something to do with his having to leave for a year? Or had it been a year? She tried to recall exactly what he'd said and realized she might have assumed the time period.

Where had he been and what constituted an unavoidable reason?

Chapter Seven

Wyatt fought for mental equilibrium. When he'd noticed that the ladder was listing to one side with Cora partway down the rungs, he'd hurried to lift her down, never once thinking how she would feel to be swept off her feet in such an unceremonious way. When she'd turned to confront him, exuberant color had stained her cheeks.

His own face had stung with embarrassment and his throat had closed off, making it impossible to explain why he'd done such a brash thing.

He had about regained his voice when Mrs. Bell had extended her invitation.

He should likely have refused her offer, but he was tired and didn't feel like making a decent meal. Besides, if they were to learn about family from the Bells, he needed to spend time with them.

He fell in beside Cora as they crossed to the house.

But the first step inside the door caused him to hesitate, Lonnie at his back. The entire family gathered in the kitchen, Mr. Bell sitting at the end of the table, Lilly and Rose carrying steaming dishes forward.

He didn't belong here. If his past should be discovered, it would bring shame and disgrace to these innocent people. And he would lose something he grew to cherish more each day—the acceptance of a normal, loving family.

He tried to back up but Lonnie pressed forward, making it impossible.

"You can sit here." Mrs. Bell indicated a chair.

Still he hesitated, then he breathed a lungful of savory scents. A homemade meal sure beat beans and biscuits, even with fresh farm produce added. He stepped forward and sat on the chair.

They all took their seats. Mrs. Bell sat at the opposite end of the table from her husband, Rose and Lilly facing him, Cora to his right and Lonnie to his left.

"We'll ask the blessing." Mr. Bell held his hands toward a daughter on each side. The twins joined hands and reached for their mother's.

Cora held her hand toward Wyatt. He swallowed a huge lump. Was this what families did? Hold hands around the table? The idea lived and breathed welcome and acceptance.

Again, he fought against allowing such feelings. But he meant to learn how a decent family behaved.

Mrs. Bell had taken Lonnie's hand.

Wyatt felt his brother stiffen, and then he grabbed Wyatt's hand and squeezed hard. Knowing how much Lonnie needed family lessons, Wyatt tried desperately to shed his caution. But he seemed stuck between wanting to guard the shame of his past and wanting to move forward and take part in family life with the Bells.

"Cora," Mr. Bell said. "Let's pray."

She placed her hand close to his plate, her fingers open and inviting.

Wyatt stared at it, felt the expectant waiting from everyone at the table. He quickly considered his options: push away from the table and run from the room, giving up a hot meal that had his taste buds working hard, or hold hands with a young woman who had made him laugh, bossed him about and offered him something he couldn't remember ever having—acceptance.

He took her hand and bowed his head. Her warm fingers curled around his. A thousand emotions erupted inside him with such force he thought they'd explode from his skin—longing as deep as the deepest mine, hope as wide as the ocean and an emotion he could only name as anger. Anger at the way he'd been raised. At a violent father who had pushed Lonnie to the breaking point.

The year Wyatt spent in prison had irrevocably changed him, making him less trusting, and it would always change how others viewed him.

He even admitted a shred of anger toward his ma, who had seemed unable to stand up to her husband, and who had simply been a shadowy figure in the background. Though, he soothed his ruffled feelings, it hadn't always been so. He remembered far better times, but they'd been swallowed up by the bad things that followed.

Mr. Bell said, "Amen."

Wyatt didn't know who jerked away faster—him or Cora. The girls passed the food around and chattered up a storm, making it unnecessary for Wyatt to make conversation. The conversation also made it possible for him to cork the bottle of his agitated emotions.

"Ma and I are almost finished cleaning the garden shed," Rose said.

Beside him, Cora spread butter on a thick slice of homemade bread. "Good to hear."

Wyatt also buttered on his bread and bit down. His taste buds thanked him profusely. "Sweet-cream butter. It's very good."

"Cora's specialty," Lilly said. "People come from miles around to buy her butter. And her cheese."

"I can see why." Right then and there, he decided he could live on freshly baked bread and sweet-cream butter the rest of his life. But the meal offered more than that—mashed potatoes and rich gravy, new carrots bathed in butter, cooked green beans fresh from the garden and roast pork.

A few minutes later, he cleaned his plate and leaned back. "Thank you. That was an excellent meal. I'm trying to remember when I've had better." He tapped his chin. Sure did beat the unpalatable rations they'd lived on for the past week. As a child, every meal had been off flavored by the fear of what their father would do. "Nope. Can't recall a time. How about you, Lonnie?" The boy had eaten a goodly amount and then some.

"Sure better'n what you make." The words had slipped out unguarded, and he ducked his head as if expecting Wyatt to take objection.

Wyatt laughed. "Sure was." How he wished Lonnie would stop acting as though Wyatt was about to whip him.

The others chuckled.

"We still have dessert," Cora said, and from the cupboard Lilly brought a chocolate cake so rich it was almost black. Mrs. Bell cut generous slices and served each with spoon-thick cream.

Wyatt's stomach thought he'd died and taken it to heaven.

From the barely audible sighs at his left, he knew Lonnie felt the same. Their ma had seldom bothered with what she called "fancy baking." As her strength dwindled, and her interest in life faded, so had her efforts at preparing meals.

Once they were all finished, the girls took away the dishes and poured tea for everyone while Mr. Bell opened a well-worn black leather Bible.

"We always have a time of Bible reading after supper," he explained to Wyatt. "I hope you don't mind joining us."

He felt Mr. Bell's silent waiting and knew the man was asking Wyatt where he stood on faith matters. He didn't mind telling. "Mr. Bell, I am a firm believer in God's grace. I'd be honored to be part of your Bible reading time."

Mr. Bell considered him unblinkingly for a moment, then nodded.

Wyatt couldn't tell if his answer had satisfied the man or not.

"We are reading the last chapter of Matthew," Mr. Bell said. "'Lo, I am with you always, even unto the end of the world.'" As the older man continued reading, the words refreshed Wyatt's soul as much as the food had refreshed his body.

"We'll pray now." The Bells again reached out and held hands. This gesture no doubt knit the family members together. He wasn't likely to be woven into this family, but he and Lonnie could do something similar.

He reached for Cora's hand, again feeling a warm rush of emotions threatening to blow away his control.

Rather than try to understand what it meant, he focused on Mr. Bell's prayer as he asked God to bless all sorts of friends and neighbors. When he said, "Bless the Caldwells," Cora's fingers squeezed Wyatt's hard. She'd said the Caldwells didn't welcome the farm in the middle of their ranch.

Seemed she wasn't quite as concerned with their well-being as her pa.

Upon Mr. Bell's "amen," the family pushed from the table.

Wyatt and Lonnie did the same. "Thank you again for a wonderful meal and your hospitality." Wyatt backed toward the door with Lonnie at his side.

"No need to rush off," Mr. Bell said. "Stay and visit awhile."

Wyatt glanced about the room. The evening sun flashed through the window and splashed light on the back of Cora's head as she leaned over the table to gather up teacups.

She turned and smiled at him. "Of course, we expect you to help with the dishes." She tossed each of them a towel.

And as easy as that, he decided to stay.

Red-headed Rose had her hands in a basin of soapy water and handed him a plate to dry. Lilly took a dish of scraps out to Grub. Mrs. Bell lifted a basket from a nearby shelf and began to darn a sock while Mr. Bell sat at the table, scratching away on a piece of paper. Wyatt glanced at what the man did. Seemed he worked on a design for that four-in-one hoe. Wyatt knew there was a serious flaw in the design. It weighed too much to be practical. Would Mr. Bell find a solution?

Cora took the dishes from Wyatt and Lonnie as they dried them and put them into the cupboard. Their hands brushed each time and Wyatt's skin grew warmer with each touch.

"We're done." Rose carried the wash water outside and dumped it on the flowers.

"I'll take the slop to the pigs," Lilly said.

"Can I help?" Lonnie asked, and received an invitation to join Lilly.

Wyatt stood near the kitchen cupboard wondering if he should wait for Lonnie or excuse himself.

Cora took the towel from Wyatt's hand and went outside to hang it to dry.

He followed her out of the house. He moseyed over to the corner of the garden and leaned against the post.

Cora joined him there. "Lonnie seems to have forgotten about the rabbit."

"I hope so." Wyatt tried to think how to express his appreciation for her family's kindness, but everything he thought of sounded like an invitation for her to ask more about his family. He'd said about all he meant to say on that subject. His teeth creaked as his jaw clenched. There were so many secrets to protect. He would never forget the sight of Lonnie standing over their bleeding father, trembling, tears running down his face.

He shuddered.

Cora no doubt took it to be because of Lonnie and the rabbit. "He is so tenderhearted. I believe that means he can become a strong, confident man who is no longer afraid people will treat him as his father did."

Wyatt forced himself to relax. "He's young. He can change." With good examples like the Bells to teach him. Unless someone learned the truth of their past. He silently vowed that if anyone discovered he'd been in jail, he would never reveal it was Lonnie who had beaten their father.

Cora touched his arm. "God led us to find Lonnie this afternoon. I truly believe He directs our every step. Remember that verse in Jeremiah where God says His thoughts to us are for peace and not evil, to give us an expected end?"

An expected end? Wasn't that a warning not to think he could change anything?

He hadn't asked the question aloud, but she addressed it anyway. "Pa says the expected end means the kind of end we can expect from God. So it means good things, blessings, His tender care."

Wyatt couldn't take his eyes from her glowing face as she spoke. His heart caught her faith and swelled with joy at what God had promised. "You believe so deeply."

She nodded. "The more I choose to believe in God's love and goodness, the more blessed I feel." She smiled up at the sky. "Sometimes I could dance for joy."

He'd like to see that. He'd like to dance with her. What better time than now, he thought as he reached for her.

But Lonnie jogged toward them just then and Wyatt stepped back. He realized how foolish it would be to let his guard down. "We'll be going now," he said to Cora. "Good night."

He and Lonnie made their way back to the campsite. "We need to give the horses some oats." If he fed them well while they rested they would be in good shape for more travel when the time came. His insides twisted at the thought of leaving. He shook his head hard. Had he so quickly forgotten who he was?

Wyatt paid special attention to Fanny. "She'll have that foal any time now."

"Lilly let me help feed the pigs," Lonnie called from where he fed the horses. "They're so sweet. At least, the baby ones are. Do you know Lilly names each of them and they come when she calls?"

"Uh-huh." He had a hard time keeping his attention on talk of pigs when his thoughts hovered between hope and despair.

"Lilly says they're a lot smarter than people think." Lonnie continued to chatter about the pigs as they tended the horses and while they prepared for bed. At least he seemed to have forgotten the incident on the prairie.

Later, as they lay side by side in their bedrolls, Lonnie sighed. "Do you think I'm broken inside like Cora talked about?"

So the incident hadn't been forgotten after all. Wyatt considered his answer carefully. "I think our pa was broken. We might be broken a little because of that, but didn't she say sometimes people don't realize they aren't normal? So they don't know they need fixing."

"I guess."

Wyatt continued, silently praying Lonnie would understand he could one day become whole. "The Bells seem nice, don't they?"

"Uh-huh."

"The sort of family we wished we had. Maybe if we watch carefully we can learn to be like them."

"Did you like how they prayed together?"

"It was good."

"Cora's nice, don't you think?"

"They all are." Though he'd taken little note of Rose and Lilly. Natural enough, he reasoned, seeing as he spent most of his time working beside Cora.

"But Cora seems extraspecial. She's so smart and kind and—I don't know. Just real nice."

"Indeed." He could add more description—beautiful, full of faith, generous, determined, loyal—

That stopped him. Her loyalty belonged to her family. She'd do everything she could to protect them.

He flipped to his side and tried to find a comfortable position. Tried desperately to ignore the mocking words in his head.

He posed a risk to their security and acceptance. She'd defend her family against him if she learned he was a jailbird. He'd grown used to the idea that people would shun him because of his past. Had figured he could survive without their approval. But he hadn't figured on meeting someone like Cora who made him want to start over with an unblemished slate.

He flipped to his other side and groaned. No matter how hard he tried to make it happen, he knew his heart would bear a permanent wound when she found out the truth and—

He couldn't even think how she'd react.

How he'd continue to breathe and eat and walk.

Cora and the twins retired to their bedroom. She saw Lilly and Rose exchange knowing looks.

"What?"

Lilly perched on the edge of her bed. "He makes you laugh."

"Don't I usually laugh?"

Lilly nodded. "But you sounded real happy talking to him in the garden."

Cora tapped Lilly's arm. "I'm always happy."

"But not that kind of happy. Aren't I right, Rose?"

The pair nodded.

"Honestly, I have no idea what you mean."

"We know you don't, which is really sad."

Cora wouldn't admit there was a hint of truth to their observations and didn't reply.

Rose sighed. "It was kind of fun telling our stories, wasn't it?" She glanced from Cora to Lilly and back again. "I like having company."

Cora tipped her head. "I never thought of it before." They attended church every Sunday in Bar Crossing and each Saturday went to town to sell their goods and buy supplies, but their friends very rarely visited the farm. No doubt they didn't want to get involved in the feud the Caldwells wouldn't abandon.

She and Anna, the preacher's daughter, always found plenty to talk about when they got together. Though, on closer examination, Anna did most of the talking.

It *was* nice to have visitors on the farm, but she didn't want to admit how much she enjoyed Wyatt's company. Not even to herself. "Life is simply fun if you let it be."

The twins agreed.

The three of them crawled into their beds and opened their Bibles to read a passage—something Ma had taught them. At first, she'd read to them, but as they grew older they were each presented with Bibles of their own. In the flyleaf of each Ma had written a blessing. Although Cora knew the words by heart, she turned to that page first. "To the daughter of my heart:

You are strong and bold in life. May you also be strong and bold in your faith. May our love hold you close all the days of your life." Their parents had given each of them a special verse, and Ma had penned Cora's below the blessing. "Proverbs 3:5-6: Trust in the Lord with all thine heart; and lean not unto thine own understanding. In all thy ways acknowledge him, and he shall direct thy paths."

She breathed in the words, let them settle deep into her heart with a comforting touch. Throughout the day, she'd discovered surprising longings and desires welling up. Always when she was around Wyatt. When he touched her. When he revealed tenderness and strength at the same time.

She needed to keep her thoughts focused on God's will and God's ways and not be drawn aside by her silly reactions to a man she barely knew.

She read a few verses and closed the Bible. Rose turned out the lamp and the twins' deep breathing soon informed her they had fallen asleep. Cora lay awake thinking of Wyatt and Lonnie. What could she—all of them—do to help the pair?

The next morning, she waited until breakfast was over, the dishes done and the twins had left the house to do chores.

"Ma, Pa, can I talk to you?"

Her parents returned to their chairs. She sat between them.

"Ma, remember how you said that God had brought Wyatt and Lonnie here so we could help them?"

Ma explained to Pa what Cora meant.

Cora continued, "Maybe we could help them more by

having them join us for dinner and supper." She turned to Pa. "They need to see how a good father behaves."

Pa smiled at her praise.

Then her parents looked at each other. They never spoke a word and yet she knew each somehow understood what the other was thinking.

Cora always marveled at how they could communicate this way.

Pa spoke first. "We know so little about them."

Ma nodded. "Only enough to know they've been badly hurt." She turned to Cora, who was about to point out that Wyatt had said their father beat them. "Yes, he's told you about his father. But my concern is that badly hurt people can sometimes be dangerous."

Cora stared. "You think Wyatt or Lonnie might hurt us?" She couldn't believe it, though her only evidence as to his goodness was the way her heart jumped when he touched her and the tenderness he showed toward Lonnie. And Lonnie? Why, he couldn't even hurt a rabbit.

Pa touched her hands. "If I thought Wyatt presented a danger to us I wouldn't let him stay. But I fear you might grow too fond of him."

She ducked her head to avoid his probing stare. She'd warned herself of the same thing, but nevertheless had grown more fond of him than she cared to admit. Not that she meant it to get out of control.

Pa continued. "I just don't want to see you get hurt again."

She nodded. "I think I've learned to be careful about trusting a man."

Ma shook her head. "I don't think that's what Pa meant. It's okay to trust, but only when you know the truth, the whole truth."

"No dark secrets. No mysterious past. No unanswered questions." She listed the things she considered necessary.

Pa patted her hands. "Exactly. You're a sensible girl. I know you'll follow your head and act wisely."

"I believe you're correct in suggesting we ought to invite them to share our meals," Ma added.

Cora thanked them both for their wisdom and left to do her chores. She was sensible. She would offer help to Wyatt and his brother, but she'd also guard her heart.

When she went outside, Wyatt and Lonnie were already working on the barn, nailing the loft floor into place. She should be helping them but had the cows to tend first.

Wyatt looked up and waved. His hat shadowed his eyes but his smile flashed. Her heart picked up its pace in response. Too many unanswered questions, she reminded herself, but smiled as she continued on her way. She hurried through her chores so she could join Wyatt working on the barn.

Wyatt and Lonnie, she corrected herself.

But it wasn't Lonnie's smile she wanted to see more of.

She sought Pa's words of advice and pushed them to the forefront of her thoughts.

Somehow, with loads of determination, she'd work with Wyatt, she'd help them both and she'd keep her thoughts and heart firmly under control.

How hard could it be?

Chapter Eight

Later, Cora hurried up the ladder so fast that Wyatt called down a warning.

"Careful. There's very little floor for you to stand on." He reached out a hand and held hers firmly as she climbed to his side. He didn't immediately release her hand, and she didn't think to pull away as she looked into his dark eyes and smiling face.

Lonnie pounded a nail. The sound made her remember her purpose in being there. To help, she reminded her stalled brain.

"You started early," she said.

"Yup. I wanted to get some solid footing up here before you came." He continued to smile at her, making it difficult to tear her gaze away. "I don't suppose I can persuade you to leave the work to us?"

"Why would you want to?" Her tongue felt stiff, making her words slow.

"What if you get dizzy? What if your foot slips?"

His concern delighted her. When did anyone ever worry about her like that? Pa was protective but thought her self-sufficient. The twins looked to her for direction much of the time. Ma was affectionate but had taught her to be independent. And her papa—well, he hadn't concerned himself about her safety even when she was five.

She realized that Wyatt waited, as if thinking she might take herself down to the ground. She laughed. "I won't fall."

"Promise?" A smile lingered on his lips, but his gaze was dark and demanding.

"I promise."

His eyes said he would guard her and make sure she didn't stumble. And then he blinked and the thought was gone.

She wondered if she'd only imagined it. How foolish she was getting, and only a while after assuring her parents she would be wise. But somehow she struggled to keep her wits about her when he looked at her with his dark eyes full of feeling.

She jerked her attention to the task before them. "Let's get this done. Tomorrow is Saturday and we go to town." She picked up a hammer and a handful of spikes and began to nail a plank into place. "We take a supply of cheese, butter and eggs, and trade them at the store for things we need." She pounded on the nail. "Ma will likely take some garden produce, too. She sells out of the back of the wagon. We do all right, you know?" She rattled on without giving him a chance to answer. "Sometimes the ladies bring their complaints and ask for one of her medicines." *Pound, pound, pound.* The noise made further conversation impossible.

Wyatt set another board in place and knelt beside her to hammer in nails.

She sat back and watched how easily they went in for him.

Noticing she had stopped work, he turned to her, two spikes protruding from his mouth. He took them out so he could talk. "Something wrong?"

"Only that it takes me three times as long to drive a nail home."

He grinned and flexed his arm. "So you're willing to admit I'm better than you?"

She sighed dramatically. "At pounding in nails, I have to concede you're better."

His eyes narrowed. "That's all?"

She pretended to consider the question seriously, then shook her head. "Can't think of anything else. Of course, I'm willing to admit it might be because I know so little about you."

His expression tightened. His eyes grew cold. "There's nothing to know."

"Really? I can think of a lot of things." Would he tell her if she asked some of the many questions she had? Seeing the tension in his tight jaw, she guessed he wouldn't. She examined the nail in her hand as if it might supply answers. She could drop the subject entirely or she could probe just a little. Perhaps make him realize it wasn't dangerous to answer questions.

"Where did you grow up?" she asked.

He shrugged. "Mostly in Kansas."

"Was your father a farmer?"

"Of sorts. But mostly he raised horses."

"So that's why you want to ranch and raise horses?"

He nodded his head. "All that's left of his breeding stock is the few head I have. It's good stock, and I hope to improve it." He pounded in spike after spike, making further questions impossible.

"Help me set this plank," he called to Lonnie.

The boy was perched on the last board, his feet dangling as something beyond the barn held his attention. He smiled slightly and appeared relaxed.

Cora followed the direction of his look. He must be watching the pigs.

Lonnie jumped up, a guilty look on his face. "I'll help." He scurried to adjust the board and hammered nails with much more vigor than accuracy.

"Slow down," Wyatt said, without a hint of rancor in his voice.

Lonnie stopped and sucked in air. "I'm sorry."

"Nothing to be sorry about. Take your time. We're not in any sort of race."

Lonnie nodded and his movements grew deliberate.

Cora ducked her head to hide her reaction. The poor boy was so leery of everyone, including Wyatt. That seemed a little strange, but then she didn't know what it would feel like to duck every time Pa lifted his hand, so maybe the reaction was normal.

An hour later, Wyatt sent Lonnie to get a bucket of water.

Cora rolled her shoulders.

Wyatt watched her. "Are you sore?"

Her instinct was to deny it. Normally she would. She'd pretend she didn't hurt and would work without complaining, but something in his voice and in his look made her answer honestly. "My arms aren't used to this kind of work."

"Then why not let us do it?"

She shook her head without considering it. "I wouldn't feel right about that."

"Why?"

She couldn't tell him it was because she liked working with him, liked watching the way he moved, the way he instructed Lonnie, the sureness of his every action. Her cheeks grew warm at her wayward thoughts. "I kind of like helping," she finally murmured.

He got a silly grin on his face and she knew her answer had pleased him.

Maybe he even shared the same pleasure in working with her.

The idea brought an answering smile to her lips.

Wyatt drank the water Lonnie brought and returned to the job of making a floor. He couldn't stop smiling. Cora liked working with him. And he liked working with her. He would not think any deeper than that.

They worked until dinnertime. He hurried down the ladder to hold it firm as she made her way to the ground. His heart stalled every time she stepped on a rung. If she caught her foot in her skirts or leaned too far to one side…

He and Lonnie were about to head to their camp when she stopped them.

"Ma's expecting you to join us."

Wyatt looked at Lonnie. Did he detect in his brother's eyes the same mixture of eagerness and reluctance he felt? Then he calmed his thoughts. This was the opportunity he sought to teach them both more about healthy family life.

"Thank you." The three of them fell in step as they crossed the yard.

The meal was more hurried than supper the previous night. Mr. Bell did not read from the Bible, but they held hands around the table as they prayed. And, most important, Lonnie did not seem to mind. Neither, Wyatt confessed to himself, did he as he held Cora's.

They enjoyed a generous feed of huge slices of golden bread and thick pieces of cheese. Raw carrots and freshly picked peas crunched in contrast.

Lonnie sighed his pleasure as he finished. "Good food. Thanks, Mrs. Bell."

Mrs. Bell patted Lonnie's hand. "Glad you enjoyed it."

Lonnie snorted. "You should see what Wyatt feeds us."

Wyatt groaned. Was the boy going to point out his deficiencies as a cook at every chance he got? "I never had a chance to practice cooking."

At the reminder of one reason why Wyatt had had no such chance, Lonnie ducked his head.

Wyatt tried to think of a way to make it clear he didn't mean just the past year. "Ma didn't like anyone messing about in her kitchen." He squeezed Lonnie's shoulder, hoping to signal he didn't mean to remind him of jail.

The meal ended and the younger ones returned to their chores.

"Ma and Pa will have a nap," Cora said. "You're welcome to do so, too, if you want."

Lonnie choked back a snort.

Wyatt ignored his brother's reaction. "I haven't had an afternoon nap since I was three."

"Just offering," she said. "No shame in taking a break

from your labors. Pa says it makes him more vigorous for the rest of the day."

"Uh-huh," Wyatt said.

"Sure you don't need a nap?" Lonnie jeered.

"I'm absolutely certain. Now, be sure *you* don't fall asleep and tumble off the roof," Wyatt said as they returned to the job.

Lonnie and Cora both laughed.

Wyatt grinned as he bent to hammer in nails. He'd made his little brother laugh. Lonnie had allowed physical contact.

His pleasure lasted throughout the early part of the afternoon. But as the sun beat down mercilessly on them, and sweat dribbled from his face, he tried to think of a way to suggest they forget about the project for a few hours. He'd come right out and give his opinion of working in the hottest part of the day, except he didn't want to look like a slacker. Now, if she'd suggest it...

"Push the plank into place," he told Lonnie as Cora sat back, wiping her face on a handkerchief.

Lonnie moved as though his limbs had turned to lead.

Wyatt understood how he felt, but the boy didn't complain. No doubt because he feared retaliation from Wyatt.

"That's good." Wyatt sat down beside Cora and Lonnie flopped to the finished portion of the floor. On the ground, in the shade of the house, Mrs. Bell, Lilly and Rose sat shelling peas. He'd do most anything to get out of the blazing heat, but not unless Cora suggested it.

She didn't. They continued throughout the hot afternoon, though their movements grew slower and more sluggish as the hours passed. Lonnie kept them supplied with water. A bucket disappeared quickly between three people drinking copious amounts and he and Lonnie pouring it over their heads.

Cora splashed it on her face.

"Sure is hot." Lonnie fanned himself with his hat.

"Finally," Cora said with feeling. "I thought no one would ever complain, and I wasn't about to be the first."

"Well, I'm hot." Lonnie sounded defensive.

"So am I," Cora said. "Aren't you?" she asked Wyatt.

"I am baked, fried and toasted."

"But are you hot?" Her voice was bland but her eyes twinkled.

He laughed. "I didn't want anyone to think I couldn't handle it."

"Well, I've had enough. Let's get off this fry pan."

Lonnie was down the ladder before she finished her sentence.

She scrambled to her feet but jerked to a halt and tumbled forward.

Wyatt grabbed her, his heart thudding in his ears. He held tight as he struggled to his feet on legs that had turned to butter. He pulled her back to the floor beside him. "The heat is making you dizzy."

Her eyes had widened to the size of dinner plates and she held on to him with both hands.

She sat safely on the loft floor, but he couldn't release her any more than he could tear himself from her gaze. It demanded a dozen things from him—his protection, which he'd freely given, but also the truth about his past, his time in prison, his hopes and fears and failures—things he could not allow her to know. He tried to close the emotional door that had been flung wide-open when he'd thought she was about to fall to the ground. A door that concealed the secrets he must guard the rest of his life. But the door jammed and he could not close it.

She swallowed so hard he figured it must hurt. "I wasn't dizzy."

"You almost fell."

She withdrew her hands slowly. Their eyes held each other's. "My skirt is caught."

"Your skirt?" He echoed her words without understanding her meaning.

She blinked and shifted her gaze to her feet. "Yes. Between the boards."

He forced his brain to start functioning. Indeed, the hem of her skirt was caught, jammed between two boards he and Lonnie had pushed into place.

At the realization of how one bit of carelessness could have been the cause of a disaster, he sucked in air in a futile attempt to calm his pounding head.

"Wyatt?"

The concern in her voice made him concentrate. "I'll get it. Don't move." He pried the board away enough to pull the fabric free. But he made no move to climb down from the loft. If Cora's limbs were as shaky as his, they wouldn't be safe on the ladder.

"Thank you for catching me." She stared at the hem of her skirt.

"You gave me quite a scare." Would she notice the tremble in his voice that he couldn't hide?

"Me, too."

To keep from touching her, Wyatt pressed his hands to the new boards. If only he had the freedom to pull her close and comfort her. But he didn't, and never would, because he would never be free from the sting of his past.

She sucked in air. "I owe you for saving my life."

He tried to snort, but it sounded more like a groan. "Let's hope you wouldn't have died."

She faced him, but he kept his gaze riveted to the spot where she almost fell. "Wyatt, if you need or want anything, feel free to ask. If I can, I'll give it to you."

Slowly his gaze sought hers and he fell into the darkness of her eyes and the sweetness of her invitation. He had needs and wants. Acceptance despite his past, someone who trusted him, believed in him, loved him. His throat tightened. His heart ached with longing. If only she could give him what he needed.

He forced himself to take slow, steadying breaths. Grabbed at reality and pulled it back where it belonged—in his head and in his heart. "Thanks. I'll be sure to let you know if there is." It was time to leave behind this sweet moment and he pushed to his feet. "Do you feel ready to crawl down the ladder?" He held out a hand to pull her to her feet.

She grabbed his hand and let him help her. She stood facing him without moving.

"Are you feeling dizzy? Weak?"

She shook her head. "I'm fine." She headed for the ladder.

He stepped around her. "Let me go first so I can help you." She didn't protest as he descended, one rung at a time, and waited on each to help her down.

They reached the ground and he stepped aside.

Lonnie straightened from petting Grub. "What took you so long?"

"My skirt was caught in the boards." Cora smiled at

Wyatt, her fingers pressed to her throat as if she tried to contain the memory of her fright.

Only it wasn't fear he saw in her eyes. What was it? Gratitude? Or something more? Something that grew from having shared a moment full of raw emotion? How could he tell? He was ill equipped to read the silent message contained in her eyes. He'd grown up with a mother who grew more distant with the passing years, a father who had one emotion in varying degrees, and he'd spent a year with men who calmly said one thing and meant another without revealing any emotion.

Mrs. Bell called out to them, "I've got fresh lemonade. Come and have some."

They traipsed across the yard to plunk down in the shade of the house, where it was several degrees cooler than on the top of a half-finished barn. Lilly poured them all lemonade and Wyatt drank eagerly. So did Lonnie and Cora.

A smile tugged at the edges of his heart and teased his lips.

Cora noticed. "What are you grinning about?"

"Us." He turned to explain to the others. "We about melted up there, but none of us wanted to be the first to admit the heat was getting to us."

Lilly and Rose gave all three of them considered study.

"Who was first?"

"Me." Lonnie sighed. "Those two are too stubborn to admit it."

The twins laughed and Mrs. Bell tsked.

Cora looked around. "Where's Pa?"

"He went to check on his fruit trees. Wouldn't be

surprised if he found a shady spot and fell asleep." Mrs. Bell's voice rang with affection.

The peas were done and the Bells seemed content to rest in the shade. So Wyatt followed their lead, quietly observing them. They were so relaxed around one another. Even Lonnie sat with Grub at his side, as relaxed as he ever got. Which meant he slid his gaze from one to the other as they talked, alert for any sign of tension.

Wyatt leaned back to watch. How long would it take for Lonnie to realize this family didn't operate that way?

Grub trotted off, found a stick and dropped it at Lonnie's feet.

"He wants to play," Cora said.

"With me?"

Wyatt understood that Lonnie wondered if he had permission to play with the Bells' dog.

"Seems he's chosen you," Cora said. "Go ahead. Throw the stick for him."

Lonnie did and laughed as Grub tripped over himself in his rush to chase it.

Wyatt's muscles relaxed. Guess he, like Lonnie, needed to learn that people could be trusted to be kind.

How long would it take him to learn it?

Mrs. Bell took the peas inside. The others continued to lounge in the shade.

Lilly got to her feet and stretched. "I'm going to take the pea shells to the pigs."

Lonnie stilled. "Can I go?"

"Certainly. Come along. Grab that basket."

Rose joined them and the three carried the baskets of peapods to the pigs.

Only Cora and Wyatt remained.

"We go to town tomorrow," she said.

"Yes." She'd already mentioned it.

"If I go, I can't help with the barn."

"That's fine." He'd be happy enough if she kept her feet firmly planted on the ground.

"Guess I don't have to go." She sounded disappointed.

"Why wouldn't you?"

"I couldn't leave you working alone."

"Lonnie will be here."

She brightened. "Or you could come with us. Yes. Why don't you? You'd get to see our little town. Besides, you and Lonnie deserve a break."

Town was the last place he cared to be. Too many curious people. But if he refused, he had no doubt she would opt to stay home, too.

He simply wasn't ready to see her on the loft floor again.

"A trip to town might be a nice change," he finally said.

He could only hope no one in town asked questions of him or cared enough to look for answers.

Chapter Nine

Cora sat with her sisters on quilts in the back of the wagon, crowded in amidst the vegetables and other things they'd brought to sell and trade.

Wyatt and Lonnie perched at the end of the wagon. They'd get dusty in the cloud that rolled up from the wheels.

Ma and Pa rode on the wagon seat, as always.

They rumbled across the rocky ford of the river. The Bell farm was three miles from town—an easy walk. The girls had walked it to attend school and they often walked to church, but on Saturdays they took the wagon to carry in their produce.

The wagon rattled past several ladies who lifted their hands in greeting. Cora smiled at the way they eyed the wagon, trying to see what vegetables Ma had to sell.

They passed a livery barn where several men conducted business. Next to that was a blacksmith shop. Cora pointed out each business, though likely Wyatt could read the signs for himself.

They came to a pretty white church with a steeple.

"That's where we go to church," Cora said.

Then Pa turned the wagon down another street. False-fronted wooden buildings were crowded by impressive brick structures. Cora wondered if Wyatt noticed how the town seemed determined to escape its early frontier beginnings and move into regal permanency.

She watched him, saw he studied each business they passed, so she didn't point out the lawyer, newspaper office, freight station and three mercantile stores. Pa stopped in front of Frank's Hardware and Necessities, where they did their business, and got down. He trotted to Ma and assisted her to the ground.

Wyatt and Lonnie jumped down. Lonnie stared at the store, his eyes searching. What did he want? Cora wondered as Wyatt helped each of the girls down. The twins hurried to their ma's side but Cora waited for Wyatt.

"I could use some help getting supplies at the feed store," Pa said.

Wyatt needed no more urging. He jumped up beside Pa and Lonnie climbed back into the wagon, his gaze lingering on the display in the store.

Cora turned to see what held so much interest for the boy. Just the ordinary tools Mr. Frank sold—an array of shovels, some leather goods—nothing to hold a young man's attention that she could see.

She followed Ma and the twins into the store and breathed in a myriad of scents. Linseed oil on the dark floorboards. Canvas rolled up in the back. Tangy dill from a barrel of pickles. A jumble of tools and cast iron ware occupied one corner and another held ladies' wear. The store was crowded from the roof to the floor and from wall to wall.

Cora stuffed back unreasonable disappointment. Yes,

she'd hoped to show Wyatt around the store and then the town, but of course he'd sooner spend the time with Pa.

Her visual assessment stalled at Anna Rawley, Cora's best friend since grade three. Anna saw her and waved her over. Rose and Lilly followed on Cora's heels as they crossed the floor, edging past the coffee grinder and a display of pitchforks.

Two other young ladies left off the examination of a new shipment of buttons and joined them, Nancy White and Mary Ann McHaig. Nancy lived with her family across from the school and Mary Ann had recently started up a milliner's shop and wore a specimen of her work—a fancy affair in green satin, frothy feathers and big bows.

Rose pointed to it. "Very nice. How is your business doing?"

"Flourishing," Mary Ann assured them. Her smile faded. "Though I would sooner have my uncle back." Her uncle had been her guardian, and upon his death several months ago she had inherited money enough to start her own business.

Cora squeezed her arm. "If you get lonely you can always come and visit us." Silently she thanked God that she had her sisters, and Ma and Pa Bell.

The town girls were full of news about who had been seen with whom and the newest merchandise in every store, all of which interested Cora and her sisters. She and her sisters likewise told their news, including the arrival of Wyatt and Lonnie and their need to rest their horses until Fanny foaled.

She knew the moment Wyatt stepped into the store. She felt his eyes without even turning in his direction. A smile curved her lips as she shifted to look at him.

Wyatt stood alone in the doorway. Ma had gone across the street to speak to a friend she'd spied. Pa had no doubt gone to fetch her.

She'd never taken into account how tall Wyatt was until she saw him framed by the screen door. He stood with his fingers tucked in the front pockets of his trousers and his hat tipped back, which allowed her to admire his dark brown hair. He'd gotten it cut. That surely explained why she studied him so thoroughly.

His bottomless eyes met hers. A smile barely touched his lips but filled his gaze.

He tipped his hat forward and strode toward her.

She jerked around, breathing slowly, hoping to calm the wild fluttering of her heart.

When he reached them, Rose and Lilly shifted so he could join their circle. He favored each girl with a smile and greeted each of the young women in a charming fashion.

Cora's lips tightened as Anna and the other two town girls preened like a trio of peacocks.

"Girls," she managed in a neutral voice, "I'd like you to meet Mr. Wyatt Williams." She left it at that, then introduced each of the girls.

"This is the man visiting at your farm?" Nancy sounded as if she'd run all the way from Fort Benton.

Anna nudged Cora. "The cowboy with the herd of horses?"

Cora was beginning to wish she hadn't mentioned anything about him. In truth, she'd said very little, but Rose and Lilly had run over with information.

Mary Ann leaned forward and offered her hand. "I own the new milliner's shop. I guess you won't be needing a new bonnet for yourself. But perhaps for your wife..."

He grinned. "I don't have one."

Mary Ann beamed. "Or your mother."

Wyatt's grin lingered, though Cora thought it lacked the usual amusement. "I think my ma would have little use for a fancy bonnet even if she was still alive."

His response made her want to cheer. Why would any woman spend good money on such foolish things? But she'd seen enough women wearing elaborate hats to know not everyone shared her opinion.

She couldn't fault his manners, though he remained aloof despite the girls' attention.

"Mary Ann was about to tell us some interesting new about the Caldwells." Cora hoped to distract the girls from practically falling over themselves trying to impress Wyatt.

Mary Ann nodded, sending the feathers on her bonnet into a furious dance. A little curl of black hair fluttered across her cheek. Her dark eyes rounded. "I hear Duke Caldwell is returning."

"His name is Douglas." Duke was his nickname, which Rose refused to use. "I thought he was gone for good."

Lilly nudged her in the ribs. "You only wish it were true."

Anna tsked. "You don't really want that!"

"I sure wouldn't," Mary Ann said, fluttering her eyelashes at Wyatt.

Nancy nodded agreement.

Cora had noticed Mary Ann's particular interest in men before, but now it had grown downright annoying. "We can only hope he'll be kept busy and maybe keep the Caldwell cowboys busy enough they won't bother us."

"He was always unkind to us, as I recall." Rose adjusted her gloves as she spoke, worrying them until Cora caught her hands and stilled them. Rose sighed. "Just like his father. I don't expect we'll see any changes. Certainly not for the better."

Lilly nodded, her face tight with worry. "It might get worse."

"Here's Pa," Cora said, grateful for the diversion. She whispered to the girls as they crossed the oiled floor to join their parents. "Don't repeat your concerns about Duke to Ma and Pa. They'll worry needlessly."

They conducted their business, Mr. Frank taking the cheese, butter and eggs and noting the amount in his little notebook.

Ma ordered syrup, cocoa and a few other items they were low on.

Cora watched Lonnie, who was now studying the display in the window. She turned to Wyatt, saw he, too, watched his brother. "What has him so interested?"

Wyatt shook his head. He poked his head outside and called to his brother. "Lonnie, let's get some candy."

The boy jerked as if he'd been lassoed at a full gallop. He drew in a shuddering breath and hurried in to the candy display. Between them, Wyatt and Lonnie filled a bag rather generously, Cora figured.

"I'm done here," Ma said, and led them outside. Pa helped her to the wagon. She turned to study the girls as Wyatt helped them into the back. "Is something going on I should know about?"

Ma could always see through any secrets the girls

tried to keep. Cora knew there was no point in trying to hide the news.

"Mary Ann says Duke Caldwell is coming home."

Pa grunted. "The younger Caldwell returns. Maybe Philadelphia has had enough of him."

Ma faced forward, her shoulders stiff. She did not like the feud between the families. "Neighbors should get along. You never know when you'll need help from each other."

"Sadly, the Caldwells do not share your philosophy," Cora said.

Wyatt sat on the back of the wagon, looking as self-satisfied as one of Lilly's cats at milking time.

Cora pretended to adjust her skirts so she could study him. Had he enjoyed the attention the girls had paid him?

Ma and Pa chatted as they journeyed home. Pa seemed satisfied with his purchase—new wooden planks that filled the air with a piney scent.

Ma nodded and made agreeing noises at the appropriate times as Pa talked, but Cora wondered if she really listened to him. Was she worrying how Duke's return would affect them?

Cora turned to her sisters. "Did Mary Ann say when Duke is expected to arrive?"

Rose snorted. "Too soon for my liking."

"You've never forgiven him for teasing you about your red hair, have you?"

"That was only one of many things he did."

Lilly interrupted before Rose could itemize Duke's faults. "According to Mary Ann, Mrs. Caldwell said he was making a leisurely trip, stopping to visit a few places. They are anxious for his return, but Mary Ann didn't know a specific date." She turned to Rose, her expression so guileless few would guess she meant to tease her twin sister. "Rose, did you hear when he would arrive?"

Lilly and Cora darted amused glances at each other. Rose and Duke had their own personal feud going on, and the sisters didn't mind reminding Rose of it.

"I don't care." Rose managed to look glum.

"Nice town," Wyatt murmured as they drove away. He settled back, pulled out the bag of candy and passed it around.

They crossed the river and turned homeward. She sat up and looked toward the farm. Out of habit, she ran a practiced eye about the place, mentally checking each pasture, the orchard, the sheep—

Whoa. She jerked her gaze back. The sheep pasture stood void of the little wooly animals. She rose to her knees. "Where are the sheep?"

At her question, Pa and Ma strained forward.

Lilly jumped up and pressed to their backs. "The pasture is empty."

Rose leaned around Ma.

Wyatt crowded close to Cora's back, not touching, but she breathed the lemony scent of his freshly groomed hair.

"There." He pointed past her, his arm brushing her shoulder, sending startled awareness up her spine and down to her fingertips.

The small flock huddled at the water's edge a hundred yards farther down, half-hidden by the rocks and a scraggly bunch of bushes at the river's edge.

Lilly staggered toward the back of the wagon.

Cora and Wyatt both reached for her at the same time and steadied her.

"Sit down and wait until Pa stops," Cora ordered.

Lilly jerked to one side and then the other to escape their grasp but finally sank to her knees. "It's those Caldwell cowboys again. If any of the animals are hurt—" Her voice broke.

Cora turned to Wyatt, knowing full well her concern filled her face. "Why must the Caldwells constantly harass us?"

Wyatt touched her arm. "We'll get them all back safely."

She nodded, grateful for his reassurance and comforting touch. She could not remember a time when she didn't feel she had to be the one to stand strong to protect her family.

She shook away the foolish thought. She would never let harm come to them so long as she could prevent it.

Wyatt hung on to Lilly. He figured if she could, she would launch herself out the back with no heed for life and limb. Were these girls intent on killing themselves over the farm and their animals? Over family? Someone ought to inform them they were of more value to family and home alive than dead.

Before Mr. Bell pulled the wagon to a halt, Wyatt jumped to the ground. He reached up and helped Lilly down. She grabbed up her skirts and ran toward the bleating sheep.

Wyatt turned back in time to help Cora alight. "Does this happen often?"

"If not this, then something else." Her words were tight, as if it hurt to move her jaw.

Rose jumped to their side. “Come on, you two. Lilly needs help.” She raced to her sister. “Now, now, Lilly. Don’t fret. We’ll get them all back safely.”

“The poor things.” Lilly’s hands fluttered helplessly.

“I’ll take Ma to the house,” Mr. Bell called, the wagon rumbling away.

Wyatt watched them depart. The man was likely grateful for an excuse to escape the near hysteria of his one daughter.

He turned to Lonnie, who had the look of a trapped animal. “It’s okay,” Wyatt said softly. “You can help or go to the house with Mr. Bell.”

Lonnie looked about. “I’ll help him unload.” He scurried away and Wyatt turned his attention back to the girls.

“We’ll get them all back,” Cora said as she hurried to Lilly’s side.

Lilly sobbed hard.

Wyatt pressed the heel of one hand to his forehead. If all three of them started weeping he’d… He wasn’t sure what he would do, but being locked up with a bunch of angry men sounded safer at the moment.

He dismissed the thought as quickly as it came. Surely crying lasted for only a moment. Being locked up was endless.

He kept to Cora’s side as he took in the scene. Some of the sheep were in the river. He figured all that kept them from being swept downstream were the rocks that corralled them. Other sheep stood in the bushes.

Heedless of her dress and shoes, Lilly rushed into the stream. “They’ll drown.” Only the weight of the water around her legs slowed her frantic hurry.

“Sheep can swim,” Cora said. She turned to Wyatt.

"She'll drown herself before she'll let something happen to one of those creatures."

Wyatt didn't stop to think about his actions but plunged in after Lilly, calling to Cora over his shoulder, "You stay there and pull them from the water when I shove them in your direction." The cold made him gasp. The water sucked at his legs.

He grabbed the nearest ewe and shoved her toward Cora, who helped the animal climb the rocky bank to safety.

Meanwhile, Lilly had her hands full trying to persuade another animal to back away from the rocks so she could push it to Cora. The animal bolted, was caught in the current and would have been carried downstream if Wyatt hadn't reached out and snagged it.

In a few minutes, all the sheep stood on grassy ground. Wyatt helped Lilly out of the river and then began to scramble over the slippery rocks.

Cora held a hand out to him. Without hesitation he let her help him out of the water, but he dropped her hand as soon as he stood on two feet. He needed to keep his distance from her. Each time he saw her it grew harder. He thought of the moment he'd stepped into the store and seen her dark blond hair hanging in a braid down her back. She'd met his gaze, her eyes dark and watchful across the cluttered shop. She'd stood surrounded by five young women, but none of them were half as beautiful as she, and their expressions revealed nowhere near as much character. Cora was a force of nature—strong, independent, protective. Her family came first with her. The thought swept through his mental wanderings, leaving him with one solid surety. Nothing would ever entice her away from her sisters and the Bells. Nothing would be allowed to endanger them in any way.

The bracing thought enabled him to ignore how warm and firm her hand had been in his.

"It's cold." He shivered.

"Thanks for helping get the sheep out." She favored him with a sunlit smile that slipped right past his defenses and plopped into his heart like a stubborn squatter.

She cast a troubled look at the wet sheep bleating in a huddle nearby. "Lilly would have been devastated if one of them drowned."

Poor Cora, always trying to protect her sisters from anything bad. What would she do if she failed or thought she had? "Where did Lilly go?" Cora searched for her sister, though she must be as cold as he.

They saw her at the same time, tromping through the bushes. "The sheep are caught in the branches."

Ignoring his wet clothes and waterlogged boots, Wyatt went over and helped free the animals.

Cora worked at his side. "Lilly, they're unharmed. All we have to do is get them back to their pen."

Rose shepherded each animal back to the pasture as it was freed.

Finally, the last ewe was back, the lambs bleating after them. The smell of wet lanolin filled the air. The warm breeze dried the edges of Wyatt's shirt, but his trousers hung heavy about his waist and his feet stood in boots full of water.

The four of them stood together in the gap of the fence. The posts were tipped over.

"I know those posts were in solidly." Cora ground

the words out. “But those Caldwell cowboys know how to make it look as if they had nothing to do with it.”

Wyatt looked for signs in the ground, but the sheep had trampled away any clue. His fists curled; his insides tightened. This was beyond causing trouble. It was vindictive. Mean-spirited. Harsh. The sheep might have drowned if the Bells had been gone longer. He couldn’t abide someone bigger, tougher and more powerful treating those weaker and more vulnerable this way. It reminded him too sharply of his father.

“Why don’t you—” He meant to ask why they didn’t go to the sheriff or approach the boss at the Caldwell ranch, but his question was cut off by a howl from Lilly.

“Lambie Four is missing.”

“Lambie Four?” Wyatt turned to Cora for an explanation.

“She numbers them when they’re born. Doesn’t give them real names until they’re weaned.” She shrugged. “Don’t know why.”

Wyatt didn’t miss the way her shoulders slumped forward. Or how her arms hung at her sides.

“Poor Lilly.” Her voice dripped with sympathy. “The animals are so precious to her.”

He touched Cora’s hand. “Maybe the lamb is still out there. Come on. Let’s look.” He returned to the bushes. But no little white lamb was caught in the branches.

He pressed his lips tight. The Caldwells were cruel people. He turned and came face-to-face with Cora.

“Don’t you think we would have seen a lamb if it was there?” she asked him.

“Of course you would have. I didn’t mean otherwise. But I’m not about to give up and provide those two more reason to cry.” He tipped his head toward the twins.

Rose held Lilly in her arms, her sister's head pressed to her neck. Their muffled sobs hit him harder than an iron fist. Women shouldn't be made to cry. They should be protected, though—he darted his gaze to Cora—if she heard him say so she would likely inform him she didn't need protection.

Cora stared at the river. "It might have drowned."

Remembering how the sheep caught in the current had passed him, he grabbed Cora's hand. "Or it might have been carried downstream. Let's see."

Her fingers, warm and strong, gripped his. "Oh, please, God. Let it be alive."

His muscles tightened as he silently echoed the prayer. He could understand why Cora felt so strongly about protecting her sisters. He wanted to do the same for her. Strange thought from a man who'd known little but darkness and violence in his life.

They trotted along the bank of the river. Bushes reached the water's edge in places and Wyatt clambered down to examine them, both relieved that he didn't find a dead animal and disappointed he hadn't found Lambie Four alive and well.

Half a mile later, Cora caught his arm. "We might as well go back." She rocked her head back and forth. "I don't know how I'm going to deal with Lilly." She plunked down on a nearby rock. "I try to protect the girls, but how am I to shield them from the Caldwells? From the hurtful teasing like Duke hands out?" Her hands hung between her knees and she stared at the gurgling water.

Wyatt sat at her side. "You live on a farm. Isn't birth and death part of the experience?"

Cora spared him a pained look. "But not senseless like this."

He nodded, understanding the difference, and sat as dejected as she. He looked past her, avoiding the anger in her face. He knew the look wasn't directed at him, but the set of her mouth made him nervous. In his experience, anger led to uncontrolled actions.

She sucked in air. "I'm going back to console Lilly and fix the fence." Her expression softened and he relaxed. Her anger seemed short-lived and controlled.

The breeze snorted down the river. Despite the heat of the sun, he shivered in his damp clothes.

The breeze bent the willows growing along the water. Something flashed. He squinted. Was it his imagination or had he seen a bit of white? "There's something in those bushes." He hurried toward them.

"What is it?" Cora kept pace at his side. She watched the bushes, trying to catch a glimpse of whatever he'd seen.

"I don't know, but I thought I saw a bit of white."

She sucked in air as if he'd promised her a sure thing.

"I can't be certain." He no longer saw it.

They reached the willows. "You wait here." He slid into the water.

"I'm coming, too."

"I'm already wet." He waved her back, hoping she would heed his suggestion. The last thing he needed now was to worry about her. He already felt as if his heart was near to shattering with all the emotional upheaval of the afternoon.

She clung to a tree, almost falling into the water, but remained on shore while he pushed into the bushes.

That was when he saw it. A little lamb caught in the

branches, bobbing in the flow of the water. Wyatt drew his mouth back and hid his reaction when he could detect no movement from the animal.

"Did you find anything?" Cora called.

"I think so. Just a minute." He wanted to pretend he hadn't, but he couldn't lie to her. Besides, she'd demand to see for herself. He parted the bushes and untangled the limp creature. His insides boiled that someone had deliberately caused this needless death, not to mention the pain and sorrow for Lilly and the frustration for Cora that she couldn't protect her sisters from such agony.

He edged back toward Cora.

She saw the lamb and her face lit up. "You found it. How wonderful."

Unable to tell her the truth, he cradled the creature close as he made his way to the bank. Cora held out a hand to help him from the river.

He turned so she couldn't see the lamb and knelt. But he couldn't release it, couldn't let her see the truth.

She pulled at his arms. "Let me see."

He shook his head.

Sitting back on her heels, she stared at him. "You mean…?"

He nodded and slowly, reluctantly lifted his head to see her reaction. If only he could spare her this. Spare all of them. He sat back, staring at Cora. Instead of sadness, her eyes flashed hardness, punching a hole in his sympathy. She bolted to her feet and stalked toward the river. He half rose, but she spun around, her fists bunched at her sides, and he settled back, withdrawing at the fierceness of her look.

"I would like to march over to the Caldwells and

toss this poor dead lamb on their table. I wonder how they'd like that."

"I can't think they would." He watched her carefully, not sure how she'd handle her anger.

Cora dropped her gaze to the lamb in Wyatt's arms. "Poor little thing." She sucked in air as if preparing for battle. "Poor Lilly. Well, there's nothing for it but to go home and tell her the news."

He shifted his weight back on his heels to push himself up. The lamb shifted as he moved. And then it shifted again. He sank back to the ground and stared. "Cora!"

"Come on. Let's get this done with."

"Cora, come here."

"What's wrong with you? You object to carrying a dead lamb? Maybe you don't like sheep."

He ignored her accusing tone. "I like sheep just fine. But I don't think I'll be carrying a dead lamb."

She pushed him aside. "For goodness' sake. Give it to me. I'll carry it."

The lamb bleated weakly.

Cora fell back, landing on her rump, her eyes so round that Wyatt nearly laughed.

"It's alive?"

"That's what I was trying to tell you." He grinned at her.

"God be praised." She sprang to her feet and threw her arms about him. "God be praised." Her words were muffled against the hollow of his shoulder.

He didn't move. Didn't raise his arms to hold her. Couldn't. She only hugged him because of her joy over one live lamb. She didn't realize what she did. Any more than she knew how warm and inviting her arms were.

Or how her hair tickled his nose and made him want to bury his face in it.

His heart beat at an alarming rate. As if he'd swum a mile in the cold river. Or climbed the tallest mountain. Or run all the way to town carrying a heavy pack.

He blinked hard. He was an ex-con. He ought to remember that.

She stepped back and tipped her head to consider him. "You're ice-cold."

A weak grin touched his mouth without reaching his eyes or coming anywhere near his heart. "I've been in the river twice now."

The lamb bleated again and tried to stand up.

"Maybe he was only cold." She patted Wyatt's check, sending tension to his eyes and hope to his heart. "You are a hero, Wyatt. Wait until the girls learn what you've done."

He shook his head. "I didn't do anything." He didn't expect Rose and Lilly would throw themselves into his arms, but if Cora did it again…

He swallowed hard. He couldn't let himself get too drawn to this family. His past could hurt them. Especially if Jimmy Stone showed up. Wyatt knew the man wouldn't hesitate to hurt the Bells if he thought it would hurt Wyatt. He needed to remember that.

Needing to escape Cora's gratitude, he turned to the lamb. "Lambie Four, I presume."

Cora chuckled. "I'm sure he's pleased to meet you."

"He's awfully weak." He scooped the lamb into his arms. "We'd better get him back to his mama."

"Which one?" The words gurgled from her throat. "The ewe or Lilly?"

Wyatt laughed as every remnant of tension slipped from him. "I expect they will both fuss over him."

Cora patted his shoulder. "I expect they will. Best you be prepared for gratitude and joy."

He gave an exaggerated shudder. "Please tell me they don't cry when they're happy." He tried to concentrate on the unfamiliar smell of wet sheep, paid attention to the ground before him so he wouldn't trip and drop the lamb. He thought of how waterlogged his feet were. He would have to hang his boots by the fire tonight to dry them out.

"Wyatt, what's wrong?"

He shook his head. "Nothing." Except all this crying and hugging was so unfamiliar he wasn't sure how to react. Should he enjoy it as much as he did? At least the hugging part? "Did you know wet sheep smell like damp clothes?"

She laughed. "'Cause it's the same thing. Wool on the critter becomes wool in a garment."

He knew that, of course. He released the air in his lungs quietly, lest it draw attention to the fact he'd acted so strangely.

Cora patted his cheek. "Wyatt, you're a hero."

"So you said, but don't believe it. I'm just an ordinary man."

She snorted. "No man thinks he's ordinary."

Her statement made him plumb forget his past and his need for caution. "Really? How do you know this?"

She quirked an eyebrow at him. "From my vast experience with men, of course." She held his gaze, her eyes wide.

Except he didn't believe her. She was far too innocent and fresh to have had a lot of experience with men. On top of that, he knew firsthand how carefully Mr. Bell watched his daughters. Wyatt tipped his head back and roared with laughter. "Your vast experience! Now I've heard it all." He hooted again.

She shrugged and grinned as if pleased with herself. "You sound as though you doubt me."

He shook his head while his chuckles continued to erupt. "Oh, not at all," he choked out.

They drew close to the farm. Mr. Bell and the twins were repairing the fence. Rose glanced up and saw them. She called to Lilly, who stared at the white bundle in Wyatt's arms, her eyes wide.

"He's okay," Cora called, and Lilly raced toward them.

Wyatt couldn't miss the joy in her face. He shifted his attention to Cora, who beamed at her approaching sister, then flicked him a smile that touched him like a gentle caress and turned his heart to a quivering mass that longed for such approval every day of his life.

Lilly reached them with Rose at her heels.

He realized that laughing with Cora, receiving her hugs and approval, had soothed some part of him inside that had hurt all his life. Something he'd not been aware of until he felt the lightness when it was gone.

For a heartbeat he wondered if she had the ability to heal other wounds. Wounds left by his angry father, by a year of sharing his life with criminals who cared nothing for his feelings other than to mock if they thought they'd found a tender spot, and by the hurt heaped on him by cruel comments and rejection from people he had considered friends and neighbors.

He'd gladly let Cora be the one to heal him. Only he didn't want to bring disgrace or danger into her life.

Chapter Ten

Cora wondered if she'd ever felt so alive. Knowing the lamb was safe and then hugging Wyatt in her excitement… Something had shifted between them at that moment. The joy of making him laugh, seeing the tension in his eyes disappear, was rivaled only by that of returning Lambie Four safely to Lilly.

Wyatt released the lamb to Lilly, who took it to the ewe. She dried the little one with her skirts and no one protested. Together she and the ewe hovered over the lamb, petting and comforting it.

Rose stayed close as well, reassuring herself that Lilly was going to be okay now.

Cora stole a glance at Wyatt. He stood with his hands on his hips, his stance wide, grinning at Lilly. He whispered to Cora, "Two mamas, just like you said. That little one is getting his fair share of care, I'd say."

She laughed. "I expect it will last for days, weeks." She tossed her hands in the air as if exasperated. "Months more than likely."

Pa joined them. "The fence is repaired." He looked

Wyatt up and down. "Looks as if you should find some dry clothes."

Wyatt glanced down. "Guess I should, at that."

But before he could make one step toward his camp, Lilly and Rose spoke to each other, nodded and trotted to him.

Rose hesitated, but Lilly didn't lose a moment. She hugged him hard. "I'm so grateful to you for finding him. I can't believe the rest of us were ready to give up so easily. It shames me."

Rose patted Wyatt's arm. "We are so grateful. If there's anything we can do for you, name it."

Cora smiled gently. Her sisters' joy had been restored and that was all that mattered. Then she noticed how easily Wyatt patted Lilly on the back and grinned at Rose. Why had he stood stiff and awkward when she'd hugged him? It had only been a gesture of joy and gratitude, but still. Would it have hurt him to respond just a little? She turned away from the trio and stared at the repaired fence.

Her anger and confusion focused on the damage the Caldwells had done. Perhaps they'd intended for the whole flock to drown. She kicked at a clump of sod and sent it sailing over the fence.

Wyatt touched her shoulder. "Don't let them get to you. Everything is back to normal. Now I'm going to get out of these wet things." He patted her shoulder in a fatherly way and trotted toward the barn.

Cora's insides boiled. She'd had a father who left her. She had Pa, who took real good care of her. She didn't need a fatherly pat from Wyatt. And he was wrong. Things weren't back to normal. Thanks to his presence on the farm, things might never be normal for her again. He made her long for things she couldn't allow herself. Her place was here on the farm, watching over her sisters. Besides, hadn't she learned her lesson about trusting any man but Pa? Twice she'd been hurt by men with no regard for her feelings. First her papa and then Evan. There would not be a third time.

Not that Wyatt had in any way suggested he might have feelings for her. It was only her own silly reaction to an emotionally fraught moment that had even made her think such things.

She was far too practical to let her thoughts get out of control.

Between them, Cora and Rose persuaded Lilly to leave the lamb long enough to change into dry clothes.

Lonnie wandered over. "Where did everyone go?"

Cora explained about finding the lost lamb. "Wyatt has gone to change."

Lonnie's face wrinkled in worry. "Is he okay?"

"He just got wet. He's fine." She didn't add that he had been rather cold, and she chafed her arms where his skin had chilled hers. Her heart longed to take care of Wyatt—wrap him in a cozy woolen blanket, rub his hands and arms until they glowed with warmth, give him hot, sweet tea.

She closed her eyes, sucked in air and forced a reminder into her brain. She had no right to be imagining such intimacies.

Wyatt returned a few minutes later in dry clothes, though she knew his boots would still be wet inside.

She half expected Lonnie to rush to his side, but the boy hung back. He'd picked up one of the kittens and held it close. His eyes went to Wyatt, then darted away.

How strange. It was one of the many unanswered

questions about the pair that warned her she must be cautious.

Yet despite what her brain said, she struggled to keep from watching Wyatt's every move. In helping rescue the sheep, he'd revealed so many different facets of his character—tenderness, caring and determination. Combined with all she'd already observed and the way she'd seen him with fresh eyes at the store, it created a very appealing package. He was a man of honor and character.

A man with a past he refused to talk about.

She'd hugged him. Out of gratitude for the rescued lamb. But she'd felt much more than gratitude. There was a fluttering in her heart as she tried to identify her emotions. Admiration and concern. When she'd realized how cold he was, her nerves had tensed. What if he got sick?

Looking back, she realized how foolish it was to be so concerned. He was a tough cowboy, used to riding long hours in any weather. A little soaking wouldn't hurt him.

Please, God, keep him safe.

It was a prayer that she might have said for anyone. Except she'd never before prayed it for anyone outside her family.

Ma called them to come to the house.

Cora gladly turned away from the pair and pulled determination into her thoughts. She had her head on straight and meant for her heart to follow.

Lonnie trailed along behind Wyatt, carrying the kitten.

"Ma doesn't allow cats in the house," Cora warned.

Lonnie pulled to a halt. "I'll stay out here with it."

He sank to the grass and trailed a bit of string for the kitten to chase.

"You all need a good strong cup of my red rot tea." Ma guided them toward the table.

"Red rot tea?" Wyatt asked, swallowing hard.

Cora hid a smile as he glanced toward the door, his eyes wide, his shoulders tensing.

"Best thing to ward off a chill from your dunking." Ma waited for everyone to sit, then poured tea into cups and passed them around.

Wyatt sat with his hands under his knees staring at his cup. He turned to Cora. "Red rot?" he whispered.

Lilly could not stop talking about her sheep and all they'd suffered, so the others did not hear his question.

Cora leaned closer. "Would you sooner be sick?"

He contemplated the tea. "Maybe."

"Would it help to know that the plant Ma uses to make the tea eats ants?"

He jerked back. "You're joshing." He gave her such a doubting look she pressed her hand to her mouth to keep back a laugh.

"No, I'm not. It's a carnivorous plant with excellent medicinal qualities."

By now, the rest of the family had grown still and was listening to the conversation. Lilly and Rose sucked in their lips to stop from laughing.

Wyatt sat back in his chair and stared at the tea as if it might bite him.

Cora cleared her throat so she could speak. "Not to worry, though. Ma puts a few other things in with it to tame it."

Lilly and Rose no longer tried to hide their amusement and giggled.

Ma smiled gently. "Wyatt, it's perfectly harmless. Don't let these girls tease you so. Why, people come from miles around for a supply of red rot tea each fall. It keeps them healthy and fights off chest infections."

Pa sipped his drink. "Ma's right. Look at me. An old man now and never sick with a chill. All thanks to Ma's medicinals."

Cora turned to her pa. "You aren't old." It bothered her to think of him in those terms.

He patted her hand. "I'm sure not as young as I used to be."

A shiver snaked up her spine. "Don't you even talk about getting old." She didn't want to think of losing either of their parents. Not for a long, long time.

"Age is not something I can control," Pa said. "But no need for any of you to fret. I'm healthy as a horse."

Cora studied him a moment. She couldn't recall him being sick a day since he and Ma found them. Reassured by the knowledge, she turned back to Wyatt. "Don't tell me a big strong cowboy like you is afraid of a little cup of harmless tea."

He squinted at her. "How harmless can something called red rot be? You're sure my insides won't disintegrate?"

Cora shrugged. "Who knows? I suppose it depends on how tough you are." She drank from her cup and gave him a daring glance. "Maybe you aren't as tough as us Bells. Especially as, apart from Pa, we're all females."

As if to prove their toughness, Rose and Lilly lifted their cups and drank. Even Ma gave him a challenging look over the rim of her cup.

Wyatt's gaze went from Rose to Lilly to Ma then

to Cora. Finally, he considered his cup. He edged one hand from under his knee and grasped the handle gingerly, as if even touching it carried risk. He shuddered and slowly lifted the tea to his lips.

She laughed, and at the exact moment he swallowed she said, "Might be your last moment on earth."

He sputtered but it was too late. His eyes widened. "It doesn't taste bad."

The Bell family chuckled.

But Cora couldn't resist one last tease. "Let us know if your stomach starts to hurt or you begin to bleed from your pores."

Wyatt squinted at her, informing her he didn't believe a word of her warning.

"Cora," Ma scolded. "Stop tormenting the poor man."

Wyatt gave her a superior look. "Your ma is defending me." He set his cup down and shifted, making his chair squeak. He glanced around the table. "I hope you don't mind me asking, but why don't you report this mischief to the sheriff? Wouldn't that put an end to the Caldwells bothering you?"

Five cups clattered to the table. Five pairs of eyes stared at him. Cora had told him the sheriff could do nothing.

"Or go to this Mr. Caldwell and ask him to stop his cowboys from doing this?"

Lilly shook her head. "It might make things worse. The Caldwells might get more aggressive."

Rose planted her fists on either side of her cup and pursed her lips as she looked around the table, spearing each of them with her gaze. "The Caldwells aren't the only people with a right to own land."

Cora looked at her sister. Rose always wanted things fixed: have the Caldwells put in their place, get Ma's remedies neatly noted in a little book, learn the facts about who their birth family had been and if any of them lived. Perhaps even search for them. In Cora's opinion, Rose simply asked for more hurt, more reminder of how little they mattered to their birth father if she pursued the subject.

Cora would protect her younger sisters from feeling the devastation of such rejection.

Pa pushed back from the table. "While Ma makes supper, we'd best get some work done." He trod toward the door.

Cora listened to his footsteps. Did they seem heavier, slower than the last time she gave it thought? She shook her head. She only considered it because of his reminder that he grew old.

Lilly grabbed Ma's hand before she could push to her feet. "The sheep had a good soaking. Those that didn't have been under a lot of stress. Ma, do you think some of this tea would help them? Maybe keep them from getting sick?"

Ma sank back and studied Lilly. "Sometimes we do all we can and still don't get the result we want."

Yes! Exactly what Cora wished Rose would accept. She shot her redheaded sister a look and gave a little nod. *Listen to our wise ma.*

Rose only widened her eyes to inform Cora she didn't plan to change her mind. Rose could be so stubborn. So single-minded. To her own harm.

"But I must do all I can," Lilly beseeched Ma.

"Of course you must, but how are you going to get a dozen ewes and their lambs to drink tea?"

Lilly shrugged, misery in her eyes and posture.

Ma patted Lilly's hand. "I have a tincture that has the same medicinal qualities. I'll get it for you."

Ma hurried to the garden shed where she kept most of her herbs and healing plants.

Rose grinned. "There you go, Lilly. Your sheep will be just fine. Do you want help doctoring them?"

Lilly smiled at her twin. "I won't be able to do it on my own." She darted a glance toward Cora and then Wyatt.

"We'll help, too," Cora said.

The twins trotted out to get the tincture from Ma.

Cora faced Wyatt. "Do you object to helping with the sheep?"

His eyebrows rose. "Should I?"

"I don't know. Seems cowboys often hate sheep."

"Cowboys have the reputation of hating farms and farmers. Do I act like I do?"

She shook her head, mesmerized by the teasing gleam in his eyes. She forced her tongue to work. "You aren't like most cowboys I know."

His grin flashed. "And with your vast experience with men, you've known hundreds, I suppose?"

She gave an airy wave. "So many I couldn't begin to count them."

"And not one of them has cared for sheep?"

"Not a one." Her smile flattened as she thought of the Caldwell cowboys. "In my vast experience—" she tried to sound nonchalant "—they would like to see all sheep drown in the river."

His grin fled. "That was downright stupid and callous and—" He lifted his hands in a gesture of defeat.

"I can't even begin to say all the things I feel about that dreadful deed."

Cora admired his passion and ushered them outside. "You are not like any cowboy I ever met."

He thrust his shoulders back and held his chin high. "I take that as a true compliment."

As they walked out together, a wonderful warming feeling spread like sweet honey throughout Cora's insides.

Wyatt looked about. "Where did Lonnie go?"

Cora saw him first. "He's over by the pigpen."

Wyatt called to him. "We're going to help Lilly with the sheep. Do you want to come?

"Mr. Bell is going to show me how to make a rope."

"Okay."

Cora smiled. Pa would do more to heal Lonnie's fear of men than anyone she knew.

They had reached the fence of the sheep pasture and she stepped away from Wyatt's side. She enjoyed his company far too much for her own comfort. She would do well to listen to the same advice she wished Rose would heed. A person could be the cause of their own hurt if they didn't take care.

Hadn't she promised Pa and Ma and herself that she would not be hurt by Wyatt? She had no intention of being too free with her trust.

Grub sat outside the fence and jumped to his feet, wagging all over when he saw they were venturing into the pasture.

"No, you stay here, boy," Cora said.

"Wouldn't he be a help?"

Cora snorted. "You heard how good he is at herding turkeys. He's even worse at herding sheep."

"I have to ask why you keep such a useless dog."

She gave him a wide-eyed look of shock. "Why, that should be obvious. It's because he's so cute."

Wyatt roared with laughter. "He's the ug—"

"Don't say it," she warned him.

He stifled a chuckle as he closed the gate behind them.

In the pasture, Lilly and Rose held a sheep as Lilly inserted a dropper in its mouth and held its jaws until it swallowed. Only then did she glance up. "If you two can catch them and bring them to me one at a time, it would sure go a lot faster."

Rose marked the treated sheep with a little colored chalk and turned it loose.

"You know how to catch sheep?" Wyatt murmured.

"Sure. Reach out and grab it and drag it to Lilly."

He leaned back on his heels and grinned at her. "It sounds as easy as catching a little pig."

She rolled her eyes and pretended to ignore his reference. Inside, she chuckled at the memory of their first meeting. "How hard can it be?"

"If you say so. Grab that one. She's close."

They lunged for the ewe, but she bleated and trotted away, leaving Cora with had a handful of wool.

She sat on her rump and stared at the animal.

"You're going at it all wrong," Lilly said. "Just call them to you and hold each one under their chin. It's not hard."

Wyatt groaned. "Seems I've heard that before."

Under her breath, Cora murmured, "I don't much care for sheep."

Wyatt choked. "And you accused me of not liking

them. As if it was the worst possible crime a man could commit."

She ignored him. This teasing brought her perilously close to the invisible line that she would not, must not, cross.

He nudged her with his foot.

Still she ignored him.

He pushed her over.

She gasped and stared up at him. "Why'd you do that?"

He planted his hands on his hips. "Why did you pretend you liked sheep?"

She scrambled to her feet and gave a dismissive toss of her head. "I never said anything of the sort."

"You might as well have."

She shrugged. "I can't help it if you make huge assumptions."

He took a step toward her.

Not caring for the look in his eyes, she edged away and considered the sheep. "We'd better get to work."

He growled, "I should have brought my rope. I could lasso them."

"Go around them," Lilly called. "All you have to do is herd them my way. I'll call them."

As they moseyed around the animals, Lilly called, "Watch out for the ram. He's harmless but he likes to butt."

Wyatt jerked, looking around for the animal. "Cora, watch out."

The urgency in his voice sent tremors up her spine, but before she could turn, something hit the backs of her legs and propelled her forward.

"Cora." Wyatt could barely push her name past his teeth as the ram hit her from behind. He raced forward, intending to beat the animal off with his bare hands if he must. But the ram trotted off, his head high, as if pleased with his actions.

Cora lay facedown in the grass.

Wyatt squatted at her side. He reached out, wanting to roll her over and make certain she was okay but afraid she might be too injured. “Cora.” He touched her shoulder gently. “Cora, say something.”

Her ribs expanded in a great gasp. She lifted her head, spit out grass and rolled to her back to stare up at him.

“I don’t like sheep,” she muttered.

He chuckled, more from relief than any other reason. “Good to see you alive and kicking.”

She sat up and groaned. “I’m not kicking, but if Lilly wasn’t so blame fond of these horrible, smelly creatures, I’d sure be tempted to kick a ram.”

Suspecting she didn’t mean a word of her threat, he watched her closely. “I tried to warn you, but it was too late.”

“Seems to be the story of my life.”

There was a whole lot of information hidden in those few words, but now was not the time or place to ask about it. “Are you hurt anywhere?”

“Only my pride. Imagine my chagrin to be knocked over by a silly ram, especially in front of a cowboy.” She closed her eyes and managed to look pained. “Why is it you always see me at my worst?”

“I can’t imagine what you mean.” He couldn’t recall a time when he’d seen anything but her best.

“I’m sure you can. First, you find me falling on my face chasing a little pig. Then I trip on my skirt and almost fall from the barn. Now I'm falling on my face over sheep."

"Best moments of my life." He held out a hand to help her up.

She looked ready to slap it away, then accepted defeat and grabbed on.

He pulled her to her feet and kept hold of her hand even after she was upright. He looked into her eyes and smiled. "Yup, best moments of my life."

"Oh, you." She pushed him hard.

He staggered back but kept his feet. "What was that for?"

She shrugged. "You figure it out."

He grinned. He liked teasing her. Liked seeing her chasing little animals and helping her sisters. Guess he liked most everything about her.

He spun away and reached for one of the ewes.

It mattered not if he liked anything or everything about Cora. Indeed, if he cared the least little bit about her, he would leave this minute, before he brought shame and censure to her and her family.

He looked toward the river and the campsite he and Lonnie shared. Fanny hadn't foaled yet and couldn't travel. Even after she did, they'd have to wait until the foal was strong enough before they moved on.

With a sigh of resignation, he bowed his head. How was he to give his horses a chance to rest, allow Lonnie to learn about normal family and yet protect the Bell family from being affected by his reputation?

How was he going to keep his secrets locked away? Even more important, how would he keep his heart safe?

Chapter Eleven

Cora accompanied her sisters to their shared bedroom to prepare for church.

Pa had informed Wyatt that the Bells attended church every Sunday. He hadn't come right out and said the words, but his meaning was clear—Wyatt and Lonnie were expected to attend, as well. Poor Wyatt had looked as if he wanted to sprout wings and fly away. Lonnie had shrunk back into the shadows, so Cora hadn't seen his expression, but his actions had said it all. They'd both acted as though church attendance threatened their safety.

Cora could think of no reason why anyone would think such a thing unless they were afraid of someone or something. But what could they possibility be afraid of? It wasn't as if they were evil men with their likenesses on a wanted poster. She'd seen enough of them to be certain of that.

Their father was dead. They couldn't be expecting him to turn up at any moment.

So who or what did they fear?

If only he would answer the question should she pose

it to him. There were so many things she didn't know about him. Reason enough to cling to her guardedness, she told herself.

She turned her attention to selecting a dress.

Every other day of the week she wore cotton dresses, some stained and mended. Normally, she didn't give much thought to what she put on, so long as it was practical and allowed her freedom to work. She had two dresses saved for Sundays. She'd always thought the dark red one looked rather nice on her. But it was heavy satin with a high collar that would suffocate her in the summer heat. The other one, a cotton in blue-and-white stripes, would be cooler. She had worn it every Sunday for the past month without giving it a thought, but now she stared at it. The simple style seemed a little childish.

She realized Rose was watching her and brushed her hand over the skirt as if removing specks of dust.

"Something wrong with your dress?" Rose asked.

Cora shook her head. "It's fine."

Lilly and Rose moved closer and studied the gown.

"You could wear that lacy white shawl Anna gave you last Christmas. That would make it look nice," Rose said.

"And why not pin that lovely brooch Ma gave you to the neck?" Lilly added.

"Why in heaven's name would I do that?" Yet she already pictured how those two additions would make the outfit more grown-up.

"To look nice," Lilly said.

Rose nodded. "After all, you know Mary Ann and Nancy and half the young women in Bar Crossing will be flocking to Wyatt likes bees around Ma's flowers."

"And why would I care about that?" Cora couldn't decide if she should be cross or amused.

"I like Wyatt," Rose said. "I wish he would stay here."

Cora gave Rose a look of disbelief. "You are begging for pain and sorrow if you grow too fond of him. That man has deep, dark secrets. Who knows how they might threaten our family?" She hadn't meant to blurt out her own concerns. She pressed her point with another shake of her head, then turned to Lilly. "You two need to learn you can't count on any man hanging around."

The two backed away and stood shoulder to shoulder, denial and stubbornness drawing their mouths into tight lines and narrowing their eyes.

Lilly sniffed. "You always think every man will leave you just because our real pa did."

Rose nodded. "And Evan."

"Thanks for the reminder." Cora slipped the blue-and-white dress over her head. "But it isn't me who needs reminding. It's you two."

Rose and Lilly silently consulted each other. Lilly shook her head but Rose turned away. "Cora," she said. "Why won't you tell us anything about our parents?"

"What's to tell? I was five years old. About all I can remember is staring after a wagon and waiting for it to come back. I know our father was on that wagon, but that's about all I remember." All she cared to remember. "He didn't care for us then. We don't need him now." The girls looked teary eyed so she added, "Then Lilly started to fuss, and all I thought of was how to take care of you two." She smiled at them.

"It's still all you care about," Rose pointed out.

"But we're grown up now. Besides, you must remember something."

Lilly tapped Rose's arm. "Let it be. You know she's not going to tell you anything, and maybe she's right. Maybe we're better off not knowing."

"There you go." Cora arranged her hair in a floppy roll around her head. How did Anna make it look so easy? "Rose, listen to your sister."

The girls turned back to preparing for church, but Cora felt their restlessness. Rose wanting to know who their parents were and why their father had left three little girls behind. Lilly wanting to avoid information for fear it would hurt.

Cora took the suggested brooch and pinned it at her throat. The silver of the oblong embossed brooch looked quite fine. She glanced at the shawl wrapped in tissue on the shelf of the wardrobe and dismissed the idea of wearing it.

Rose noticed her hesitation and picked up the shawl. She draped it over Cora's shoulders. It was as light as morning dew and lacy as the first frost of winter.

"You look great," Lilly said. "Wait a minute." She retrieved her best straw bonnet from the top shelf. "This will be perfect."

"I couldn't," Cora protested. "It's your favorite."

"Nonsense. What are sisters for if they can't share?" Ignoring Cora's objection, she tied it on Cora's head then turned her to the looking glass.

Cora stared at her image.

"You look very nice," Rose said. "I'm sure Wyatt will think so, too."

"I'm not wearing this so Wyatt will notice." She reached for the strings of the bonnet, intending to remove the hat, but her sisters pushed her to the door before she could accomplish it.

"This isn't about Wyatt," she murmured as they left the room.

"Uh-huh." The girls might make agreeing sounds, but they obviously didn't mean it.

She wanted to argue but they reached the kitchen and she wouldn't say anything in front of Ma.

Ma waited, wearing her usual dark blue dress and matching bonnet. Cora tried to recall if she'd ever seen Ma wear anything else for church.

"Pa is ready," Ma said, pulling on black gloves. "It's time to go."

Pa waited at the side of the wagon to help Ma up.

Wyatt stood at the back, Lonnie behind him.

Cora stared at him. He cleaned up nice. He wore black trousers, a black-and-white striped shirt with a black string tie at the collar and a brown leather vest.

"Oh, my!" Lilly whispered.

"Good thing you fancied up a bit," Rose murmured near Cora's ear.

Cora ignored them both and waited as Wyatt assisted her sisters into the back of the wagon, where Pa had spread an old quilt for them to sit on. Then Wyatt reached for her hand. Even with gloves on, she felt the warmth of his touch. He'd slicked his hair back with something lemon scented that had the power to turn her brain to mush.

She climbed into the wagon box and sat beside Rose, spreading her skirts to keep them smooth.

Wyatt waited for Lonnie to climb up, then jumped in and pulled the tailgate closed to keep out dust. He settled between Lonnie and Lilly, facing Cora, his black-clad legs stretched out. He'd polished his boots until they gleamed.

How was she to ignore him as they rattled toward town? Three miles of torture. She shifted her attention to the scenery and kept her attention on the view.

Rose patted her arm. "Cora, tell us about the time you rescued Evan from the mad cow."

Cora sent her sister a look rank with protest. It wasn't the kind of story she cared to share with Wyatt.

"Oh, yes, do," Lilly echoed.

Wyatt looked interested. "Who is Evan?"

Cora signaled her sisters to be quiet but they ignored her.

"Evan Price was her beau." The twins rattled off the information like well-oiled gears working together. "He left to go looking for gold."

"He wasn't the man for our sister."

Cora closed her eyes and hoped the twins wouldn't say any more about her and Evan. She felt foolish enough that she'd trusted the man. She surely didn't intend to repeat her mistake. Her resolve allowed her to face Wyatt and his teasing grin.

Rose continued with the story. "I think it began when Evan thought he would hurry Cora along so they could go to the church social." She turned to Cora. "Isn't that right?"

Cora barely nodded. They knew the story as well as she.

"One of the cows had just freshened—"

"Bossy," Cora said. She turned to Wyatt. "Bossy can be very cranky."

"How cranky?" His eyes sparkled.

He was enjoying this far too much. "Let's just say she doesn't care for strangers around her newborns."

Rose said, "We tried to warn Evan, but he said he knew how to handle animals."

"Of course, we didn't see what happened to start with," Lilly added. "But when we heard Cora yell, we rushed out. There was Evan, perched on top of the fence, waving his feet wildly." She turned to Cora. "What did he do?"

Cora rolled her eyes. "I've told you before."

"I know but we weren't there."

A chuckle rolled up Cora's throat. It pleasured her a little to picture Evan up on the fence, begging her to rescue him. "He walked up to where I was milking Maude. Bossy's calf was nursing. He didn't even look at her. I doubt he saw her. He saw me and got all huffy because I wasn't ready to go. I didn't listen to his fussing because I saw Bossy jerk her head up at the sound of a stranger. The calf had skittered away. I knew he was in danger and tried to warn him. 'Evan,' I said. 'You best be getting behind that fence.' Of course, he thought I meant he should wait out of my way and started to argue. Bossy caught him in the rear end with a head butt. Did he ever get over the fence in a hurry then! I had to push Bossy away from him and persuade her he wouldn't hurt her baby."

Rose and Lilly laughed. "It was quite a thing to see."

Cora snorted. "In hindsight, if I'd known he meant to go looking for gold I might have left him there to fight his own battle."

Wyatt grinned, though she detected a glint of something else in his eyes. Perhaps he felt he had been warned. She regarded him steadily to let him know she didn't take kindly to people hurting her. Or worse, one of her family.

They arrived at the church and Pa stopped the wagon.

She allowed Wyatt to help her down because it would be foolish not to. As Ma said, pride goeth before a fall and she didn't care to provide proof.

As they walked toward the church, they saw Mary Ann and a cluster of young women huddled together, watching and chattering.

Cora sighed. Mary Ann had no doubt told all her friends about the cowboy staying at the Bells'. Mothers of eligible young ladies also studied the visitor.

Lilly chuckled. "Seems we're attracting a lot of attention today."

Rose snorted. "I don't think it's us." She gave Wyatt a pointed look.

"Me?" he said. He'd left his hat in the wagon and ran his hand over his hair. "Is my hair sticking up? Do I look funny?" He glanced down at his outfit. "Don't my clothes fit properly? The man that sold them to me said they did, but perhaps he only meant to make a sale."

The three girls stared at him.

"Are you serious?" Cora asked. Surely he understood they looked because his hair looked fine, his clothes fit fine and he looked good enough to eat.

"What?" How did he manage to look so confused?

Cora couldn't believe he was serious. "Wyatt, you're joshing, aren't you? They are looking because they like what they see."

He stared at her, then a slow grin curled his lips and lit his eyes. "They're admiring how fine I look?"

"Yes." She'd as much told him she thought he looked

rather nice. Heat stung her cheeks and she knew she surely glowed like a ripe apple.

"The mothers are plotting how to get you to marry their daughters, and the young ladies are wondering if you'll accept an invitation to dinner."

Amusement fled and his jaw muscles tightened. "The answer is no."

She wasn't pleased at his instant refusal. It wasn't as if she'd grown fond of him.

Seeing as it was Sunday and they were about to enter the church, she had to be honest with herself. Maybe she'd grown just a little fond of him.

They trailed into church and sat in their regular pew. Somehow Cora ended up between Rose and Wyatt. How had her sisters managed that?

Mary Ann followed them down the aisle and paused to speak. "So nice to see you again, Mr. Williams."

"Nice to see you, too." He introduced Lonnie.

Mary Ann barely gave poor Lonnie a look as she practically swooned at Wyatt's feet. The half-dozen girls with her sighed. When had her friends ever been so blatantly foolish?

Mary Ann fluttered her eyelashes. "Will you be visiting long, Wyatt?"

"Not long."

"Maybe we can plan a social while you're here."

Cora barely constrained a groan.

"I wouldn't think I'll be here that long."

Thankfully the bevy of girls moved on and settled into pews. Several of them turned and smiled in Wyatt's direction.

But he had opened the hymnal and was turning the pages.

Cora breathed slowly. In and out. In and out. Church was not the place to let petty emotions rage through her. She glanced around the congregation, seeing familiar faces in familiar places. She frowned at Mr. and Mrs. Caldwell sitting front and center. At least they had the dignity not to look back at the Bells. And later, out of habit, the Caldwells and the Bells would exit without crossing paths. It had been that way for eight years, and she didn't expect it would change in her lifetime.

Anna's father took his place behind the pulpit and the service began. Pastor Rawley announced the first hymn. Rose shared her hymnal with Lilly, which left Cora to share with Wyatt.

He held the book toward her. As she grasped the corner, their fingers brushed, and awareness of his warmth and solidness and handsomeness sent a jolt up her arm, branding the inside of her heart.

He smiled at her then. She swallowed hard, hoping he hadn't noticed her reaction.

Then the wheezy organ pumped out the hymn and they turned forward to join the singing.

At first he didn't sing, and she recalled his earlier confession that he growled rather than sang. She jabbed him in the ribs.

When he glanced at her, she nodded toward the hymn book, silently suggesting he should sing.

He shook his head and rolled his eyes.

She managed to keep singing despite the bubble of laughter in her throat and ignored the little glances Mary Ann tossed their way.

Wyatt let the familiar words of the hymns fill his heart. Sitting in church with Cora holding the hymnal between them and listening to her sing at his side felt right and good and refreshing.

Those silly girls giggling and glancing at him had annoyed Cora. Just as they annoyed him.

The sermon was based on the passage, "No man, having put his hand to the plow, and looking back, is fit for the kingdom of God." Before the last amen, Wyatt's resolve had returned. He had vowed to move far enough away that his past couldn't follow him. He'd promised himself he would not let anyone he cared about be hurt by being associated with a jailbird. He dared not forget it.

The service over, he joined the general exodus, glad he could escape before Mary Ann reached him.

The Bells paused to speak to their neighbors but carefully kept to one side of the yard.

Cora leaned toward him to explain. "See that man and woman over there? The ones dressed in such fine clothes?"

He nodded.

"That's Mr. and Mrs. Caldwell."

His eyes widened. "You attend the same church?" Wyatt looked at Mrs. Caldwell more closely. A regal woman with steel-gray hair, she wore a fancy bonnet, perhaps one of Mary Ann's designs, and a velvet cape that was surely too warm for the present weather. Her expression could only be described as pinched, though Wyatt had no way of guessing if she always looked that way or only when she must be in the presence of the Bells.

Mr. Caldwell wasn't a big man but nevertheless carried an air of authority and power.

"It's the only church here. It's either go to the same

one or don't go to any, so we've all decided to ignore each other on Sunday for the sake of worship."

He studied the idea. Somehow it didn't seem right. "Doesn't the scripture say if you have something against your brother you are to make it right before you come to church?"

"It doesn't say exactly that, but how are we to make peace when they want our land badly enough to try to drive us off?"

They had walked ahead of the others and stood by the wagon.

Mary Ann and her entourage headed in their direction.

Wyatt groaned. "Any hope we can leave before your friend starts asking me more questions?"

Cora waved to her sisters and they trotted over. "We'll all get into the wagon. That way Mary Ann will realize we don't plan to stay and visit."

Wyatt gratefully helped the girls into the back, waited for Lonnie to jump aboard, then climbed in, pulling the tailgate closed. He wondered what Lonnie thought of attending church, but the discussion would have to wait until they were alone.

Mary Ann slowed, waved prettily and pouted a little.

Wyatt silently begged Mr. Bell to hurry along. But the man made his way slowly toward them, his wife at his side, as they spoke to several neighbors.

Finally they climbed onto the wagon seat and headed out of town. Wyatt let out a huge sigh.

As they passed the livery barn, a swarthy man ducked into the shadows.

Every nerve in Wyatt's body jerked. He pulled his hat low and squinted at the man. Was it Jimmy Stone?

He shook off the thought. No, this man was heavier. Though if Jimmy wanted to find him, he could. It wouldn't take a skilled tracker to follow the trail a herd of horses left behind. And Jimmy had vowed revenge.

Wyatt sank back against the side of the wagon. He was only letting his fear of discovery—it never quite left his mind—make him unnecessarily nervous.

Later that evening, when he and Lonnie were alone, he turned to the boy. "What did you think of church?"

Lonnie shrugged. "It was okay." He grinned. "The girls sure did like you."

Wyatt groaned. "I hope they stay away. Young ladies are always full of demanding questions."

Lonnie sat back on his heels. "I never thought of that. What if they find out?"

"We'll just have to be careful of what we say." He tried not to think of the man he'd seen as they left town. It couldn't be Jimmy Stone. Could it?

Chapter Twelve

The next morning, Cora, Wyatt and Lonnie resumed work on the barn. Having had a serious talk with herself the night before, Cora concentrated on pounding in spikes and refused to let her mind wander to thinking of Wyatt as handsome, kind, gentle, helpful—

Whoa. She wasn't going to think like that anymore. No. If she couldn't keep her mind occupied with measuring where to place the spike and hitting it with each blow then she'd think of less positive things.

Such as how Wyatt had pulled his hat down when they'd passed the livery barn yesterday. As if he didn't want anyone to see him. How could he be concerned about that when he'd gone to town Saturday and church on Sunday? Most everyone in the community would have seen him by then.

Suspicion scratched at her thoughts.

Everyone except for those just passing through. Maybe the man she'd glimpsed near the livery barn knew Wyatt. If so, why didn't Wyatt greet him?

Many questions but no answers.

And as she'd told Ma and Pa, she'd guard herself and the family from a man with unanswered questions.

By midafternoon the floor was completed, and the three of them admired their work.

"Next, we'll tackle the roof," Wyatt said.

She felt his gaze on her and turned to meet his look. "What?"

"Are you sure I can't persuade you to let Lonnie and me do it on our own?"

"Huh?" Lonnie had been watching Lilly feed the pigs.

"We could manage on our own, don't you think?" he asked Lonnie.

"I guess." Lonnie's attention had already drifted away as he watched Lilly.

Cora refrained from pointing out how often Lonnie's attention had wandered. Usually to observe the pigs.

Lilly noted Lonnie's interest and called up to him, "I found the other batch of kittens. Do you want to see them?"

Lonnie scampered down the ladder before Wyatt could say a word.

Cora laughed at the confounded expression on Wyatt's face. "He likes the animals every bit as much as Lilly does. She gets a lot of satisfaction out of tending them. Not just the pigs and the sheep, but also the cats and their yearly batches of kittens. She hates to give the little ones away, but kittens from the Bells are known to be good mousers and are in high demand."

"I promised him we'd have pigs when we find a place to settle down."

"Have you decided where that might be?"

He shook his head, his eyes revealing nothing but secrets.

If she needed any reminder of the distance that separated them, he provided it at every question.

She shifted her attention to Lonnie and Lilly as they went to the cow shed to find the kittens. It reminded her of their first kittens on the farm. "We moved out here when I was twelve. Even though I liked the thought of living on our own farm, I didn't like change and I was sad. One day, Ma brought home a kitten for each of us. I remember how mine comforted me." That gave her an idea. Something that might help Lonnie get over his bouts of worry and fear. "Lonnie loves the pigs."

"He sure does."

"I would like to offer him two little ones in return for his work." Perhaps the pigs and the pleasure of working to earn them would comfort him as much as the kitten had comforted her.

Wyatt shook his head. "Our work here is to pay for the feed for the horses and our meals."

"I could ask him to do some other chores."

"Such as?"

"Feed the pigs."

Wyatt laughed. "He already does that. No, in order to be fair, it would have to be a job that needed doing."

She pressed her finger to her chin and considered the matter. "There's always something to be done." She refrained from pointing out that Lonnie often got distracted while helping with the barn, so he wasn't really doing his share anyway. "Like picking potato bugs off the plants. Or cutting the grass around the trees in the orchard."

He nodded. "So long as he does enough work to warrant earning the pigs."

"I'll see that he does. Do you want to tell him?"

"It's your deal. You tell him."

"Let's tell him together."

He helped her down the ladder and they crossed to the shed where Lilly and Lonnie sat cross-legged, each holding two kittens while the mama cat hovered nearby.

Lonnie looked up and guilt blanched his face. "I'm only going to spend a minute or two with them."

Cora again wondered at the tightness in him when he spoke to Wyatt.

Wyatt spoke gently. "I'm not here to scold you. Cora has a business proposition for you."

Lonnie turned an eager look toward Cora.

She stole a glance at Wyatt, and if she didn't miss her guess, he was hurt that Lonnie seemed to trust her more than him. If only she understood the reason. Could it be that Lonnie thought Wyatt would act like their father if angered? But she'd seen no evidence of raging anger, even when he corrected or instructed Lonnie. But there had to be some reason for Lonnie's odd behavior around Wyatt.

For now, she had a deal to strike with Lonnie. "Every year we sell most of the pigs."

Lilly sighed. "I hate that we do, but we can't afford to feed them all winter long. Besides, there are new ones in the spring."

Cora continued when Lilly gave her a chance. "I see you like pigs, and Wyatt says you want to raise them when you get your own ranch." No reason why it should hurt to think of them moving away, but she couldn't deny a stabbing pain in her heart.

"Has he changed his mind?" Lonnie's voice carried a bitter edge.

"No. Not at all. In fact, he and I have discussed letting you do extra chores around the place in exchange for two of these little pigs."

Lonnie transferred the kittens to Lilly's lap and bounced to his feet in one swift movement. "Really? You mean it?" He looked from Wyatt to Cora and they both nodded.

"If you think it's a good idea." Cora wanted to hear him continue to express his pleasure as openly as he did at the moment.

"Wowee! Do I ever! Thank you." He grabbed Cora's hand in a hard grip and pumped her arm up and down.

"You're welcome. Be sure to thank Wyatt, as well."

Lonnie faltered for barely a second, but his joy would not be thwarted. He slapped Wyatt on the back. "Thank you, big brother. Come on, Lilly. Help me choose which ones I want." The pair trotted over to the pigpen.

Cora grinned after them. "That went rather well, I think."

Wyatt's face wore a look of wonder and amazement as he stared after his brother. He nodded without speaking.

Sensing how Lonnie's customary fear around him hurt Wyatt's heart, Cora pressed her hand to his upper arm. "He's cautious of trusting people. Who can blame him when he's been hurt over and over by the very person who should have protected him? Give him time. He'll learn to trust—" She thought to say trust *you,* but perhaps that was too direct. "He'll learn to trust others in time."

Wyatt nodded again.

They didn't return to work on the barn before supper, but Lonnie trotted over to ask what chores he could do and Cora put him to work picking potato bugs off the plants. To his credit, he didn't complain about the disagreeable task.

Rose and Lilly sidled up to Cora. "Sure glad he likes the job," one of them said. "'Cause we don't," the other added, and they both shuddered.

The next two days Lonnie scampered up the ladder, eager to get done the work on the barn so he could do chores to earn his pigs.

Cora wondered if Wyatt had spoken to him about paying more attention to the building of the barn or if the boy was motivated of his own accord.

During the hot afternoon sun, and because she had other things to attend to, she insisted they take a break.

Lonnie scurried to do whatever jobs she assigned him.

She had to smile at his eagerness.

Pa, aware of her bargain with Lonnie and supportive of it, came to her side as she watched him scouring the potato plants for more bugs. Besides that, he had swung a sickle and mowed a patch of grass in the orchard. Once it was dry he'd stack it in the cow shed.

"He's a hard worker when motivated," Pa said.

"Certainly is." Her gaze went toward the path that led to Wyatt and Lonnie's campsite. Wyatt had gone there an hour ago to check on Fanny.

"I wonder if Fanny is okay," Cora said.

"Seems she should have delivered by now. Perhaps you should run down there and see if she needs help. Come and get me if she does."

"Okay, Pa." She trotted to the camp.

She hadn't been there since the first day and was surprised how neat and tidy the place was. She'd seen cowboy camps on occasion, and they were usually anything but clean.

The horses cropped the grass contentedly. Wyatt had moved the rope corral to give them ample grazing. A couple of the horses whinnied at her approach, then ignored her.

She didn't see Wyatt anywhere and edged along the herd. There he was. He signaled her over, holding a finger to his lips to indicate she should approach quietly.

Tiptoeing and moving slowly so as to not disturb the mare lying nearby, she moved to his side.

"Look," he said.

"Oh." A newborn foal lay on the ground.

"It was just born," he whispered.

The mare struggled to her feet and turned to lick her baby, cleaning it and encouraging it to stand.

The newborn put one front foot and then the other in place, lurched to its feet and fell as it failed to get its hind legs in place.

Cora held her breath, willing the little one to get up.

It struggled twice more, then took a break.

The mare waited beside it. Then the mare licked the baby again until it staggered to its feet and lurched forward on incredibly long, wobbly legs, nuzzling as it looked for milk.

Cora dashed away tears with her free hand. When had she taken Wyatt's hand? Or had he taken hers? All she knew was they held on tightly and neither made any move to break free.

"That was beautiful," she murmured.

"My first foal." His words resounded with awe.

"May it be the first of many, and may they be as perfect as this one."

He looked deep into her eyes, letting her see clear through his thoughts, except all he allowed her to see were his hopes and dreams of a successful ranch.

Far away from here, if he followed his plan.

She slipped her hand away. "What will you call her?"

He studied the little one, apparently unaware they no longer held hands.

For a heartbeat she regretted breaking the contact. But only for the length of time it took for her thoughts to register in her brain. He made it clear he meant to leave. He refused to share his secrets and she knew there were plenty. Truth be told, she knew little about this man.

Except his generosity, his gentleness with his brother and with animals and his honor in wanting to help to pay for feed that others might have accepted without offering anything in return.

"I think I'll call her Bell Flower. Because she was born on the Bell farm and you three girls are like flowers in a summer bouquet."

She added one more asset to the list. He was poetic.

He tipped his head to look into her face. "Do you like it?"

Feeling responsible for the uncertainty in his voice, she met his eyes. "I like it very much."

His gaze went on and on, laying claim to her thoughts, forbidding them to recall her reasons for caution. It went past her fears and her doubts to a tender spot inside that she kept covered, hidden from view. A spot that yearned to be touched in an affectionate way. To be protected through every danger. To be loved until life was no more.

She knew she had good reasons for keeping that place tucked away, but at the moment there seemed no reason at all and she could only smile with an open heart.

He touched her cheek. His gaze dipped to her mouth and then lifted to her eyes.

"Wyatt, Cora, are you here?" Lonnie, Lilly and Rose called them.

"They will all want to see the newborn."

"Yes, they will."

But neither of them moved.

The others called again. The mare whinnied, protective of her baby.

Cora sighed. "We'd better go warn them to be quiet before they start a stampede."

"Yes, we should."

Still they continued to look at each other, then he nodded and took one step away.

She blinked. What had just happened? How had she been mesmerized like that?

"Are you coming?" Wyatt waited for her, and she hurried to join him.

They reached the others, warned them to be quiet and led them back to watch Fanny and Bell Flower.

"Oh, the baby is so sweet," Lilly whispered.

Everyone agreed, but after a few minutes, Wyatt indicated they should leave the pair alone. They made their way back to the campsite and sat on logs pulled into a circle.

Rose and Lilly talked at once, joined often by Lonnie, oohing and aahing about the baby.

"I think my pigs are just as cute," Lonnie finally said, reducing the whole lot of them to laughter.

Cora jerked to her feet. “Come on, girls. Pa will wonder where we’ve disappeared to.”

The twins rose more slowly. “He’ll understand. After all, we’ve not seen a newborn foal before.”

“You’ve seen calves and pigs, kittens and puppies born,” Cora pointed out.

“It’s not the same,” Rose insisted.

“No, it’s not,” she agreed. “Besides, can one ever get tired of seeing the beginning of new life?” She smiled around the circle but her gaze rested on Wyatt. “A reminder that we can start fresh. Every day is a new beginning.” She hadn’t meant to suggest he should start over, build a new life, leave behind whatever secrets dogged him. The words had come out without such forethought.

But perhaps he would consider it.

And if he did? Would she be willing to open her heart to him? Trust him?

She wasn’t sure. Wasn’t it easier and safer to guard her thoughts and heart and mind?

It wasn’t until after he and Lonnie lay in their bedrolls that night that Wyatt got a chance to think through the events of the day.

The birth of Fanny’s foal had changed his relationship with Cora. Or at least it would if he let it. They had shared a special moment. He’d allowed himself to open his heart to her in a way he’d never done before. And then she’d offered him the hope of starting over.

But she didn’t know what she offered or to whom. He was a man convicted of a crime and could not accept the hope of a new beginning.

“Are you awake?” Lonnie asked.

"Yes. Are you?"

Lonnie laughed. "No, I'm talking in my sleep."

Wyatt grinned. He loved it when Lonnie relaxed enough to joke and laugh with him. "What's on your mind?"

"So many things don't make sense. Like how nice the Bells are. But what would they think if they found out the truth?"

Wyatt had no answer. "I hope they never do. You know what people are like when they learn about me. I wouldn't want the Bells to have to deal with that." All the name-calling, the refusal to do business with anyone who associated with a jailbird and the accusations every time someone lost something.

Lonnie grunted. "Me, either." He perched up on one elbow. "It's nice for a while, though, isn't it?"

"It surely is." But Wyatt knew deep inside that he couldn't keep his past hidden forever. There was always the threat of someone journeying through who would recognize his name or face and recall the story of his going to jail. All he could hope for was to stay until Fanny and Bell Flower were ready to travel.

Please, God, keep the truth concealed until we can leave and then after so the Bells are never touched by my past.

He would leave as soon as possible, but he meant to enjoy every minute of the few weeks it would take for Bell Flower to get strong enough to travel.

Surely there was no harm in that.

He closed his mind to the warning bells jangling in his head.

Chapter Thirteen

The rafters were in place by early afternoon the next day. It was time to start building the roof. Wyatt eyed the height and slope and swallowed hard. How was he to persuade Cora to stay on the ground and let him and Lonnie do the work? He'd mentioned it three times yesterday and she'd scoffed. But he simply couldn't think of her in such a dangerous place.

"No one is going up there until I make some footholds." He climbed the ladder and nailed boards into place.

From his vantage point he saw a wagon crossing the river. Five minutes later, he called, "You got company coming."

Visitors weren't unusual. Three times in the past week someone had come for one of Mrs. Bell's medicines, or eggs or milk or any of the various things the Bells sold.

Until now, the arrival of callers had set his nerves to twitching. Each time he feared it was someone to inform the Bells they harbored a jailbird who was not welcome in the community. But today he breathed a prayer of thanks. This wagonload of people might be enough to keep Cora on the ground for the rest of the afternoon.

He recognized Anna, Nancy and three other young ladies from church whose names he didn't recall. Apparently this was to be a social call. All the better.

The wagon drew to a halt before the house. "Hello, Cora," called Anna.

Cora sighed loudly enough that Wyatt heard her from his perch atop the roof. "Hello, girls."

Wyatt wondered if the visitors heard the resignation in Cora's voice. If so, it didn't deter them. They hopped down, patted their skirts and adjusted their bonnets. One young lady removed her hat to reveal a mass of golden curls. She looked around, spied Wyatt on the roof and waved.

Five pretty faces turned in his direction and smiled.

He ducked away and hammered nails, successfully drowning out anything they said.

"Rose, Lilly, we have guests," Cora called, and the girls left the garden where they'd been picking beans.

Wyatt saw a lot more eagerness in their faces for the interruption than Cora had expressed.

Lonnie had watched the proceedings from the ground but now climbed the ladder. "Suppose they're going to have a tea party or something?"

"Do you want to join them?" Had Lonnie noticed that one of the girls was a younger sister?

"Nah."

Rather a halfhearted response, but Wyatt let it go. He meant to make the most of this time with Cora otherwise occupied and he placed boards and nailed them in place as quickly as he could with Lonnie struggling to keep up.

The young ladies and the Bell sisters spread quilts in the shade of the trees next to the house. He could have wished for them to go around the corner out of sight so they couldn't all watch him, but such was not to be the case.

Cora brought out a tray of glasses filled with lemonade and Rose passed around cookies.

Eight heads tipped together and laughter reached Wyatt. He told himself it was normal girlish behavior, but he couldn't help wondering if they found him amusing.

Cora rose and crossed toward the barn.

Wyatt watched her every step. His lungs tightened as she approached the barn. Had they sent her on an errand? He guessed they had, and guessed, as well, that it involved him in a way he might not like.

Cora reached the bottom of the ladder. "Wyatt?"

He slowly turned to look down at her. "Do you need something?"

"Yes. You."

The girls giggled.

Pink raced up her neck and pooled in Cora's cheeks. "My visitors accuse me of having bad manners by not inviting you to join us. So would you both please join us?"

He should refuse. There was the roof to finish. Besides, he had no desire to share the afternoon with a bevy of giggling females, but Cora appeared to need help in dealing with her friends. "Thank you. We accept your invitation."

She nodded and stepped back as Lonnie descended the ladder.

Wyatt climbed down more slowly. At the bottom he

whispered to her, "I'm hardly clean enough to join your friends." Perspiration soaked his back. He swiped his arm across his face to dry it.

"They'll no doubt be impressed by your muscles and sweat." She rolled her eyes.

He grinned at her. "Is that what young ladies like?"

"If so, you're all set for success."

Their gazes locked. Did he read admiration? Reluctant, if so. But he also detected uncertainty. Why? Then it hit him. She thought he might enjoy the admiration of those young ladies.

"Success if I want admiration, but not if I much prefer conversation and sharing of similar tastes." He wished he could express himself better, explain to her that her honesty and hard work were a lot more appealing to him than giggling admiration.

She smiled, the tension gone from her eyes. "Let's see if you can't enjoy a bit of each."

He accompanied her to the tea party where Lonnie hovered, waiting to be invited to sit down.

"Ladies," Cora said. "You remember Wyatt and Lonnie from church." Ignoring their wide-eyed admiration, she introduced her friends. Besides the two he recognized there was a Miss Sally Jones, as well as a Miss Inez Burroughs and her younger sister, Ellen, who smiled sweetly at Lonnie.

Cora indicated they should sit.

Wyatt sat next to her and took the offered glass of lemonade and two cookies.

"Where are you from, Mr. Wyatt?" one lady asked.

"Kansas," he said. They might want more information but he didn't mean to provide it.

"Are you planning to settle here?" Nancy asked.

"Going north." The same answer he'd given Mr. Bell.

The questions continued to fly. Where north? Why? Did he have a wife and children waiting for him? Had he been in the army?

"Army? No. Why would you think that?"

Sally, who had asked the question, shrugged. "I thought the way you carry yourself, your short answers—" She shook her head. "It made me think of my uncle who was a soldier."

Lonnie's hand halted half to his mouth with a cookie. His shoulders tensed.

Wyatt didn't want anyone to look at the boy and wonder at his reaction, but he struggled to control his own movements. Did something about the way he talked and moved provide clues that he'd been in jail? He'd hardly think it would be similar to being in the army.

Cora, who'd watched in silence as he fielded the many questions, spoke to the young women. "Is there anything new in town?"

The preacher's daughter, Anna, bounced with eagerness. "Indeed, there is much news. Someone stole a bunch of stuff from Mr. Frank's store."

Miss Nancy interrupted. "The cash box was stolen from the feed store."

"Two houses were broken into, and silver and jewelry taken," Miss Sally added.

Cora looked shocked. "Really? There have never been robberies in Bar Crossing before that I know of."

"That's what everyone is saying."

"No one in town would do something so awful," Anna said. "My father says it must be a stranger doing it."

Wyatt kept his eyes lowered. Bad enough to be

among those under suspicion because he was a stranger, but he'd be found guilty without evidence or a trial if anyone discovered his past.

Fortunately, no one pointed out the fact that he and Lonnie were strangers, and the conversation moved to other things. Wyatt wanted to excuse himself and return to the barn, but when he pushed to his feet, the girls protested.

"You aren't leaving us?"

"Please stay." Cora's tone revealed nothing. Did she want him to stay for her sake?

He'd stay only because she asked him.

The ladies remained for three hours, as if there was nothing more important in anyone's life than sitting in the shade.

Finally, Nancy, who seemed to be in charge, pushed to her feet. "It's time for us to leave. It's been so nice visiting with everyone."

Wyatt rose as soon as she moved and nodded to her and to the others as they left.

Only after they rumbled from the yard, calling more goodbyes, did he let his gaze go to the barn. It waited patiently for boards to be nailed into place.

Cora let out a long sigh. "Ma needs our help." The girls gathered up quilts, glasses and the remnants of the afternoon and traipsed indoors.

"Supper will be ready shortly." Cora paused to inform him, then disappeared inside.

Lonnie had already gone to see the pigs.

Wyatt jammed his hands in his pockets. What was he to do with himself? It hardly seemed worthwhile to climb the ladder. He wouldn't have time to fit a board into place.

He barely finished the thought before Cora called out, "Supper."

Wyatt aimed to get his brother, but he saw the boy was already headed for the house.

They joined the others.

The meal was rushed, as everyone seemed eager to do the work that had been neglected over the afternoon, but they still took time for Bible reading. Wyatt enjoyed this pool of calm at the end of the day.

Mr. Bell had barely said "amen" before Cora bolted to her feet.

"The cows are getting impatient to be milked."

He realized they had been calling softly and followed her outside. "Do you need help with the milking?"

Her eyes widened. "You can milk a cow? I didn't think cowboys considered the chore manly enough for their status in life."

"I heard that somewhere, too, but I milked cows once upon a time." Years ago, when his pa still had a prosperous farm, before he started selling off stock and moving around. "Don't suppose I've forgotten how."

They brought the two cows in from the pasture and left the dry one. Each one went to a stall in the shed.

"Well, let's see if you remember." Cora handed him a bucket and pointed him to the smaller cow. "You milk Maude, she's the gentler of the two."

He grabbed a stool, and he and Cora sat at the haunches of the cows. The *squish, squish* of milk going into the pail filled the silence. A motley-colored cat with a right-angle crook in its tail appeared, and Cora sent a stream of milk that it caught neatly.

"Where's Grub?" Seemed to Wyatt he should have been at the milking.

"He's mooching at the kitchen. Lilly will give him treats. Do you know she makes cookies for him?"

Wyatt snorted a laugh. "Cookies for a dog?"

"Not the kind you'd like. Believe me. I was once foolish enough to taste one. Ptooey. But Grub loves them."

She aimed another squirt of milk toward the cat. Wyatt made a smacking sound to get the cat's attention and sent a squirt its way. He laughed when it was right on target.

Cora stood, set the milk bucket to the side, let her cow out of the barn and returned to stand at his side. "Are you finished?"

He wasn't, but he wasted no time stripping the cow's udder of the last of the milk and turning her out with the other. He followed Cora to the house.

Lilly pulled what looked like cookies from the oven. He was thankful he'd been warned and wouldn't be sneaking any cookies from that tray.

Cora nudged him. "Milk goes in the workroom." He accompanied her there and poured the milk through the straining cloth.

"Could I offer you a cookie when we're done here?" Her innocent tone did not fool him.

He barked a laugh.

She grinned. "I guess you'll check every cookie carefully from now on before you bite into it."

"I'll make sure you take a bite first." He smiled at her.

The mischief in her eyes stirred his blood and made him wish for days and days of nothing but teasing and joy. His throat tightened. He couldn't stay, no matter how enticing the idea seemed. He must get far enough away that his past would never catch up with him, someplace where no one knew him or cared a fig about him.

Her hands stilled as the moment lengthened into something soft and alluring.

He sucked in warm air laden with the smell of fresh milk, cheese and a heartbeat of sweetness from the woman before him. His resolve threatened to crumble like dust.

"I need to take care of my horses." He bolted from the room, calling a hasty "Thank you and good night," and trotted to the campsite.

Lonnie thundered after him. "What's the hurry?"

Wyatt slowed his steps. "The day got away, what with company all afternoon."

"Didn't you enjoy it?"

"I wanted to get the roof built."

Lonnie shrugged. "We've got lots of time. Didn't you say it will be a month before Fanny and the foal can travel?"

"Yeah."

"So what's the harm in a little socializing?"

Wyatt stared at his brother. "Is this the same person who wanted to leave a few days ago?"

"That was two weeks ago. But now I got reason to stay."

"Like some young gal?"

Lonnie blushed. "I have to earn enough to buy two pigs. Remember?"

"Oh, right. That. You didn't get much done toward that today, what with all the socializing."

"I'll make up for it." Lonnie trotted on ahead.

Wyatt thought to warn the boy of the dangers they faced by staying. Not only to themselves but to the Bells and anyone else associated with them. They needed to put more distance between them and their past. But he couldn't ruin Lonnie's mood. It was the first time he'd seen him so content about staying and so ready to associate with others. Another reason to be grateful for the delay in their travels.

Before he caught up to Lonnie, alarm bells filled Wyatt's brain. Every delay increased the risk. But even worse was all this socializing. People would grow more demanding about his past. Lonnie might let something slip.

He'd simply have to excuse himself from any more of it.

It should be simple enough. From what he'd observed, it wasn't as though the Bells entertained a lot or visited others. He had no call to go to town on Saturday and could find some excuse to miss church.

How hard could it be?

The next morning, Cora put on her oldest dress and headed for the barn as soon as the chores were done. Wyatt and Lonnie had arrived a few minutes ago and were nailing boards to the rafters.

At her approach, Wyatt came down the ladder. "Cora, for my peace of mind, please stay off the roof."

The pleading look in his eyes caused her determination to waver. "But I have to help." Even to her own ears, she sounded less than convincing.

"It's far too dangerous with those long skirts."

She looked down at her dress. "I could borrow a pair of Pa's trousers."

Wyatt hooted. "Can I listen while you ask him?"

She grinned in acknowledgment. "Pa would have a fit, wouldn't he?"

"I expect so."

"That leaves me little choice, then." She took a step toward the ladder.

"Cora, please reconsider." He caught her arm, sending a jolt through her nerves and making it hard to remember why it mattered that she worked on the barn if he cared so much.

"Hey, Wyatt, I need another board," Lonnie called.

His words were all the reminder she needed. They were working to pay for feed for their horses and the meals the Bells provided. However, building the barn was not their responsibility. They'd be moving on. North somewhere. She'd be here with an unfinished barn if she didn't do her share.

"I'll see that the barn is built." She'd promised herself the day Pa fell from the ladder. She'd drive every nail by herself if she couldn't get help. "I thank God He sent you to help, but it's still my job."

"Why not trust Him to provide enough help that you don't need to take risks?"

She met his gaze. Was he asking her to trust God? Or him? She tried to read past the appeal in his dark eyes, but he had closed his thoughts to her probing. Disappointed, she turned away. How could she trust a man who shut himself off from her? As to trusting God… "I trust God to protect me." And give her strength.

Wyatt let out a long sigh as if she taxed his patience. He muttered something under his breath. Sounded as if he said, "How hard can it be to convince her?" Then his gaze slid by her and his eyes widened. "Looks as though you've got more company coming."

She turned to shade her eyes and watch three wagons approach. "What's going on?"

"I'll let you figure it out." He climbed up the ladder and started hammering furiously.

"Wyatt?" What was wrong? He should be happy that more visitors had descended on them. Wouldn't it ensure she couldn't help?

The wagons drew closer. Ma and Pa and the twins lined up to watch.

"Why, Pastor Rawley," Pa said, stepping forward as the first wagon drew to a halt. "What brings you our way?"

Mrs. Rawley sat beside him in the wagon. Anna and two men rode in the back. The second wagon had four men in it, and the third two women and two men. Some of the people were from nearby farms; the rest were from town.

Cora could not think what they wanted.

Pastor Rawley jumped to the ground. "My Anna came home yesterday to say you were putting up a barn by yourselves. Now, we all know that isn't a job for a family to do alone. So we decided to do the neighborly thing. We've come to help."

The others stepped to the ground, each man carrying the tools they'd need.

Mrs. Rawley and the other women approached Ma. "Now, we know you weren't expecting a crew, so we brought along food for the noon meal."

"Bless you," Ma said. "Bless you all."

"I see you've done a great deal already," Pastor Rawley said.

The men moved to the barn and Wyatt slowly turned to greet them.

Cora couldn't figure him out. For a man who thought she should trust God to provide help to get the barn done, he certainly seemed reluctant when all this help appeared.

Anna caught Cora's hand and dragged her away. "Isn't this wonderful?"

"Indeed." Cora gave her friend a little squeeze. The barn would be finished in no time. Wonderful news.

So why did she feel as if she'd been robbed of something special?

She would not answer the question.

But as the sound of hammers on nails and saws through wood filled the air, she couldn't shake the feeling.

She helped move two tables under the trees and set out the food.

"Stop staring at him," Anna said.

Cora jerked her attention back to filling a dish with bread-and-butter pickles. "I'm watching the progress on the barn. I can't believe how fast it's going." The roof was almost finished.

"Uh-huh. But I have to say, he is worth taking a long look at."

"Who?" Though there was only one person to be considered.

"Why, your Wyatt Williams, of course."

"He's not my—"

Anna patted her arm. "If you say so."

Rose and Lilly joined them.

Cora hoped they were too late to overhear Anna's silly comments. But she forgot to hope Anna wouldn't repeat them.

"She's not staring at Wyatt," Anna said.

"Of course she is. Just like the rest of us."

"Rose." Cora couldn't believe her younger sister. "Have you no shame? If Ma heard your comments she'd confine you to your room."

Rose laughed. "Do you suppose she looked at Pa that way once upon a time?"

They all looked toward Pa. Ma sat with the other women, shelling peas as she watched the progress.

"I expect she did," Lilly said.

A little later, Ma called out for everyone to come eat. The men gathered around the table. Wyatt, Cora noted, came last.

Pastor Rawley said grace and then, one by one, the crowd filed past the table, filling their plates with a wide variety of food. The ladies must have planned this the previous evening, as they'd brought fried chicken and potato salad, along with several kinds of vegetables.

Lonnie made no secret of examining the array of desserts. "You sure there's going to be lots?"

One of the men said, "Not if I get there first."

Wyatt laughed along with the others.

Cora's heart beat more smoothly than it had all morning. Perhaps she'd only imagined that Wyatt objected to the visitors.

Everyone settled on the grass except Pa, who sat on a chair next to Ma.

Cora wanted nothing so much as to sit next to Wyatt, but it would be unseemly. When Anna whispered in her ear, "Let's sit over there," and pointed to a spot close to Wyatt, Cora shook her head. "I'm going to sit beside the twins."

Anna pouted a little but followed Cora.

After the food was put away, Cora looked longingly

at the garden, but she could hardly turn her attention to hoeing while they had company. She suggested they go for a walk along the river, but Anna begged off.

"My shoes are too tight."

Cora silently groaned. "What do you want to do, then?"

"Sit here and watch. And don't tell me you don't want to do the same thing."

Cora quirked an eyebrow. "I guess there'd be no point if you have your mind set on believing otherwise."

"Exactly." She plopped down in a spot that allowed them a view of the men shingling one side of the barn. Of course, one of the men was Wyatt, Lonnie at his side.

Cora observed for several minutes and began to notice something. She sat up straighter so she could see better.

Anna nudged her and laughed.

Cora ignored her and kept her attention on Wyatt. The other men talked and laughed and called to each other. Wyatt did not.

Why had he withdrawn?

Chapter Fourteen

The barn stood with its roof finished. Apart from doors and the interior, it was done.

Wyatt admired the job along with the rest of the men. They filed past and shook his hand, and he thanked each one. They hadn't been helping him specifically, but he was grateful Cora wouldn't feel bound to climb up to the roof to help.

Their arrival had been a surprise—a mixed blessing, to be sure.

He'd meant to avoid meeting any more people and instead was surrounded by them. Friendly, inquisitive people who wanted to know everything about him. At first, he'd been able to answer without revealing anything of importance. The men liked to hear of his horses. When he said he was headed north, several offered suggestions for a good location.

But when the talk turned to the robberies occurring in town, he knew he'd better watch his every word.

The men loaded up their wagons and in short order they were driving their horses out of the yard. Wyatt had been aware of Cora's concerned looks all afternoon. As if she wondered at how he'd pulled away from the conversations around him. He'd seen the determination on her face and guessed she meant to question him. But he could not give her an answer. At least, not one he cared to share.

He decided the best thing would be to pass on supper and return to his camp, even though his stomach growled at the thought. Before he could escape, Cora appeared at his elbow.

"I expect you're relieved to see the barn done."

"Uh-huh. Aren't you?"

"Of course I am."

They were both talking to avoid saying what they really wanted to say. He wished with all his heart he could tell her the truth. Would she run away from him if he did? Or would she comfort him with words and touches?

At the thought, his mouth dried so much that he almost choked.

"Let's go for a walk," she said, and headed for the river.

He meant to say no. He knew a dozen reasons he should refuse. Instead, he walked at her side.

"It's nice that you have friends to help," he said. *Would you accept me as a friend if you knew the truth? Would they?*

"Both Stu Maples and Mr. Frank said no one would help because of the Caldwells. I guess they were wrong."

"It seems the Caldwells have less power than they think." These people were willing to stand up to the Caldwells. Would they be as ready to stick by the Bells if they were associated with a jailbird?

As they walked, Cora paused occasionally to caress wildflowers.

He glanced at the flowers, but they weren't as beautiful or beguiling as Cora. Had she thought him silly to say the Bell sisters were like a summer bouquet? A long-forgotten memory sprang to mind and it tumbled from his mouth before he could put the brakes on his words.

"These flowers remind me of a time when Lonnie was about three—which would make me eight. Our pa had just moved us to a new farm with his horses. Lonnie and I were out exploring and we found a whole meadow of flowers." He remembered the vivid colors. "Bluebells and purple spiky things and little red flat flowers and tiny white lacey ones." He smiled as he recalled the details of that day.

"Lonnie laughed and spun around like crazy in the flowers. Said they were as pretty as a rainbow. A butterfly flitted about and Lonnie tried to catch it. He called it a butter bee. You know, mixing up butterfly and bumble bee." He smiled clear to his socks as he thought of the joy of that moment.

"Of course, we picked an armload of flowers and took them home to Ma. She found a Mason jar and filled it and put it in the window. 'Now it's really our home,' she said."

His smile disappeared and his insides turned brittle. He did not want to remember what happened next.

Cora slipped to his side and rubbed her hand up and down his arm, easing some of the tension. "It sounds like a beautiful day."

He nodded. He kept his gaze focused on the horizon, knowing if he looked at her she would see his pain and he would pull her into his arms, seeking her comfort.

"Something happened to turn it into a bad memory, didn't it?" she asked quietly.

He sucked in air until his lungs could hold no more, but it didn't release his heart to beat with normal regularity.

"Wyatt." Her voice was soft as the brush of butterfly wings. "What happened?"

A shudder shook him from head to toe.

Her arm pressed about his waist and steadied him.

"Pa was in a rage about something. I suppose he was angry he'd had to sell the old farm, though it was nothing to do with me. Or Lonnie." He swallowed hard. "He came in as Ma was arranging the flowers and grabbed me. Cuffed my ears for wasting Ma's time." His head had rung the rest of the day.

"I'm so sorry." She pressed her cheek to his arm.

"That wasn't the worst part."

She held on to him.

He knew he should hold himself tight, not let go of his emotions lest they drown him. But he raised his right arm, wrapped it around her shoulders and breathed deeply of wildflowers.

"He slapped Lonnie so hard—" His voice tightened. "So hard Lonnie fell to the floor screaming. Ma tried to stop him, but he pushed her aside and said if she ever interfered again he would boot her out on the road."

He'd forgotten that Pa had said that. Remembering it helped him understand why Ma never did anything to stop the beatings.

"Wyatt, I am so, so sorry for both of you. That isn't the way God meant for families to be."

"I know. I see how your family is. You're very fortunate to have them." He pressed his cheek to her head and let her comfort wash through him.

"Thank goodness you and Lonnie had each other. You take good care of your brother."

Wyatt released her. "Seems Lonnie thinks I'm like Pa. I'm not, you know. I'm not."

She caught his hand. "I think he knows it. He's just afraid to trust."

"I'm his brother. He should trust me." He couldn't disguise the pain in his voice. Didn't even try.

"I guess some hurts take a long time to heal."

"I guess so."

She tugged at his hand. "Wyatt?"

Slowly he brought his gaze to hers. In her eyes he found a store of comfort and understanding, and he allowed himself to soak it in.

"What about you?"

"Me? What *about* me?"

She smiled gently, chidingly. "What about your hurts?"

"My hurts?" At first he didn't understand, then he realized he'd let his barriers slip and she meant to step into forbidden territory. He pulled his hand away. "I'm fine. I'm older. Been away from home for a bit so I got over Pa's meanness." In prison he'd met people even more cruel than Pa and learned to stay out of their way, though he'd never stood by while they'd picked on someone smaller or weaker. Guess that grew out of his attempts to protect Lonnie from their pa. Jimmy Stone turned out to be more vindictive than Pa had even been.

She grabbed his shoulders and faced him squarely.

He settled his gaze on a lacy flower over her right shoulder.

"I don't know if you truly believe that or not. But I don't. Wyatt, I see before me a man with a whole lot of secrets and hurts. You need to let go of them and let people care about you."

His gaze met hers. Soft and inviting, full of comfort.

"Cora." The word grated from a tight throat. "You don't know what you're asking." No, that said too much. "You don't know what you're talking about." He stepped away, put enough distance between them so she couldn't reach for him. Heaven help him, if she wrapped her arms about him and asked the source of his hurt, he might well blurt out the whole ugly truth. *Would you still be so sure people should care about me?*

Would you care about me?

He couldn't live with the alternative—having her turn her back on him, knowing others judged her because of him.

"We need to get back." He waited for her to fall into step with him but made sure to keep a good, safe distance between them.

When they reached the house, Rose stepped outside.

"I was just about to come looking for you," she said. "Supper's ready."

"Thanks, but I need to check on Fanny. Make sure she's okay. Tell Lonnie there's no need to rush back." He strode away without a backward look, even when Cora called his name.

A can of cold beans and some jerky would have to suffice. At the least, it'd serve to remind him to guard his heart and his words more closely.

Saturday dawned with a festive feel in Cora's mind. The barn was almost finished. She sang as she milked the cows. Today they would go to town. She meant to steal a few minutes of Wyatt's time and take him around on her own. She planned to show him the house they used to live in, now occupied by another family. They'd go by the school and the little grove of trees in the back of it where she and Anna had spent many happy hours.

She hurried through her daily tasks so they could get away in good time. Yet part of her watched the trail that would bring Wyatt and Lonnie up from their camp. What was taking him so long? He usually arrived before she finished the chores, but today the milking was done, the milk put to cool, the wagon loaded with produce to take to town and still neither Wyatt nor Lonnie had appeared.

She was about to suggest that someone should check on them when a figure loped toward them. Lonnie. But where was Wyatt?

Lonnie reached the wagon. "Wyatt says he can't go to town. He says he's neglected the horses and wants to tend to their needs today."

"That's fine," Pa said. "Is there anything he wants me to pick up for him?"

"He didn't say." Lonnie shifted from one foot to the other.

"Did you want to come?" Pa asked.

"Can I?"

"Certainly. Unless Wyatt needs you."

"He said I could go if I wanted." Lonnie scrambled into the back of the wagon and sat beside Cora.

Cora smiled a welcome even though her heart felt as if it had been gouged with a handful of spikes. But perhaps this was another way to get through to Wyatt. She'd go through Lonnie.

But as soon as the thought came, she dismissed it. She would not use such devious methods. Instead, she joined in the general chatter with her sisters and Lonnie. All the while, more than half her brain and most of her heart lingered back at the farm.

If it wouldn't be inappropriate and forbidden by her parents, she would have asked to stay behind, as well. But all she could do was laugh and smile through the day. She did her best to do so, but a day in town had never felt so long.

Or so unwelcome.

They arrived back at the farm in time to prepare supper.

Ma said what Cora longed to hear. "Lonnie, bring your brother up for supper. I don't like to think of him eating on his own when we have such abundance."

Lonnie ran to do her bidding and Cora ducked her head over the salad she prepared lest anyone see the anticipation on her face.

But if she hoped for a chance to talk to Wyatt alone after supper, she was disappointed. The girls were full of news from town that they were eager to share with him. Neither of them appeared to notice the distance in the back of his eyes.

The evening flowed past until Ma and Pa announced bedtime, and still she hadn't had a moment alone with him.

She crawled into bed, pulled the covers to her chin and closed her eyes. *God, how can I help him deal with his inner hurts? Oh, I know I am powerless to help him in any way, but I do want to see him open up. Please help him, and if You can, please use me to help him.*

Tomorrow was Sunday. She prayed Pastor Rawley

would have words to minister to the brokenhearted, meaning Wyatt. That Wyatt would have ears to hear the words and readiness to apply them to his life.

She sat straight up in bed. What if he refused to go?

The moonlight through the curtains revealed both girls looking at her.

"What's wrong?" Rose asked.

"What if Wyatt chooses not to attend church tomorrow?"

"Why would he do that?"

"Why didn't he go to town with us?" She didn't wait for an answer. "I get the feeling he's wanting to leave." Or at least distance himself from them—or her. She swallowed the thought as if it were bitter gall.

Lilly sat up. "Surely not. Fanny and Bell Flower aren't strong enough yet."

"You're right, of course." She lay down, not comforted in the least.

"I expect he'd come if you ask him nicely." Rose's innocent-sounding words didn't disguise the teasing.

"I agree," Lilly said. "Ask him."

She would.

And the next morning she did. And he agreed.

She smiled all the way to church.

Wyatt had meant to find an excuse for staying home Sunday. But when Cora came to the camp, looking like a pretty blue flower and asking him to accompany the family, he couldn't say no.

Nor did he regret it.

Pastor Rawley spoke about the prodigal son. "I know some of you have prodigal sons or daughters. Are you ready and willing to welcome them home? Perhaps some of you are prodigals. Return to those who love you. It is never too late or too early to start over again. To receive the love and acceptance offered you. Often the first step is the hardest. But I urge you, don't keep running. Isaiah 55:7 says, 'Let him return unto the Lord and he will have mercy upon him.'" The pastor then went on to admonish each one to be prepared to welcome and accept prodigals. "Make this church and community a place where repentant sinners and returning prodigals find a home."

Wyatt listened to every word, his heart hungry for such acceptance. Would he find it in this community if they knew the truth? He believed the pastor would live up to his words. But what about the others?

For the first time since his release from prison, he allowed hope to creep into his heart.

Hope rooted and grew throughout the day as the Bell family lazed about on a warm, sunny Sunday.

Cora suggested a walk and he readily agreed, wanting to talk to her about the sermon.

"I'm glad you came to church with us," she said as they wandered along the river.

"I am, too." They paused to watch a crow and a sparrow dueling in the air, amazed at the boldness of the smaller bird. Then they continued on until they reached a row of boulders and sat down.

"What did you think of the sermon today?" he asked.

"I agreed with every word. People should be accepted for who they are. Backgrounds shouldn't make any difference if the person is honorable and good."

His heart did a happy flip. "Even if the person carries a bad reputation?"

"If the person is ready to leave that behind, people

should accept that and allow that person to start over."

She turned to study him. "Are we talking about anyone in particular? You, perhaps?"

He took one step into dangerous territory. "The past can't be erased."

"It can't even be forgotten." She stared down at her hands twisting in her lap.

She had a loving family and belonged in a supportive community. He couldn't imagine she'd ever done anything she'd be ashamed or embarrassed about. "What's in your past you want to forget?"

Her posture pulled at his heart. Why should the subject distress her?

She looked at him with her brown eyes bleeding pain. "I want to forget that my papa left the three of us in the middle of the prairie and rode away, never to return."

As he stared at her, his heart drained of all feeling. With each beat it filled again—with shock, surprise and wrenching sorrow. He could not ignore her pain and sidled closer to wrap an arm about her shoulders and pull her against his side.

"Tell me what happened."

"I remember my mother. Before she died, she made me promise to take care of the twins. I remember a man. I guess he was my father. I am no longer sure of my memories, but in my mind I think I see a man lift us from a wagon to the dusty ground and then drive away. I do remember staring after the wagon until it disappeared. And standing on tiptoe watching for its return. We waited and waited. Lilly started crying and then Rose. They always cried at the same time. I assured them Papa would come back. After a few hours I quit saying it and told them I'd take care of them. I don't know how long we were there. I know we fell asleep holding each other. We woke with the sun on our faces and resumed our post watching for Papa. The Bells found us and took us home and adopted us."

Though her words were spoken with cold precision, his heart threatened to burst from the pain he knew she tried to disguise.

"I was five. The twins were three." She shivered.

He pressed close, offering his strength.

She leaned into him, accepting it and reached for his hand.

"I refused to go with them at first. Said our papa would come back and find us gone and he wouldn't like it. But they persuaded us we could wait at their place. They lived in Bar Crossing at the time. For months, years in fact, I looked for Papa. One day I thought I saw him, and my heart almost leaped from my chest. I raced over to him and threw my arms about him, but when the man looked at me I knew it wasn't my father. I was eight years old by then, and that's when I knew he was never coming back. From then on, the Bells were my only family. I owe them my life and the twins' lives. They have been ideal parents."

The final words came out strong and bold, yet she held his hand with such force he knew fears and uncertainties lay beneath the surface.

He recalled how she'd said some hurts take a long time to heal. Maybe there were some hurts that never healed.

She let out a breath that seemed to come from her very depths. "There are people who think less of us because of our background."

"Why, that's plain stupid. It wasn't as if you were in

any way responsible." Maybe the community wasn't as accepting as he hoped.

She nodded. "Pastor Rawley said exactly that in one sermon. Oh, he didn't mention us by name, but I'm pretty sure he had us in mind. 'Friends,' he said in his gentle way. 'Judge not that ye be not judged.' Then he told a story about a missionary who did such wonderful work and said many a society had rejected him because his father was in jail for beating a man."

Wyatt's insides tensed, though he gave no outward appearance. Had she guessed his secret? Reason prevailed. Of course she hadn't. But her words offered him hope.

Impossible hope, all things considered.

She chuckled. "I'll never forget his words. 'Do not judge a man by his past but by his future, not by his failures but by his dreams and possibilities.'"

Wyatt breathed in each word. "It's idealistic."

"Yes, it is, but it's far better to reach for the ideal than to wallow in the unchangeable. Our pasts cannot be changed. Our future is a blank slate. We choose what goes on it."

"So you're saying to forget the past and move forward?"

She shifted to face him squarely, their hands still entwined. "Maybe I can't forget the past. It hurts to think my real father would abandon us. But I'm determined to put it behind me and press on."

The intensity of her gaze burned through his resistance and threw open the locked doors of his heart. He longed to be able to live without the burden of his past weighing him down.

Was it possible?

He touched her cheek and smiled. “You make the future look bright and free.”

She trailed her finger down his cheek. “It can be.”

Could it? Could he face his past here, in this family, church and community? Could he find acceptance?

Or would such a choice invite more of what he’d experienced and worse, in that it would affect the Bell family?

He could not risk that.

Seemed he had no choice but to stick to his plans.

He got to his feet and pulled her up. She clung to his hand as they retraced their steps, and he didn’t even try to slip from her grasp. He told himself it was only to comfort her after learning about how she and the twins were abandoned.

But how could he deny himself the same comfort?

He couldn’t stay, but how would he make himself go? Dare he allow himself to hope his past would never catch up with him?

Chapter Fifteen

After breakfast the next morning, Ma said, "Mrs. Rawley informed me the chokecherries and serviceberries are plentiful in the hills."

"We're going berry picking?" The twins grinned.

Cora smiled at them. "It's work, you know."

"But fun work," Rose said.

They crowded for the door and pushed through in their hurry to prepare for the outing. And crashed right into Wyatt.

"Whoa." He steadied them. His hands felt warm and firm on Cora's shoulders, reminding her of the emotional upheaval she'd been through yesterday. She'd found such comfort and strength in his arms that she'd almost turned to his chest for more.

Even now, her heart ached to feel his arms around her. Instead, she struggled to keep her reaction hidden.

She'd never confessed to anyone how it hurt to be left by their papa, but yesterday, when he'd talked about leaving the past behind, the words had tumbled out as if she'd been waiting all her life to tell someone. When he'd offered his comfort and strength she knew this was the person she'd been waiting to tell.

His sympathy had helped her realize how little it mattered that her real father had proved untrustworthy. She had a wonderful life here with her sisters and Ma and Pa. The past had no claim on her.

Now all she could hope for was that he'd also choose to put his past behind him—whatever it was—and be willing to—

What?

She closed her eyes and admitted what she hoped for.

She wanted him to be willing to start over right here in the Bar Crossing area.

"What's all the excitement?" he asked, bringing her back to the present moment.

"We're going berry picking," the twins chorused. "And you and Lonnie are coming with us."

Cora could have hugged Rose for saying what she hesitated to say.

Lonnie grinned. "I ain't never been berry picking."

"You'll like it," Rose promised.

"I guess I will," Lonnie said.

Wyatt had looked ready to refuse the expedition, but at Lonnie's eagerness he relaxed. "It sounds like fun."

Pa brought the wagon to the house and the girls helped Ma bring out a box of food, jugs of water and every bucket and basket they could lay their hands on.

Lonnie looked doubtful. "You expect to pick a lot of berries."

"It's fun," Lilly assured him.

Grub wriggled about, begging to accompany them.

Lilly patted his head. "You stay here and guard the place."

Cora and Rose laughed.

"He's not a very good guard dog," Cora explained to Wyatt. "But we hope when people see him they think twice before causing trouble."

At that, she glanced about the farm and searched every inch of the horizon. No sign of any Caldwell cowboys. Maybe they were too busy to bother the place today while the Bells were away.

Dismissing the concern, she took the hand Wyatt offered and stepped into the wagon box. The others climbed aboard, pushing aside baskets to make room for a place to sit.

She sat with Wyatt pressed to her side. "It's a perfect day for picking berries," she said. "Sunshine, a little breeze and no sign of rain."

They trekked west toward the hills, following a faint trail left by others. They passed some berry bushes, but Pa said there'd be better picking further along. A few minutes later he pulled the wagon into a little clearing.

Before the wheels stopped turning everyone grabbed a bucket and scrambled from the wagon.

"Come along," Rose said to Lonnie. "I'll show you what to do."

Lilly followed them.

Wyatt grinned at Cora. "Guess you'll have to give me berry-picking lessons."

"I don't mind. Not in the least." She realized she just stood there smiling at him and told her feet to start walking. In a few minutes she found a place where the serviceberries were big and plentiful. "Pick the purple ones. I try to keep from putting leaves or other garbage in the pail. Makes it so much easier to sort and clean the berries for canning."

He started picking berries at her side. As they worked, she moved left and he moved right.

"I love canned serviceberries," she said.

"I haven't had any in a long time, but I remember having them with thick cream. I liked the nutty taste."

"It's an almond flavor."

He didn't reply. The only sound was the plink of berries in the bottom of her bucket, which ended as she added more and more berries.

"Did your ma can berries?" Would he tell her more about his past?

"She did some." A beat of silence. "But then she got pretty frail."

Cora moved to where she could see Wyatt's face and detected tension around his mouth. A horrible thought surfaced. "Did your pa beat her, too?"

Wyatt's hands grew still and he slowly brought his gaze to her.

At the dark despair she saw in his eyes, she grabbed a branch full of ripe berries to steady herself.

He swallowed hard. "He didn't beat her physically as far as I know. But she feared him and he used that to control her." He shrugged, but the gesture wasn't dismissive so much as it indicated how helpless he felt.

"I'm so sorry." How many times had she said that to him? "I'm sure you did everything you could to make it easier for her."

He jerked his attention to the berries on the branches before him and picked with a decided urgency. "I tried." The words rang with failure.

He'd left for a time. A year, had he said? He'd left both his mother and Lonnie to cope with an angry man.

Why had he done so? Where had he gone? "Where did you go when you left them alone?"

His hands grew still. The air pulsed with hope and possibility. Then he shuddered. "I wish I could tell you, but it involves other people who would be hurt if I told you the whole truth."

"I see." But she didn't. How could she trust him if he harbored secrets? She closed the distance between them and waited for him to meet her gaze. She hoped she conveyed both trust and a desire to help.

"Wyatt, don't you know you can trust me? You can tell me without fear of it going further."

Every heartbeat pounded behind her eyes as she looked deeply into his gaze.

She could almost hear his pulse beat, too, as he considered her words.

Hope flicked through his eyes. He opened his mouth. Then he snapped it shut and shook his head. "I'd like to tell you everything, but it's better if I don't."

"Better for who?" She wanted to shake her hands at the sky and demand answers.

"For Lonnie." His voice thickened. "For you."

"For me?"

He nodded, all misery and regret.

"How can that be?"

"Trust me. It's better you don't know." He sucked in a shuddering breath. "Do you still believe it's possible to start fresh? Put the past behind and forget it?"

She opened her mouth, then closed it again without saying anything. She wanted to say yes. But he had a past full of secrets. That was different. At least it was different for her. She didn't know if it was possible to build a future on the unknown.

"Maybe what I'm asking is—can you trust me without knowing the answer to your question?"

She could tell he tried to keep his voice neutral, as if her answer didn't matter, but she heard the yearning and knew he longed for her to say yes. The seconds rushed by as she considered her response. Would knowing the past change what she knew about him? She'd seen him being tender, gentle, noble, kind and comforting. He'd held her and made her past less hurtful.

Could she not do the same for him?

All she had to do was speak the words. All doubts fled as she realized how much she wanted to give him the gift of her trust.

She rested her hand on his arm, warm from the sunshine and as strong as the man himself. "Knowing your secret will not change who you are or how I feel about you."

He rested his hand on hers. "Thank you." His eyes filled with brightness.

They stood smiling at each other a moment as the distant voices of her sisters and Lonnie reached them. Birds chattered in the trees. A juvenile robin swooped in to enjoy the berries.

"The birds are going to eat them before we get our share," he observed.

They pulled apart and returned to picking.

The air shimmered with hope and trust and possibility.

They picked steadily. Twice they returned to the wagon to dump their buckets in a basket. The third time they got there along with Lonnie and Rose.

"The baskets are filling up fast." Cora's satisfaction came from more-than-successful berry picking.

Ma and Pa arrived with their buckets of berries, and

all of them quickly grabbed a sandwich and a handful of cookies and ate before they returned to work.

Cora and Wyatt moved deeper into the bush where they found a patch with extralarge serviceberries and set to work. She moved quickly, wandering farther to her left, knowing that whatever they got today would provide a welcome addition to their meals during the winter months.

Her thoughts sang a happy song as she worked. Wyatt had asked her to trust him. Had asked if it was possible to start over. If he meant to stay in the area they could get to know each other better. There'd be time and opportunity for attending socials together. She wrinkled her nose. Nancy and Mary Ann would surely hover around seeking his attention. She grunted. But they wouldn't accompany Cora and Wyatt on long solitary walks or little picnics. Soon the summer busy season would end and she'd have time for such things. Wyatt and Lonnie could visit and play board games with Cora and her sisters. They could read to each other.

Her heart thrilled with what the future offered.

The leaves rustled to her right. "Wyatt?" She stepped around to see him. Perhaps she'd tell him all the things she hoped for.

Whoof.

A black bear rose up on his hind legs, as startled to see Cora as she was to see him, though she'd guarantee he wasn't a fraction as afraid.

"Wyatt!" She called his name without thinking whether or not it would anger or frighten the bear.

Whoof.

Wyatt stopped to listen. It sounded as though someone exhaled really hard. Had Cora fallen and had her breath knocked out of her? His heart kicked into a gallop. She might be hurt.

"Wyatt!" Her voice sounded strangled.

He dropped his pail to the ground and rushed toward the sound. But there were so many bushes in the way. How far had she gone?

"Cora, where are you?"

She didn't answer.

He met a wall of bushes. What direction to go? "Cora?" Still no answer.

He flung about to the right and the left. Where was she? He sucked in air and forced himself to slow down and think. The sound had come from the left. He held still, hoping to hear her. He didn't, but through the bushes he saw a bit of her straw hat and pushed past the berry-laden branches.

There she was. She was edging backward toward him.

He looked past her and saw a bear on his hind legs sniffing the air. His heart lunged to his throat and refused to work.

Cora was doing the right thing, retreating as quietly as possible, letting the bear know she was no threat and the animal was welcome to the area.

He held his breath and prayed as never before. Two more steps and he could pull her to safety.

Cora edged her foot back, caught it on a clump of wiry grass and started to go down. Her hat fell to her back and hung by its ribbons.

A silent scream tore at his throat. Clamping his teeth closed to keep from crying out, Wyatt forced himself to remain motionless. If the bear thought it was outnumbered, it would feel more threatened.

She caught herself, took one more step, and he grabbed her and pulled her out of sight into the bushes. He didn't stop moving until they were a safe distance away, then he turned her into his arms and held her tight. He buried his face in her hair and struggled to regulate his breathing.

She clung to him, her arms around his waist as shuddering breath followed shuddering breath.

Slowly his heartbeat calmed and his lungs remembered how to work. He plunged his fingers into her hair and pressed her head to his chest, close to his heart where he could keep her safe.

"You gave me an awful fright." He didn't even try to hide the croak in his voice.

She shuddered and her arms tightened about him.

"You're okay now," he soothed. "I've got you. I won't let anything happen to you."

Would she be so willing to come into his arms if she knew the truth?

He closed his eyes and wished he could tell her everything, but first he must talk to Lonnie. But how could he be certain of her reaction? He did not want to lose this connection with her. Couldn't bear to see scorn and rejection in her eyes.

He'd asked her to trust him enough to not ask to know his secrets.

Did he trust her enough to tell them to her?

Slowly she relaxed, but she didn't pull away. Her head rested below his chin and she breathed calmly.

He made no move to end the hug, either. If they could stay this way, in this place—minus the bear—

his past wouldn't matter. But time did not stand still. Life must be lived.

"We should warn the others about the bear," he murmured, reluctant to end the moment.

"Of course." She eased back and lifted her face to him. "Thank you."

It was he who should thank her, for offering to trust him. "You did everything right. Your pa will be proud of you."

"I was never so scared in all my life."

For him, it rivaled the moment he'd discovered Lonnie standing over their father, a bloodied shovel in his hand and the man beaten almost beyond recognition. He shook the image from his mind.

"Where did you leave your berries?" he asked her. "If you dropped your bucket near the bear, we are leaving it behind."

She chuckled. "I thought the bear was you."

"You think I look like a bear?"

"No, of course not, silly. I heard something in the bushes and thought it was you. I wasn't expecting it to be a bear. I left my bucket over there." She pointed.

He measured the distance with his eye. Was it far enough from the bear that it could be retrieved safely? He checked for signs of the animal and saw the furry hide farther up the hill. "You stay right here and I'll get it."

He retrieved it, then they returned to the spot where he'd left his and they returned to the wagon. Mr. and Mrs. Bell were there.

"Ma, Pa, I met a bear over there." She pointed.

"Are you okay?" Mrs. Bell grabbed her and ran her hands over her arms and back.

Mr. Bell stood very close, his eyes full of worry.

Wyatt smiled at their tender concern. "Your daughter handled it very well. She backed away quietly until she was out of sight."

"I remembered all the lessons you drilled into us, Pa."

"Good." Both parents shifted their attention to the bushes around them. "What about the others?"

"Our berry picking is over," Mr. Bell said. He cupped his hands and called the others.

Cora joined him in calling their names and Wyatt added his voice. They paused to listen.

"Coming," a distant voice answered, and in a few minutes the three of them broke into sight.

"We're done here." Mr. Bell took their pails and set them in the back. "Cora met a bear. We're going home while we're all safe." He helped his wife to the wagon seat and the others clambered into the box.

The twins each grabbed one of Cora's hands, peppering her with questions.

Cora told them the details of her bear encounter, all except the few precious moments she and Wyatt had held each other.

Lonnie stared at the three girls.

Wyatt wished he knew what the boy was thinking. Did he see the affection among the Bell family and want to be part of it?

Maybe they were safe here. Perhaps they could settle nearby and enjoy a life that included the Bells. Wouldn't it be nice to learn to live and love as they did?

Wouldn't it be sweet to spend more time with Cora?

He stared at the scenery drifting away as they followed the trail back to the farm and tried to convince himself he had nothing to fear from people in his past.

If anyone noticed his shudder, they'd likely put it down to the bear. But what scared him as much as seeing the bear facing Cora was knowing she would endure harsh comments and condemnation if anyone ever discovered he'd spent time in prison. Or even worse, Jimmy Stone if he ever discovered Wyatt's whereabouts.

Not too many people were willing to overlook that kind of a past.

Dare he hope no one would ever recognize him? He recalled his reaction to the man at the livery stables. The man in the shadows had looked so much like Jimmy Stone. Would he ever stop looking over his shoulder for the man who had vowed revenge? Jimmy was lazy. Maybe too lazy to follow Wyatt across the prairie. But he was not the sort of man to overlook a grudge.

Was Wyatt dreaming impossible dreams to think he could escape his past and Jimmy Stone?

Chapter Sixteen

The next day, Cora wanted to help Wyatt on the barn. He had the doors and stall partitions to install. But Ma needed all the help she could get sorting and preparing berries. Besides the serviceberries that were processed in syrup, the chokecherries had to be cooked. They'd put them through a sieve and then add sugar to the pulp before cooking the mixture into jam. It was hot, time-consuming work, but no one complained, knowing how delicious both would taste during the long winter months.

As much as possible, Cora sat outside the kitchen door, sorting berries where she could watch Wyatt and Lonnie work. Or if she had to be in the kitchen, she often glanced out the window.

"You can't keep your eyes off him," Rose teased.

"I feel I should be helping with the barn." It was a poor excuse and she knew everyone saw through it.

The twins had quizzed her last night about how Wyatt had rescued her. Fortunately it had been too dark for them to see the warmth that flooded her cheeks and stained them a telltale pink. All she'd said was that he dragged her away and then retrieved her pail of berries.

She was not prepared to reveal how tightly he'd held her. And how she'd held him just as tightly. Reaction to the scare explained only a portion of why they'd clung to each other.

She, for one, had welcomed the excuse to be in his arms, finding comfort and strength she'd ached for since—

Maybe since she'd told him about her papa. Or was it since he'd caught her as she about tumbled from the partly finished loft floor? Or maybe when they'd shared the awe of seeing a new foal. She couldn't say where it had started. Only that she was at home in his arms, his heart beating soundly beneath her ear.

But from the way the twins winked at each other and rolled their eyes each time they caught her looking toward the barn, she had to wonder if they guessed more than she meant to confess.

By the time the berries were done, it was late afternoon and the kitchen was so hot Cora feared Ma would have heatstroke.

"Let's eat outside," she suggested.

"Good idea," Rose said. "You set up a table for the food and we'll carry it out."

Pa helped with the sawhorses and planks that created a table.

Wyatt and Lonnie trotted over, their hair wet from soaking it in water they pumped from the well.

They gathered in a circle, holding hands.

"Let's sing the blessing, Pa," Lilly said.

So they sang the doxology. And if anyone noticed

that Wyatt's voice was indeed more of a growl than a tune, they didn't mention it.

"How much did you get done on the stalls?" she asked Wyatt, who sat beside her on the warm, dry grass.

"One more good day should see them finished."

"Done already? I never thought to see it go so fast."

"Helps to have lots of hands."

She wasn't sure if he meant the work bee of a few days ago, or the help he and Lonnie provided.

"All the help has been an answer to prayer," Pa said.

"Amen," Ma added.

Cora insisted on helping finish the barn the next day. Not that Wyatt objected. His mind twisted and turned with possibilities. Could he discover how she'd feel about a man who had been in prison without implicating himself or Lonnie? Or was he building dreams on nothing but fluffy clouds of wishing?

They stopped for dinner and then hurried back to work. The sun had barely passed its zenith when they hung the last gate on the last stall.

"Done!" She clapped her hands as Lonnie put away the tools. She went to the door and smiled at the bright landscape. Her sisters worked in the garden. Her ma sat in the shade of the house, shelling peas. Noises from the work shed indicated where her pa was.

She called them all over. "Thanks to Wyatt and Lonnie and our friends from town, we have our barn. Isn't it great?" She walked them all through and took the twins up to the loft. Lonnie followed, but Wyatt remained on the ground with her folks.

"Ma, Pa," she called from the loft door, and they

looked up at her. "This calls for a celebration. Let's go on a picnic."

Lonnie looked as eager as any of them.

Wyatt schooled his face not to reveal his own anticipation of the idea.

Mrs. Bell shook her head. "I'm too tired. But you young people go ahead if you like. You all deserve a break from the work."

"Can we take the wagon?"

Mr. Bell agreed they could. They decided to take a picnic supper and go to Chester's Pond.

Cora explained to Wyatt. "It's a pond created by a small landslide. It's a beautiful spot."

"Sounds nice." He thought the driest spot on the bald prairie would be pleasant enough to thrill him.

"I'll get the wagon," Mr. Bell said, and Wyatt went with him to hitch up.

By the time Wyatt drove up to the house, the girls had a box full of food and several quilts ready to load.

He wondered if Lonnie would sit by him on the seat, but he scrambled in beside Lilly and Rose, his arm on the box of food as if he had to make sure it wouldn't disappear.

"I'll ride with you," Cora said with a sweet smile.

He tucked the smile and her offer into his hopeful thoughts. Starting over might be possible. His heart thudded against his ribs in eager anticipation.

"Turn that way." As Cora pointed to her left, her arm brushed his and optimism walloped into him. *Don't expect acceptance until you get it.* But the warning seemed unnecessary. Hadn't she already said she trusted him?

They took a direction away from town, for which he

was grateful. Would he ever feel comfortable around others? Perhaps he'd always fear having his past revealed. Wasn't that reason enough to confess it? But how could he tell her the whole truth? It would mean condemning Lonnie, and he'd spent a year in prison to prevent that.

They followed the river for a few miles, then she pointed again. "There it is."

A grove of trees prevented him from seeing a pond, but no doubt she knew how to reach the water.

"Turn here, and then there's a trail that will take us through the trees."

He saw the tree-shrouded opening and followed it.

The twins and Lonnie crowded to his back.

As soon as the water came into sight, Lilly sighed. "This is one of my favorite spots."

"Me, too," Rose echoed.

Cora said nothing and Wyatt glanced at her. She caught his gaze and smiled so widely, so invitingly that he forgot about the water, the twins, Lonnie… everything but the joy of this moment, the anticipation of sharing the afternoon with her.

"Ahem," Rose said. "Did you forget we're here?"

He jerked away. "It's a very pretty place." What he meant was that any place was beautiful with Cora at his side, smiling so sweetly, so trustingly.

Would the truth steal it away?

He stopped the wagon and jumped down. The others scrambled from the back, but Cora waited for him to help her down. He didn't mean to hold her longer than he should, but his hands lingered at her waist as she lifted her face to him.

Perhaps she'd meant to thank him, but no words

came from her mouth as their gazes caught and held, hers so deep and burning he felt as if the sun had seared his insides.

"Come on, you two," Lonnie called, and they slowly backed away from each other.

His hands lingered, reluctant to let her go.

"Look," Lonnie called.

Cora's smile seemed as regretful as he was. But they traipsed over to join the others.

Lonnie had found an arrowhead with a broken shaft attached. "Do you think there are Indians here?" He glanced around, a mixture of fear and excitement on his face.

Lilly pulled Rose close. "There aren't, are there?"

Wyatt wished he could reassure them all that they were safe. The government had recently established a reservation for the Natives and they had supposedly gone willingly, but only thirteen years ago, Colonel Custer had been badly beaten by Sitting Bull and his angry braves.

It was enough to make them all look intently into the trees searching for Indians.

Cora laughed nervously. "Even if they left the reservation, they'd be back in the hills where there's lots of game."

Lonnie squinted into the trees. "'Less they want revenge for us taking their land."

Wyatt groaned. "Thanks, Lonnie. That's reassuring. Let me see the arrow."

Lonnie reluctantly handed it to him. "I want it back."

Wyatt examined it. "This is old. Look at how the end of the shaft is rotting. It's likely been here a long time."

"Might be from Custer's last stand."

Wyatt didn't bother pointing out that the battle had taken place to the southeast, many miles away.

Cora let out a long breath. "Just the same. Maybe we should head back home."

The twins shook their heads. "There's nothing to be afraid of."

"I can't chance that."

The twins faced her, a wall of protest. "Stop worrying about us. We're all grown up now."

"You're only eighteen."

The twins looked at each other then back to her. "Most girls our age are married. We'll likely be old maids because no one is ever good enough for us."

Wyatt laughed at the sorrowfulness of their words. "What does she do? Stand at the end of the lane and beat suitors off with a stick?"

Lilly looked guilty. "No. But she doesn't need to. She just scowls at them and they turn tail and run."

"I'd say if they aren't prepared to fight a few battles, maybe confront opposition from your family or the community, they aren't worthy of you." His words swelled within his heart. Was he willing to face opposition in order to be with Cora? More important, would she face it to be with him?

Rose nodded. "That's true." She faced Cora. "We are staying and enjoying ourselves." She and Lilly marched away.

Cora scowled at him. "Don't be encouraging them to be foolhardy."

"I didn't mean to." Were they being reckless, or was she being overly cautious? Overly protective? That might be the flaw in his hopes. Cora might be willing to face his past, but it wasn't likely she'd let anything threaten her sisters' happiness and security.

"Come on." Cora grabbed his hand. "We're going to make sure no one is lurking in the trees."

He willingly allowed her to lead him into the bushes. But she had serious searching on her mind. They looked behind every tree, parted the bushes to make sure no one hid in them, examined the ground in open areas for tracks. Crows flew from the treetops cawing their protest. A rabbit skittered away. But they saw nothing that meant a threat.

They returned to the edge of the pond. "Are you satisfied?" he asked, half amused.

"I guess so." The others circled the water, examining pebbles and bits of wood. Lonnie tried to skip rocks.

Cora sat on a fallen log and patted the spot beside her. "It's nice to see them enjoying themselves, isn't it?"

"Yup," he said, though he thought the Bell sisters always enjoyed life. It was Lonnie who had relaxed and grown happy here.

Reason enough, he decided, to risk telling Cora part of the truth and measure her response. He'd thought of several ways to broach the subject but none seemed to fit.

"Do you think you'll ever forgive your real father for leaving you?"

She continued to stare toward the others but her fingers clenched. "I don't think about him much at all. He didn't care about us when we needed him and we don't need him now, so it doesn't matter."

But it did matter. She hurt because of it and obviously hadn't forgiven him.

He realized his own fists were clenched and made

an effort to loosen them. It didn't bode well for him that she didn't forgive her own father.

Why should she forgive Wyatt? Though he'd done nothing wrong. Except keep a potentially hurtful secret. But he'd only done it to protect them all.

"Maybe he had a good reason for leaving you. Maybe he sincerely meant to return but couldn't through no fault of his own."

She fixed him with blinding accusation in her eyes. "Why are you defending him?"

He shrugged. "I'm not. I don't even know him. All I'm saying is there might be an explanation."

Her look challenged him to find one.

"Maybe he was in trouble with the law and had to run."

"A criminal as well as a man who abandons his children? I hardly find that comforting."

"What if he had been blamed for something he didn't do?"

"An honorable man would have made sure his family was safe. He'd put their needs ahead of his own."

He nodded. So that was his answer. He must put her needs, her sisters' needs and Lonnie's needs before his own selfish desires. So be it. He'd been doing so for years, so it wasn't anything new.

He took Cora's clenched hands and rubbed the backs of them. "You are absolutely right. I don't know why I thought I needed to bring it up. Guess I just like to find a sound reason for why people do things that leave us confused."

Her hands relaxed and turned palm to palm with his.

"That's very noble of you," she said, her eyes filled with sunshine. Sweetness filled the air. She so quickly put aside little annoyances, if not so readily the big things in life.

He entwined their fingers and smiled. This might be all he could have—a sunny afternoon, a few hours, memories of what might have been. He would make the most of them.

"Come join us," Rose called.

He pulled her to her feet and they walked along the edge of the pond to where the others were. Lonnie tagged Wyatt. "You're it."

Wyatt froze, and then a laugh rumbled from him. Lonnie wanted to play. Wyatt was more than ready to oblige.

The others joined in and they chased through the bushes and darted along the water's edge tagging one another and laughing.

Wyatt was it again. He had not managed to catch Cora. Each time he tried, she slipped away, dashing in a direction that left him to tag someone else. But this time he meant to catch her.

The direct route hadn't worked, so he tried another strategy. He pretended to chase Lonnie, who fled through the bushes. As soon as he was out of sight, Wyatt shifted direction and moved with as little sound as he could. To his left, Lonnie continued to batter through the trees, making a great deal of racket that served Wyatt's purpose well.

He paused to listen. Rose and Lilly whispered, giving away their position. He strained to catch any indication of where Cora might be. A rustle to his right. He moved in that direction.

She stood still, looking every which way. She tipped her head to listen.

He held his breath, but still she turned toward him. Her eyes widened with surprise. She gave a yelp and took off with him on her heels.

"I've got you."

"No," she squealed, and slipped away. She glanced over her shoulder, which slowed her, and that was all he needed to catch up. He reached out for her but tripped on a root and couldn't stop his headlong flight.

His arms caught her in his path and he turned to take the brunt of the fall.

They went down with a thud that knocked the air from him. He forced his lungs to work. "Are you okay?" His voice whistled from his throat.

She didn't answer.

He turned. Her face was buried against his arm.

"I'm okay." Her words were muffled.

Between the weight of her in his arms and the struggle to catch his breath, he couldn't move.

She shifted, then sat up. "I guess you caught me."

He sucked in air and sat up facing her. "I almost killed you doing so. I'm sorry. You're sure you aren't hurt?"

She brushed her hands over her arms. "Well, my pride might be just a little wounded that you sneaked up on me like that."

He grinned. "You sure looked surprised when you saw me."

Her grin widened to match his. "I guess I didn't expect you to be so sneaky."

"Me, sneaky? Who is the one who runs so close to someone else I have to tag them?"

She shrugged. "Strategy, that's all." Her smile didn't falter a bit.

They pushed to their feet.

Grass and leaves were stuck in her hair. He plucked them out piece by piece, aware she'd lowered her eyelids, allowing him to see only the fan of her lashes against her cheeks. A strand of her hair caught on his finger and his movements slowed as he lingered on the feel of silk against his skin. He swallowed hard, wondered if she noticed and forced himself to continue. He grasped her chin and turned her head to check each side.

Her skin was warm and smooth.

"I think that's all." His husky words revealed how deeply he'd been affected.

"My turn." Did her voice sound as thick as his?

She plucked things from his hair, each touch of her fingers sending a jolt through his brain until he thought his head couldn't contain it.

"All done." She reached around him to pick up his hat where it had fallen.

Her eyes lifted to his, full of awareness and longing.

His own must brim with the same thing, he thought. He longed to hold her next to his heart. Tell her every secret of his life.

She lowered her gaze, but before he could find solid ground, she lifted them again.

He forgot every reasonable argument about his past, his present and his future.

A persistent idea knocked at the back of his brain. This couldn't last. She'd never overlook his past and all the risks it brought to her family's safe little place.

But all that mattered right now was this precious moment of time.

He'd risk everything for the joy of right now.

Chapter Seventeen

Cora saw the longing in his eyes as clearly as she felt it in her heart. The whole afternoon had been a prelude to this moment. Running from him when she wanted to run *to* him, sharing him with the others when she wanted him to herself… Everything had accumulated until she could think of nothing else but Wyatt. Touching his hair to remove the twigs and leaves had left her unable to remember any reason she should be cautious around him.

Secrets mattered not. All she cared about was what she saw and knew of him. She lowered her gaze to his mouth, touched his lips with her fingertips.

He caught her hand and pressed her palm to his cheek.

"Cora." Her name rang like a clarion call, making her like the sound of it as never before.

He cupped his hand to the back of her head. His eyes filled with promises and pleasure, and he bent his head.

Just before his lips touched hers, he paused.

Whether to change his mind or give her time to pull

away, she couldn't tell. But she didn't intend that either should happen and she lifted her face to him.

Their lips touched. Sweetness like pure warm honey poured through her and she knew she would never feel the same.

They clung to each other, though she couldn't have said if it was a long or short time.

With a satisfied sigh, he leaned back and smiled at her. "Cora, what would you think if I settled in this area?" He rushed on as if he needed to explain. "Lonnie is happier than I've seen him in a very long time. I think he's starting to put the past behind him."

She trailed her finger along his jawline. "I think it would be a lovely idea. But I hope Lonnie's not the only one putting his past behind him. Aren't you, as well?"

"If I can't start over here, I don't know if I ever can."

She smiled at how much his answer revealed. Her heart danced to think he'd found peace and belonging here. He hadn't said so, and perhaps it was too early to wish for it, but she hoped she'd played a large part in his decision. And would play an even larger part with the passing of each delicious day.

"Who's it?" Lonnie's voice came through the woods.

"I guess we better get back to the others." Wyatt sounded as reluctant as she felt. "I don't think I'll say anything to Lonnie about my decision just yet."

She nodded. "It will be easier for him that way." Once Wyatt could say to Lonnie, "This is where we're going to live," the boy would have something solid to hold on to.

They returned to the others. She ignored the teasing grins her sisters sent her way. The game ended and they gathered round in a circle to talk.

For the first time, Lonnie spoke of his past. "My ma was so different from yours. She was weak. Or maybe frail. I don't remember cookies or cakes since I was about five." He sent a questioning look to Wyatt. "Do you?"

He shook his head.

Cora edged closer, not caring what the others thought, and squeezed his hand. "We're very fortunate. Our ma spoils us with her cooking."

Wyatt relaxed and gave her a lazy smile. "Seems you all do your share to make your home happy and welcoming."

"And productive," Rose added.

They fell into a contemplative silence for two minutes.

Lonnie spoke again. "Did you girls like school?"

The three of them said they did.

Lonnie said he kind of did, too. For a while they discussed their favorite subjects.

Cora turned to Wyatt. "What was your favorite part of school?"

He considered the question a moment. "Singing." His face was so serious she almost believed him.

Then she burst out laughing. "Did the teacher give you a bucket to carry the tune in?"

He grinned. "She asked me to stand at the back and only pretend to sing."

The others laughed.

Cora turned to her sisters. They had always liked to sing together. They nodded in understanding and the three of them began their favorite songs. Lonnie joined in on the ones he knew.

Wyatt leaned back, listening.

Cora felt his gaze on her and tried to ignore it, but she couldn't and wondered why she even tried. This afternoon was to be lived to its fullest and enjoyed, hopefully as a prelude to many such days to follow. She turned to him and sang as if no one else was there, her heart bursting with music above and beyond the songs.

His look never faltered from hers, opening his heart and his thoughts to her.

The others might be there. They might be observing them but she didn't care. All that mattered was Wyatt's trusting look and her trusting heart.

And his plan to settle in the area.

The next day, Wyatt rode away intent on finding a place to live. She knew where he meant to go but said nothing. She wondered what explanation he'd given Lonnie, but the boy didn't seem concerned.

"I need to put in some more hours to pay for my pigs," Lonnie said.

So she put him to work hauling water to the garden.

Wyatt returned later in the afternoon. He gave a barely perceptible shake of his head. He hadn't found anyplace suitable. She smiled encouragement.

They walked along the river later that evening. "You'll find something," she assured him. "God will guide you."

"I pray so."

She hoped it would be close enough they could see each other regularly and often. The future beckoned with a thousand stars.

He walked her back to the house, but Lonnie and the girls were outside so he only said a gentle good-night, called for Lonnie to join him and left.

She stared after him, wishing they could kiss again.

Not that she needed another kiss to remind her of all she'd felt last time.

Smiling, she went inside and prepared for bed. She kept her feelings to herself even when the twins teased her, wanting to know what she and Wyatt had done on their walk.

In the past few days, Wyatt had ridden every direction from the Bell farm and found no suitable land nearby. Heading out to try again, he dismounted on the trail and looked around, as if the right land would appear on the horizon.

Perhaps God meant to let him know this plan of his wasn't right. Wyatt had promised Cora he'd pray about finding a place. *God, guide me to where I should go.* He knew his open-ended prayer meant he might have to accept being led farther away than his dreams took him.

But God knew best. Even if it meant he couldn't live his dream, Wyatt would follow His lead.

A rider approached from the trail to the east, an older man with skin leathered from years of living and working outdoors. He was lean as a whip with deep blue eyes that studied Wyatt with interest.

"You lost, young man?"

"Just deciding." He didn't know what direction he should go today to look for land.

The older man swung down and walked to Wyatt with the peculiar bow-legged gait of a long-time cowboy. He introduced himself as Jack Henry. He stood beside Wyatt, studying the lay of the land. "While ya make up yer mind, why not ride along with me?"

It was an offer Wyatt didn't mind accepting. They both returned to horseback and ambled south.

"Where you from? Where you headed?" Jack asked.

"Been at the Bells'. Now I'm looking for a place to start ranching."

"Know the Bells. They's good people."

A short time later, Jack said, "This here is my place." He indicated a low ranch house and a cluster of outbuildings half a mile off the road.

Wyatt had ridden by a couple of days ago and admired the yard, but it didn't have a for-sale sign posted so he'd gone on by.

"Why not light awhile and tell me more. Do the Caldwells still object to the Bells farming in the middle of their ranch land?"

Wyatt accepted the offer mostly because he didn't have the heart to push on. And he enjoyed the old man's company.

They rode into the yard. "Nice place." Sturdy buildings. Well maintained. He told how the Caldwell cowboys harassed the Bells in the hopes of persuading them to sell their bit of land. "The Bells have turned their few acres into a beautiful productive place. I don't blame them for refusing to sell it."

Jack nodded. "A man's roots can go down mighty deep. Take me, for instance. I been here since before the Caldwells. I brought my missus out with me. She died five years ago. We never did have the family we hoped for. Say, do you want to see around?"

Wyatt accepted the invitation out of curiosity and the hope of learning from a man who'd been in the area a long time.

They rode around the place, admiring the crop of calves the man's cows had.

"I should be moving on," Wyatt said as the afternoon

lengthened. He longed to see Cora and be assured that she wanted him to stay in the area and that it wasn't just wishful thinking on his part.

Jack sat beside him, one leg bent over his saddle horn. "Son, take a look around you. Why, there ain't nothing you can't grow here—cows, sheep, crops and gardens." He paused. "And a family."

"I'm sorry you didn't have the family you dreamed of."

"It's my only regret in life."

Wyatt waited for Jack to corral his thoughts.

"I'm getting too old for all this." He pointed to the cows but Wyatt understood he meant the land and the work, as well. "You say you'd like to settle in the area." He nodded once as if coming to a conclusion. "You're the sort of man who would benefit the community."

Wyatt stared at the man. How could he come to such a verdict? One that could easily be proved wrong. He silently prayed that God would keep the truth about his past hidden.

Jack continued. "Like I say, I'm tired." He gave Wyatt a direct blue-eyed look that made Wyatt feel as if the man saw clear to the depths of his soul. "I'd be pleased if you would join me. I'd make you part owner for now. You do the work to earn your share. In time it would be all yours."

"I'm honored you ask me." Wyatt could picture himself here raising a family. Maybe sharing his life with more than Lonnie.

Hope burst forth like blossoms before the sun. "I accept your offer. How soon do you want me to join you?"

"Soon as you can. Bring those horses and let's get the herd growing."

Wyatt laughed. "I can't believe this." Doubts erupted in his brain. "Why would you ask me?"

Jack drew in a slow steady breath. "Son, just this morning I was talking to God again. Said how much I wanted to turn this place over to a younger man. And seeing as God hadn't blessed us with children, I asked Him to send along someone who would take the place of mine. I saw you there at the side of the road and knew God had answered my prayer."

"But you know nothing about me."

"Know enough. Seems God led ya here for a purpose. One that benefits the both of us."

They shook hands on the agreement and Wyatt headed back to the Bell place.

And a future as bright as the sun overhead.

He resisted the urge to make his horse gallop all the way back, but by the time he rode into the yard, he was ready to burst with his news.

Mr. Bell waved a greeting as he approached.

Mrs. Bell's face appeared at the kitchen window and she raised her hand.

He realized he needed to take care of his horse before he told his news and turned to go to his campsite, where he unsaddled his horse, rubbed the animal down, and fed and watered him—all things he did on a regular basis so they were almost second nature. When had they ever before consumed so much time?

Finally, satisfied he'd done all he needed in that regard, he trotted up the hill.

"You're just in time for supper," Rose called.

Food seemed an intrusion at the moment, but through the open door, he saw Cora setting plates at the table.

He'd not be getting a chance to talk to her until after the meal.

Lonnie bumped into him in his hurry to get to the food.

Resigned to the delay, Wyatt followed him inside and took his customary place at the table beside Cora.

When Mr. Bell held his hands out to grasp the hand of the girl on each side of him, Wyatt eagerly took Cora's hand. Would she know by the strength of his grip that he'd found a place? One he hoped she'd appreciate?

The meal took a long time as the family discussed the trip to town earlier in the day. Seemed all the news was about the continued robberies and who might be responsible.

No one knew he was a jailbird, so fingers wouldn't be pointed his way. But if the news ever came out… well, he knew what to expect.

Was he doing the right thing, subjecting Cora to such risk?

He vowed he'd tell her where he'd spent the missing year and see if she still welcomed the idea of him settling in the area.

Finally the meal ended and the kitchen was cleaned.

"It's a lovely evening," Cora said. "Would you care to go for a walk?"

He'd thought the opportunity would never come and hurried to the door.

Lonnie and Lilly headed toward the pigpen.

"I have news," Wyatt said, and called Lonnie to join them.

Lonnie came with such reluctance, his boots scraped every step of the way. "I want to help Lilly feed the pigs."

"This won't take long." He led them toward the barn, thinking after he told Lonnie, he'd go on to their campsite where he and Cora could sit and discuss the future.

At the corner of the barn, Lonnie dug in his heels. "Wyatt, what do you want?" He glanced over his shoulder. "If it's about the horses, I'll tend them after I feed the pigs."

"Very well." He smiled at Cora, his heart bursting with his news. From the way her eyes widened and filled with gladness, she guessed what he was about to report. "Lonnie, I have found a place for us. We move on Monday. It's—" But before he could say where it was, Lonnie interrupted.

"No," he shouted. "I don't want to go. I like it here just fine. No one will hurt me here."

Wyatt reached out to him. "No one will hurt you where we're going. I'll see to that."

Lonnie, breathing hard, stared at him. "I'm scared of you."

"Me?" Wyatt jerked back as if the boy had hit him. "I'd never hurt you. You should know that. After all—" He curbed what he was about to say. Now was not the time or place.

"I know you're mad at me that you went to jail." Lonnie's eyes were wild. He was unaware of what he said.

"Jail?" Cora said, the word sucked in on her breath. She stared at Wyatt with eyes as big as moons.

"I'll explain later," Wyatt said. First he had a brother to deal with.

"Lonnie, I am not mad at you. I've never been mad at you." *Please, God, help him believe me.*

"You went because of me."

"I would do it again." He didn't want to reveal that

Lonnie had been the guilty one, but he had to reassure him. "Lonnie, it was far easier for me to be there then to think of you in that place." Lonnie would have found the threats and violence impossible to deal with.

"But it was me who did it." Agony drew each word into a wail.

Wyatt gripped the boy's shoulders. A shudder raced clear through Lonnie.

He had to make Lonnie understand. "I would do it again. I couldn't have lived free knowing you were in jail. It would have been torture." Far worse than jail had been.

Lonnie's eyes clung to Wyatt. "Was it very bad?" he whispered.

He didn't answer the question, couldn't. "What made it bearable was knowing you weren't in there."

Lonnie searched Wyatt's eyes and finally saw that Wyatt meant it.

"How can you not be mad at me?"

"Because you're my little brother." He pulled the boy closer, pleased when Lonnie didn't shy away.

"Are we really moving?"

"Yes."

"Not far away?"

"Not far at all."

Lonnie nodded. "Okay, then. Can I go now?"

"Go look after the pigs."

Lonnie galloped away.

Wyatt stared at the ground in front of him. He couldn't bring himself to look at Cora. He was as an ex-con, even though he'd gone to jail for Lonnie. Would it change how she saw him?

Chapter Eighteen

Cora's mind stalled. She couldn't process this information. "This was your big secret?"

He nodded, all misery and staring at the ground.

"You went to jail to protect Lonnie, but you didn't feel you could tell me this?" Pain shot through her heart. "Did you think I would judge you?" She wrapped her arms about her and held tight. "You asked me to trust you but you couldn't trust me. Why?" She wanted to shout the question but kept her voice low so as not to draw attention from the others.

He scuffed the toe of his boot in the dirt. "I didn't want people to learn the truth about Lonnie. I still don't. He needs to be able to get on with his life, not be judged for the past." Finally he brought his gaze to her. "And I wanted to protect you."

"From what?" Her pain and uncertainty was mirrored in his eyes.

"People look at me differently. They act differently when they know I'm an ex-con."

She caught her breath, then forced words from her tight lungs. "Did you think I would see you differently?"

He didn't have to answer. She saw the flicker of admission in his eyes. And her heart answered with a stabbing pain that reached every cell of her body.

But she swallowed it. Of course he was uncertain. A pa who beat him. A year in prison. Had he ever known the kind of love and certainty Ma and Pa and her sisters gave her?

Her heart softened like butter on a warm day. "Wyatt." She pressed her hands to his arms crossed tightly over his chest. "When you asked me to trust you without knowing your secrets, I said I would. I decided I would go by what I saw and knew of you."

His eyes flooded with such yearning she couldn't speak for the span of a heartbeat, two and then a third.

"I'd seen how kind you were, how protective of Lonnie. I knew you to be noble, hardworking and a man I could honor and trust."

The doubt in his eyes faded.

"Knowing the truth has not changed my mind in the least. If anything, it's made me see you as even more noble."

His arms relaxed. He drew Cora into the shadows of the barn, where he leaned against the wall and grasped both her hands.

She lifted her face to him and let him read the truth of her words.

"You don't care that I've been in prison?"

"Of course I care. I'm sure it was an awful place."

He shuddered. "It was."

"But you did nothing wrong. You have nothing to be ashamed of. You can move forward."

He nodded, his gaze searching her eyes, drifting along her cheek and coming to rest on her mouth.

Did he mean to kiss her again?

But he lifted his face to the sky. "I almost forgot. I found a place. Do you know Jack Henry?"

"Of course."

"He's asked me to become his partner and I said yes."

Her heart leaped for joy. He still planned to stay in the area. The Henry place was not far away. The future looked as rosy as the sunset painting the sky in deep pink.

She leaned into him, wrapped her arms about his waist and hugged him. "I'm so glad."

He pressed his palms to her back and held her close. His chest rose and fell with such regularity it filled her with sweet calmness. He was staying. The future lay before them to grasp and live and enjoy.

Wyatt and Lonnie talked late into the night, seated around their campfire. Lonnie wanted details about what it was like in jail. Wyatt told him of the tedious routine, the shuffling in line like a bunch of cattle, the tasteless meals. But he didn't tell him about the bullying, the cruelty or the fear. As Cora said, he wanted to put it behind him and face the future. Even more, he did not want Lonnie to carry a burden of guilt and regret.

The next morning was Sunday and he looked forward to attending church. Now that Cora knew his past, he felt free and open before her.

They arrived at church just before service started and slipped into a pew.

The young ladies glanced toward him and quickly averted their gazes. That was fine with him. He didn't care for their attention. Perhaps they saw him and Cora as a pair now and gave up their aspirations of drawing him into their social circle.

Several people turned in their direction, then bent to whisper to their neighbors.

Wyatt tried to think what caused their interest. He glanced around the congregation and saw no one new, no one from his past. Perhaps he was only being edgy because he'd told Cora his secret.

That must be it.

He turned his attention to the preacher as he rose to greet them and announce the first hymn.

Beside him, Cora sang with pleasure and he listened, her voice a melody in his heart. He couldn't sing a note but he sure could enjoy listening.

As soon as church was over and they had shared a meal with the family, he meant to ask her to walk with him. He'd tell her every detail about the ranch. Would she be eager to hear? Had she ever visited Jack Henry and seen his house? Did she like it? Jack had said they could live in the house with Lonnie and he'd move into the smaller cabin, which suited him better.

He mentally walked through the rooms. He'd glimpsed the two bedrooms through the open doors. The kitchen was big and well equipped, though it showed signs of neglect from the lack of a woman to keep things proper. He tried to see it through Cora's eyes but couldn't imagine what she'd think. She'd no doubt love the sitting room with its big burgundy sofa and two rocking chairs. A pot-bellied stove would drive away the chill on winter nights.

The preacher said, "Amen," and Wyatt realized he had let his thoughts wander throughout the entire sermon.

He hoped God would overlook it this time.

As the family exited, Mrs. Rawley greeted Mrs. Bell, but several other ladies marched past without speaking.

"What on earth?" Cora murmured. "They have something in their craw. I wonder what."

Wyatt's heart scraped along on the bottom of his boots. "Someone must have learned who I am."

"How is that possible?"

He shrugged. "I don't know, but how else do you explain this?" Several people threw them scolding, accusing looks.

Anna Rawley hustled to Cora's side. "They're saying Wyatt is a criminal. Why would anyone say such a cruel thing? It simply isn't true."

Seeing the glance between Cora and Wyatt, Anna looked shocked. "It's not, is it?"

Wyatt nodded. "I spent time in jail."

"For something he didn't do," Cora said heatedly.

Anna shook her head sadly. "They're saying he's responsible for all the robberies around here lately."

"I was afraid this would happen." Wyatt could barely get the words past a lump in his throat the size of the good preacher's Bible.

"But you've been at the farm the whole time," Cora said. "How can they accuse you?"

The owner of the lumber yard marched over. Stu Maples, if Wyatt remembered correctly. He confronted Wyatt. "Jailbirds are not welcome here." Several others came to the man's side, nodding.

Pastor Rawley heard him and joined the gathering crowd. "A man is innocent until proved guilty."

Wyatt knew the pastor meant to be fair, but his words were as condemning as any of the others.

"Once a jailbird, always a jailbird."

Wyatt didn't know the speaker. Why were people so willing to believe the worst about a man? Especially without cause.

Mr. Bell went to Cora and she whispered to him, no doubt telling him of Wyatt's past. Would the man be willing to believe him innocent as he claimed to be?

Mr. Bell stepped to Wyatt's side. "This man is my guest. I suggest he be treated civilly."

A murmur of dissent came from the people, but they kept any further accusations to themselves.

Cora stood close to Wyatt's side. Not touching him. Not smiling at him. But confronting his accusers with a fierce look. He could feel his admiration for her growing in his heart.

The three of them walked to the wagon and climbed aboard, joining Lonnie and the rest of the Bells, who sat in shocked silence.

As they left the yard, many townsfolk turned to them with angry expressions.

Rose and Lilly patted Wyatt's arms. "Lonnie told us," Rose said. "Those people have no reason to accuse you."

He noticed Cora held his hand in a tight grip. Or did he hold hers?

They meant to comfort him, but the accusations rang through his head. *Once a jailbird, always a jailbird.* Could he never be free of that stigma?

When they reached the farm, he held back. "We'll make our own dinner."

"Nonsense," the entire family said in unison.

Cora wound her arm through his and drew him into the house.

As they sat at the table, waiting for Mr. Bell to say

grace, the man turned to each of them. "We've all heard Wyatt's story. How he was in prison but he did no wrong. I think the less that is said about it, the better. Lonnie and Wyatt deserve a chance to start fresh and I, for one, would be honored if they chose to do it in our community."

Wyatt's smile was uncertain. "I'm not sure that's possible now." This morning had changed everything.

"Oh, but you already have a place picked out," Cora reminded him. She turned to her pa. "Jack Henry asked him to be his partner. Said he'd eventually turn the place over to him." She faced Wyatt. "And you gave your word."

"He might not be so welcoming now."

Mr. Bell chuckled. "Jack sees a man for what he is and isn't swayed by what others think."

"Say you'll stay," Cora begged.

"Yes, do," the twins chimed in.

Mr. and Mrs. Bell smiled at him and he felt as if he'd been given a special blessing.

"I want to." It was all he could promise at the moment.

That afternoon, he knew he'd been right not to promise more.

The sheriff rode into the yard and asked to speak to Wyatt.

"Come into the house," Mr. Bell said.

Sheriff Thomas looked ready to refuse, then nodded. "Very well." He stood to the side and waited for Wyatt to go ahead of him.

Lonnie started to follow but Wyatt waved him away. No reason everyone should hear this.

As he sat down across from the sheriff, Cora slipped in and sat beside him.

He dared not look at her. He did not want her implicated in any way. But he couldn't ask her to leave. Her presence strengthened him.

Not that she'd likely go even if he asked.

"Several people have come to me accusing you of certain crimes," the sheriff said. "At this time, I have no evidence, but I assure you, if you're responsible I will find out."

"I've done nothing wrong."

"He's been here the whole time," Cora said.

The sheriff narrowed his eyes. "You can vouch for him?"

"Of course."

"Twenty-four hours of the day?"

"Not at night." Shock filled her words.

"Most of the crimes have taken place after dark, so I'm afraid your assurances mean nothing." The sheriff fixed him with a hard look. "I understand you did time in jail."

"I can't deny it."

"I ain't got much use for jailbirds myself."

Cora sputtered a protest.

Mr. Bell held up a hand to silence her. "Sheriff, I suggest you deal with the facts and put your opinions aside."

The sheriff rose. "I intend to do just that. Good day."

Silence filled the room. Wyatt couldn't lift his gaze from the top of the well-worn wooden tabletop.

"Wyatt, you're innocent. People will soon see that," Mr. Bell assured him.

"I wish I could be so certain." How would he survive if he got thrown back into jail? How would Lonnie? He turned to Cora. “What about Lonnie? If something happens to me—”

“He’ll have a home here, won’t he, Pa?”

Mr. Bell nodded. “He’ll be safe. But so will you. Despite his tough way of talking, Sheriff Thomas is a fair man.”

It was small comfort for Wyatt. “So long as Lonnie is okay, I can handle whatever happens.” He’d at least have sweet memories of time spent with Cora to comfort him this time.

Later, he returned to the campsite. Lonnie crawled into bed and fell asleep, his world safe with the Bells.

Wyatt sat up staring at the flickering coals of the fire. Would his innocence be proved? Would the truth about Lonnie be discovered? It would mark Lonnie just as much as jail time had marked Wyatt. Was he being fair in staying in the Bar Crossing area? Would his presence always be the cause of hurtful comments and sly accusations? Would Cora and her family be hurt by his presence?

God, show me the right thing to do. I want to stay. I want to spend more time with Cora. But I don’t want her or any of the Bells to be hurt. What should I do?

Maybe a cup of tea would help him think through his questions.

He added more wood to the fire, filled the kettle and sat back to wait for the water to boil.

A branch nearby cracked. “Who’s there?”

Two men stepped into the circle of light. He recognized them as men from town. Their hard expressions warned him they hadn’t come on friendly business.

“Howdy. How can I help you?” He hoped Lonnie

would stay asleep or, if he woke, have enough sense to be quiet and not alert the men to his presence.

"You aren't welcome around here."

"Says who?" He could have pointed out that the Bells had welcomed him but knew it wouldn't be wise. It would likely invite trouble into their lives.

"Us. And we speak for most of the citizens of Bar Crossing."

"I see. Well, sorry to say, I have made plans to stay." He didn't know why he felt the need to provoke them. Except he did. They were bullies and he had no sympathy for such.

One of the men leaned forward. "You might find you don't like it here much." His laugh lacked mirth but carried a large dose of meanness.

The larger of the two grunted. "Well, don't say you weren't warned."

They stomped away.

Lonnie slipped over to join Wyatt. "Will they hurt us?"

"They'll try to make our lives miserable so we'll feel forced to leave." He'd say no more. He didn't want Lonnie to worry. Whatever happened, Wyatt would take care of them.

"Maybe we should leave. Didn't we mean to go to Canada?"

Wyatt stared at the flames. They could leave. Or they could stay. If they left, he'd be riding away from the best thing that had ever happened to him and Lonnie—the acceptance and warmth of Cora and her family. But if they stayed, would the Bells suffer?

Was the nighttime visit from those two men a sign from God to leave?

Or was it a challenge to face his past?

He turned to Lonnie. "I was wrong to think we can outrun our past. Running is not the answer."

"Then what is?"

"I don't know." He gave Lonnie a sideways hug. "Go to sleep. I'll figure out what we need to do." Tea forgotten, he dumped out the pot of water and stared at the fire until nothing remained but coals.

Finally, he crawled into his bedroll. He knew what he must do.

He'd confront his past head-on.

Chapter Nineteen

Wyatt's mind was clear the next morning, despite his lack of sleep. He washed and shaved. He'd recently had a haircut but he might be getting another one for free soon. Might have saved himself the two bits.

He pulled on clean trousers and a clean shirt. Might as well go looking his best.

Lonnie watched him. "What are you doing?"

"I'm going to face my past." He threw a saddle on his horse.

Lonnie jerked to his feet and clenched his fists at his sides. "You're going to turn me in?"

Wyatt grabbed the boy and hugged him tight. "Never. That crime has been paid for. You can forget it." He held his brother until a shuddering breath released his lungs and he relaxed.

"Then what are you doing?" Lonnie's face wrinkled with worry. "What will happen to me?"

"The Bells have promised you can stay with them." It was his one consolation. That and Cora's continued faith in him. "Let's go."

Lonnie held back. "Where are we going?"

Wyatt led his horse and Lonnie trotted after him. "You're going to the Bells and I'm going to deal with this."

He had no idea what he'd say to Cora, but when she faced him, her eyes wide with shock, he wished he'd thought of a way to explain what he meant to do. They escaped to the privacy of the orchard.

"Where are you going?" she asked.

"I can't stay unless I can lay this matter to rest."

"Can't stay?" She turned away from him to stare past the fruit trees.

He looked at the wizened green apples on the tree before him. Hadn't he once wondered if his ways could be grafted into the gentle ways of the Bell family? The question needed to be answered to his satisfaction before he would feel free of his past.

"I need to talk to Jack. Explain this turn of events. He might change his mind about wanting me for a partner."

"And then what?" She gave him a look that pierced to the depths of his soul—accusing, begging, promising all at once. "What if he says no? Will you ride away? And if he says yes, he still wants you to be his partner, is that enough to make you stay?" She grabbed his arms and shook him. "Wyatt, what is enough to make you stay?" She dropped her hands and stepped back. "I hoped I was." Her voice trailed off into despair.

"Cora, you are. But only if I can stay here without fighting my past." He wouldn't tell her any more. No point in filling her with false hope. He pulled her close, brushed her hair back from her forehead and kissed the spot his fingers had touched. "Pray for me." He forced himself to release her and hurried away before he changed his mind.

* * *

"Wyatt." She called his name. "Where are you going? What are you going to do?"

He strode on without turning. Without answering her questions.

"Wyatt!" she screamed, but still he hurried away.

She raced after him, but he swung into his saddle and rode off without a backward look.

Cora sank to the ground. He was gone.

The twins joined her, sitting on either side.

"Lonnie said he went to put his past behind him," Rose said. "What does that mean?"

"What's he going to do?" Lilly asked.

"I don't know," Cora replied. "He's going to see Jack. Says he's going to face his past." She pounded the ground. "Then what?"

The girls pulled her to her feet and led her to the house. Lonnie hovered in the shadows.

Cora had promised that Lonnie would always have a home with them, no matter what. "Come along," she called to him. "Let's see if Ma has tea and cookies." Did Ma have a special blend to fix broken hearts?

She joined the others at the table. Heard her parents say Wyatt would do what was right. All the while her thoughts circled madly.

What was right for Wyatt? If he thought leaving was the thing to do, he was wrong. She couldn't imagine life without him. She didn't care what anyone else said about him. If they accused him of things he hadn't done, she'd face them defiantly. If they tried to drive him away, she'd tell them to mind their own business.

And if he felt he had to leave the community, she would go with him.

She would stand by his side through good and bad because—

"I love him." She blurted out the words, then clamped her hand to her mouth.

Lonnie stared.

"Well, I do," she said, bringing her gaze to her ma. Would she scold Cora?

But Ma smiled gently. "Does he know?"

"I never told him."

Pa cleared his throat. "It might make a difference."

She nodded. "But what am I to do now?"

"I think you're the only one who can answer that," Pa said.

"I need to think and pray." She excused herself and hurried to the river, where she could be alone with the vast rolling plains and the majestic mountains and listen to the tumbling of the water.

"God, I love him. I thank You for bringing him into my life." She trusted Wyatt without reservation, but a thread of fear lingered. What if he left? Just like her papa. Just like Evan. She snorted. Wyatt was not Evan or her father. He was a man willing to face difficulties and do what was right. *Thank You, God, for bringing such a man into my life. He's shown me a man can be trusted.*

If God brought Wyatt to her, did He not have a plan for how to deal with this problem? What was her role in it?

"God, show me what to do. Help people see that Wyatt is innocent of any crime in the past or present."

That was it! The answer she needed. She would go to Sheriff Thomas and explain that Wyatt was innocent without implicating Lonnie.

She raced back to the house. "Pa, Pa, I need to go to town." She explained her plan.

"You do what you must do." Pa hitched the horse to the wagon. "Just don't do anything rash."

She waved as she drove the wagon forward. She'd do whatever she needed to prove to one and all that Wyatt was not only innocent but a good man they should welcome into the community.

Wyatt found Jack in the barn examining a harness.

"I been expecting you," the older man said. "Where's that brother of yours? I've been wanting to meet him."

"I didn't bring him. There've been some developments that might be cause enough for you to change your mind about wanting us to join you."

Jack grunted. "Sounds like something we should discuss over coffee. Come to the house."

Wyatt couldn't stop himself from looking around as they crossed the yard. He'd need more corrals if he meant to raise horses and break them. Maybe add a shed to the side of the barn for Lonnie's pigs.

His fists clenched as he forced his thoughts to stop. They might never move here.

"Whatever you got to say can wait until I pour coffee." The blackened, dented pot stood on the back of the stove. Jack threw a chunk of wood into the stove and pulled the pot forward.

Wyatt thought the man had made an attempt to tidy the place since Wyatt had seen it a couple of days ago. He tried to see it through Cora's eyes.

Why was he tormenting himself with such thoughts? Yes, he wanted to share his life with her, do everything in his power to make her happy. But she'd never said anything to make him think she felt the same, and he sure hadn't spoken the words buried deep in his heart. A couple of times he'd considered doing so, but now he was glad he hadn't.

Jack set two chipped cups on the table and poured in coffee so black Wyatt thought he might have to use a spoon to get it from the cup. No milk or sugar was offered.

Wyatt hoped he wouldn't choke on the stuff that Jack sucked back with obvious satisfaction.

Jack nursed his cup. "Now tell me what's bothering you."

Wyatt began with how his father had grown mean, meaner with every passing day. How Wyatt had tried to protect Lonnie from the abuse. "I guess I was more like a father to him than our pa."

The story poured forth, every detail revealed. "Lonnie didn't handle the beatings as well as I did. Inside, I told myself the old man could beat me to death but he could never touch me. Just my body. Lonnie was different. He let it hurt him inside. Until he couldn't take any more."

Jack nodded occasionally but never interrupted Wyatt's flow of words.

"One day I was away from home and Pa flew into a rage. Near as I can figure, he went after Lonnie with a shovel. Somehow Lonnie got it from him and turned on Pa. When I found them I had to pry the shovel from Lonnie's hands. Pa was unconscious and bleeding. Someone had heard the commotion and called the sheriff. They found me with the shovel in my hands. It was easy to say I did it."

"So you went to jail to protect your brother and now

everyone says you're a jailbird and a dangerous man? That about sum it up?"

"There's a little more. The people in town believe I'm responsible for the rash of thefts." He allowed himself a beat of silence before he added, "I'll understand if you withdraw your offer."

Jack fixed him with eyes that made Wyatt feel exposed. "Huh. So you going to turn tail and run?"

"Maybe. If that's what it takes."

Jack had been tipped back on two legs of his chair but now he crashed down. "Boy, tell me one thing. Do you want to throw in with me?"

"Almost as much as I want Cora to be part of our agreement."

"Fine. I'd say you got plenty of reason to stand and fight. If you have a mind to, that is."

Wyatt nodded. "I have a mind to, all right. But I don't know if it will do any good."

"Guess you won't know if you don't try."

"Guess I won't."

Jack slammed his cup to the table. "So why are you still here?"

It wasn't until Wyatt was on the road that he thought of the answer to Jack's question. Because he didn't have any idea what to do.

Somehow he found himself heading toward town. That seemed as good a place as any to start standing. He rode down the main street. Looking neither left nor the right, he made his way to the sheriff's office.

He tied his horse to the post and strode inside as if he knew exactly what he meant to do.

Sheriff Thomas sat behind his big wooden desk, sharpening a pencil with his pocketknife. He saw Wyatt, closed his knife, stuck it in his trousers pocket and put the pencil at the top of the blotter covering the desk in front of him.

"What can I do for you?"

"I haven't come to confess to anything, if that's what you're thinking."

"Can't say as I was thinking that, but okay."

Seemed the man wasn't going to invite Wyatt to sit, so Wyatt grabbed a chair and pulled it to the desk. "I've been in jail, just like everyone says. But I'm no criminal."

"Uh-huh." The man packed a lot of doubt into a couple of syllables. "Then why were you in jail?"

Wyatt stared at the sharpened pencil. How much could he tell without sounding like a whiner and without bringing censure down on Lonnie?

"Someone got beat up. And I went to jail, but I didn't do it."

"Let me guess. You're protecting someone?"

"I'd do it again if I had to."

The sheriff shoved his chair back. "They don't send innocent men to jail. You didn't answer my question."

"Is the penalty paid?"

"I guess it is."

"So no one will have to go to jail for it in the future?" He had to know in case the truth about Lonnie got out. He'd leave and ride clear to the Yukon with his brother if he thought the boy would end up in prison.

"Can't see it happening unless that person confesses."

That wasn't going to happen. If Lonnie ever got the notion in his head, Wyatt would point out he'd gone of his own free will, and his sacrifice would be wasted if Lonnie went, too.

"That's good to know. I hope you'll believe me when I say I was innocent when I went to jail, and I'm innocent of these current crimes."

The sheriff tipped his chair back and considered Wyatt for a long moment. "You willing to prove that?"

"I'll do whatever it takes."

"Then make yourself comfortable in one of the cells while I investigate these robberies."

"You're locking me up?" He sprang to his feet. "What kind of justice is that?"

"Look at it from my side of the desk. If you are truly innocent, you'll hunker down and wait for me to complete my investigation. If you leave, what assurance do I have that you won't ride away? The thought tends to make me a little nervous."

Wyatt considered his options and finally nodded. "If that's what it will take to convince you." He followed the sheriff into the cell block with its two side-by-side cells. His nerves jangled in time to the keys the sheriff carried. He never thought he'd be back in jail. And of his own accord.

He turned his back as the sheriff clattered the door closed and locked it. He flung himself down on the hard, bare mattress and stared at the pocked ceiling. This might be the second hardest thing he'd ever done.

He'd done the first one to protect Lonnie. He did this for the hope of putting the past behind him and living in this community.

About all he could do at this point was wait and pray.

The street door opened and closed a number of times. Once he heard voices, then all was silent. Was he alone?

He stared at the cell door. Did he lie on the cot in vain? While he hoped to be proved innocent, was the sheriff collecting evidence to prove him guilty?

Was this to turn into something he'd regret?

Chapter Twenty

Cora pulled the wagon to a halt in front of the sheriff's office and jumped to the ground.

Young Robert Patton ran along the boardwalks, the thump of his shoes echoing loudly. He skidded to a halt in front of Cora.

"Ya looking for the sheriff?"

"Why, yes I am."

"He ain't here."

She hadn't considered that possibility. "Do you know where I can find him?"

"Nope. Best you wait for him to come back."

"Okay." Wait? She didn't have the patience to wait. But what choice did she have? She glanced up and down the street, but she didn't want to visit with anyone or face questions as to why she was in town on a Monday afternoon.

A trio of ladies stepped from Frank's Hardware and Necessities. One looked in her direction then leaned over to speak to the others.

Cora turned and hurried away, not stopping until she reached the church. She tiptoed inside. The place was empty. She sat on the end of the nearest pew and let the quiet fill her senses.

God, I know Wyatt is innocent. Help me be able to make the sheriff and everyone in town see it.

She sat for some time as peace and assurance filled her soul. God would make the truth clear to everyone. She had to believe it. For she doubted Wyatt would stay if he had to live with daily accusations.

But either way, before he left, she would tell him how she felt.

And if he still left…

Well, she'd been left before and she'd survived. Her insides curled like dry autumn leaves. This time would be different. She couldn't imagine the agony. She'd told herself she'd leave with him, but would he ask her? Could she ride away from Ma and Pa and the twins? If she must, she would. She would do whatever was necessary to be with Wyatt.

She sprang to her feet. She must convince the sheriff Wyatt was innocent.

Her racing feet carried her back to the sheriff's office and she burst inside. Sheriff Thomas sat behind the desk but leaped to his feet at her rushed entrance.

"Miss Cora, to what do I owe this honor?"

She hurried to the chair across the desk from him and perched on the edge. "I've come about Wyatt. Wyatt Williams. I know people are saying all sorts of things about him but they aren't true. He simply can't have robbed anyone."

"What proof do you have?"

"I know it in here." She pressed her hand to her heart.

The sheriff smiled gently. "And you consider that proof?"

"Sheriff, I love him. I know without a doubt that he's a good and noble man. What you need to understand is he is so noble he would go to jail for another person."

The sheriff nodded, his look thoughtful. "Miss Cora, I value your opinion, since you are such an upright citizen, but to prove anything, I need good, solid evidence. Do you have that?"

She thought for a moment. He'd helped on the barn. He'd taken good care of his horses. He was tender and gentle with Lonnie. He'd kissed her. Without thought, she pressed her fingers to her lips and then, realizing what she did, she jerked them away. All of those things and many more proved his innocence to her satisfaction. But they weren't the sort of thing the sheriff meant. She shook her head. "I don't suppose I could prove it to you."

"I see."

Dare she tell him why Wyatt had been in prison? But wouldn't revealing the truth about Lonnie invalidate the year Wyatt had served to protect him? She couldn't share that bit of information.

"Sheriff, I beg you to get to the bottom of these robberies. If you do, you'll certainly discover that Wyatt is innocent." She pushed to her feet. "Now, if you'll excuse me, I have someplace I need to be."

She meant to tell Wyatt she loved him no matter what.

But first she had to find him. Wyatt had said he'd go see Jack Henry. She'd go there in the hopes of finding him.

She strode from the sheriff's office and was almost trampled by two men dragging a third, who fought and cursed.

She squinted at the man being dragged. She'd seen him before. Where?

What did it matter? She had more important things to be concerned about.

"You got the wrong man," he shouted. "It's that jailbird Wyatt Williams you should be dragging here."

Those words stopped her dead. She knew where she'd seen that man before. By the livery barn. And Wyatt had stared at him as if he recognized him.

Somehow the two were connected, and she meant to find out how. She followed them into the sheriff's office.

They pushed the struggling man against the desk.

"This fella had all sorts of things stashed under his mattress." The speaker dumped coins, jewelry and paper money on the sheriff's desk.

"It's been planted," the man insisted. "It wasn't there when I left this morning."

"Uh-huh." The sheriff crossed his arms and gave the man a hard look. "So who would plant it?"

"Wyatt Williams, I've no doubt."

"Who are you and how do you know Wyatt Williams?"

"Name's Jimmy Stone and I knew Wyatt when he wasn't pretending to be such an upright citizen."

"In jail, you mean?"

"That's right." Then, realizing he'd put himself where he wanted everyone to believe Wyatt belonged, he hastened to add, "Not that I was there myself, you understand."

"If you say so." The sheriff sighed heavily. "Might interest you to know Wyatt couldn't have planted the evidence."

"Huh. Suppose he told you some wild story about being innocent and you believed him."

"I'm inclined to believe his story, seeing as he's been locked in my jail for the past few hours, and before that he was with Jack Henry. So you see, I have all the evidence I need to believe him."

Cora was grateful for the chair near the door when her legs started wobbling. She sat down before she fell on the floor.

"He's here?" she squeaked.

"Yup." The sheriff drawled the word. He tossed a set of keys to one of the men. "Unlock him and put this man in there. You," he said to Jimmy Stone, "will be tried. Best you be prepared to return to jail."

The man struggled all the way through the door at the back of the office.

Cora stared at the cells beyond. Wyatt was there? He'd been there all along? She wanted to run to him, but her legs refused to work.

Before she could even stand, Wyatt came out, followed by the two men who had assisted the sheriff.

"Thanks, boys." The sheriff waved to them as they went outside.

Sheriff Thomas leaned against the desk. "It appears to me you two have some unfinished business. I'll leave you to deal with it. Wyatt, when you're done, your horse is out back." He headed for the door then paused. "I believe the truth about Wyatt's innocence has been revealed. I suggest the two of you make the truth about your feelings just as clear." He slipped out and closed the door quietly behind him.

Cora stared at Wyatt. Did he seem older, more drawn, than when she'd seen him this morning? Then a smile touched the corners of his mouth and he looked just right. She couldn't ask for better.

His smile didn't go any further. Was he upset at her for getting involved with Sheriff Thomas?

"I had to come," she said. "I had to make the sheriff see the truth. Though I guess he was looking for it all along."

"I heard you."

For a moment she was confused by his reply, then its meaning hit her. He'd heard her say she loved him? "Every word?" she asked, her mouth suddenly dry.

"Every word." The smile that toyed with his mouth now filled his eyes, widened his lips and lit his face. "Every sweet, telling word." He pulled her to her feet.

Her gaze clung to his. Now was her chance to say the words she'd vowed to say, directly to the man himself.

But when she opened her mouth to speak, he pressed a fingertip to her lips.

"I have something to say first." He studied every feature of her face until she felt as if her skin would bloom like summer flowers.

He brought his gaze back to her eyes. "I couldn't tell you this before my name was cleared, but, Cora Bell, I love you and I want to share the rest of my life with you. Now, I know there will still be people who judge me because I've been in jail, so maybe it's not fair to ask you to share that—"

She pressed her fingertips to his mouth. "Shh. It's my turn to speak. Wyatt Williams, I love you now and forever. I don't care what others say. I know what kind of man you are."

"What kind is that?" His voice thickened.

"A noble, kind, giving, honorable, loving, protective

man. One who I know will never fail me, never abandon me, never intentionally hurt me."

He swallowed hard. "That's a lot to live up to. I'm bound to fail."

"As am I. But what counts is moving forward. We'll forgive each other when we fail and we'll grow better and stronger together." She ducked her head. Had she rushed him into more than he meant to give? "If you want it that way…."

He tipped her head so they looked full into each other's eyes. "Cora Bell, would you marry me and make me the happiest man on the face of the earth?"

"Do I have the power to do that?" she asked through her smile. "To make you happy? It seems like a tall order."

He chuckled. "Your love makes me happy. Like I've never been before."

"Your love makes me so happy I feel as if I'm going to burst. Yes, I'll marry you."

"I never knew love could feel this way." He looked awestruck, then blinked and bent his head to hers.

She wound her arms about his waist, pressed her palms to his back and lifted her face to him. Her heart beat a steady rhythm against her chest. She felt his heart's answering beat, and then their lips touched and nothing else mattered but this man and their love.

Epilogue

Three weeks later

Cora stood inside the back room of the church and smoothed the front of her ivory-colored wedding dress. At first, she'd demurred at the idea of a new dress that she would only wear once, but the twins had begged her to go ahead.

"We'll help make it," Rose had said.

"Maybe someday we'll wear it." Lilly had gotten dreamy eyed. "Wouldn't it be special if we all wore the same dress for our weddings?"

So Cora had agreed. They'd picked a simple style with a full satin skirt, leg-of-mutton sleeves and lacy accents at the shoulders.

Rose arranged the back of the skirt to her liking. "It's a beautiful gown."

Cora agreed. "I feel like a princess."

"About to marry her prince."

Cora smiled so wide it almost hurt, but there was no room in her heart for anything painful. "I'm so happy."

Somehow her sisters managed to hug her without mussing her hair or her dress.

"You deserve to be happy," Rose said.

Cora nodded. "I'm glad we'll be living close enough that I can make sure you two are okay."

The twins exchanged looks and a secret flickered through their eyes.

"What is it you're not telling me?" Cora asked. She caught each of them by the hand. "I don't want you to feel like you can't share all your secrets with me anymore."

Rose patted Cora's hand. "We know you feel responsible for us."

"You don't need to," Lilly added.

"We're grown up now. It's time for you to move on and think about your own happiness instead of ours."

"They're the same thing. My happiness would never be complete if I thought either of you was unhappy."

"We're both happy and we don't want you to worry about us," Rose said. "Promise us you'll do that."

Cora nodded, her throat tight. "I promise." She leaned over and kissed them each on the cheek. "I'll miss you."

Rose chuckled. "We'll see each other so often you won't have a chance."

"If you need any more help getting your place into shape, just let us know and we'll come," Lilly offered. She and Rose had accompanied Cora, Wyatt and Lonnie to Jack Henry's place for several days. They'd helped Jack clean out his things from the house and move them to the little cabin where he and his wife had first lived.

At first, Cora had demurred. "We'll take the cabin," she'd said. "I've no wish to displace you."

Jack had chuckled long and hard at that. "You're doing me a favor. All I need is a bed, a table and a stove. All this—" he'd waved around the room of the house where they stood "—is too much work for me."

So Cora had continued to clean the house. Her sisters had helped her wash the walls and cupboards. They'd made the wooden floors gleam. Jack had insisted he didn't need all the kitchen things, so they'd washed every pot, pan and dish, and arranged them in the clean cupboards.

Cora had let the twins help clean the smaller bedroom where Lonnie would sleep, but she'd insisted she alone would arrange the furniture of the bedroom she and Wyatt would share.

As she made the bed and hung new curtains, her heart rejoiced. When the room was done to her satisfaction, awaiting their marriage, she'd knelt by the side of the bed to thank God for their love and for the bright future ahead of them. *Bless us with happiness and a large family.*

Organ music began to play in the sanctuary of the church, pulling Cora from thoughts of her new home. Anna had insisted on playing for the ceremony.

When wedding plans had been discussed initially, Wyatt had suggested they get married at the farm with just family present. "I'm not sure the community is ready to accept me."

Cora had, at that moment, decided she wanted a big church wedding. "No more will we hide from what people think. This is our community. There are people here who accept us without reservation. The rest will soon learn that they are wrong."

Pastor and Mrs. Rawley had been thrilled at their decision to get married in the church.

"May I have the honor of providing tea after the ceremony?" Mrs. Rawley had asked.

Ma had agreed to accept her help.

Cora could hardly wait any longer for her wedding. And she didn't have to.

"It's time," the twins said, taking her hands.

They each kissed her, then slipped through the door.

Cora peeked out to watch her sisters follow each other up the aisle. Then she got her first glimpse of her groom.

Wyatt stood at the front, so handsome, so strong and noble that her heart swelled with joy.

Lonnie stood beside him. He pulled at the collar of his shirt and then stood at attention.

Beside Lonnie stood Jack Henry. He cut a striking figure in his suit. She'd grown fond of the old man in the past few weeks.

She glanced around the church, saw a goodly number of people in attendance and smiled. Just as she'd hoped, people were accepting Wyatt. *Thank You, God.*

"Are you ready?"

She turned to Pa. "I'm ready." She drank in his familiar, comforting face. "Pa, I owe you a world of thanks. You've been the best father I could ever ask for. I love you." She leaned over and kissed his cheek.

Pa squeezed her shoulder. She understood he would have hugged her, except he didn't want to disturb her dress. "I love you, too, daughter. You have been a true gift and a blessing from God." His words grew thick and he swallowed hard. "Best not to keep Wyatt waiting any longer."

They stepped to the aisle and all faces turned toward her.

Wyatt's gaze met hers and the rest of the world slipped away. She drew closer to him, feeling as though she was walking on air, and took his arm. As if from a distance, she heard the preacher's words and repeated her vows as prompted, but the only part of the ceremony that seemed real was Wyatt's kiss.

"I present to you Mr. and Mrs. Wyatt Williams," the preacher announced.

They marched down the aisle and outside to where the side yard was festooned with streaming crepe paper and flowers. She ate the tiny sandwiches and cake handed to her, clinging to Wyatt's hand to keep herself grounded.

Many people from the church and the town filed by to congratulate them and welcome Wyatt to the community. Many brought gifts, and with Wyatt's help she opened them, almost overcome with emotion at their generosity.

Finally they were able to slip away and head toward their new home, where they could finally be alone.

Lonnie would be staying with Ma and Pa for a few days, and Jack would be camping. He'd said he could hardly wait to ride into the hills without worrying about how things were at home.

Wyatt lifted her from the wagon and carried her into the house. "Here we are."

Cora clung to his shoulders. "Our future begins now."

He nodded. "No looking back." He claimed her mouth in a sweet, gentle kiss, then set her on the floor. "Cora Williams, I love you."

"I love you." She wrapped her arms about his neck and kissed him again.

He held her close. "I never thought I'd see the day when I would know such love."

She laughed with pure joy. "Our love will grow richer and sweeter every day." She'd do her best to see her words came true.

He kissed her again and she forgot everything but this wonderful man God had brought into her life.

* * * * *

Dear Reader,

I love the idea of found families. You know the sort I mean. Families who have come together in ways other than birth. That's the kind of family Cora comes from. She's found a set of parents who are everything she needs and wants. Or rather, they found her. Wyatt and his brother, however, come from an entirely different background. Family life as Cora knows it is foreign to them. So I brought Wyatt and his brother to the Bells so they could see what a loving family is all about.

It's something I feel strongly about—creating family, creating traditions, creating memories that hold us together. Perhaps this little story will help you see the value of these things, too, and if you don't have it in your birth family, I hope you'll find it somewhere or else create it.

I love to hear from my readers. You can contact me at www.lindaford.org, where you'll find my email address and more information about me and my books.

Blessings,

Linda Ford

Questions for Discussion

1. What problems did Wyatt face because of his time in jail? Do you think he'd face some of the same problems in this day and age?

2. Cora said she no longer cares about her birth father or his reasons for abandoning them. Do you believe she was as over it as she claimed? Why or why not?

3. How did she guard her heart? What reasons did she give?

4. Was Wyatt right to protect Lonnie at the cost of home and belonging? Or could he have had them even if the truth was known about Lonnie?

5. What things did Wyatt see in the Bell family that he wanted to imitate?

6. What things did Wyatt do and say that make Cora see beyond his secretiveness?

7. Do you think the Bar Crossing community will be a good fit for the Williamses?

8. Was there a spiritual lesson in this story? If so, what was it?

9. Did you find Mr. and Mrs. Bell's counseling wise and helpful?

10. What do you hope for Wyatt and Cora in the future?

COMING NEXT MONTH FROM
Love Inspired® Historical

Available November 4, 2014

HER HOLIDAY FAMILY
Texas Grooms
by Winnie Griggs

Eileen Pierce has shut herself off to life after living through tragedy. But when a stranded man and ten orphaned children seek shelter at her home, she finds herself opening the door to them—and to love.

THE BRIDE SHIP
Frontier Bachelors
by Regina Scott

Allegra Banks Howard is bound for a new life out West with her daughter. But when she is reunited with her first love—her late husband's brother—can they heal their painful past and forge a new future as a family?

A PONY EXPRESS CHRISTMAS
by Rhonda Gibson

A marriage proposal from Jake Bridges might be the solution to Leah Hollister's problems. If only he didn't already have enough on his hands between adopting his newly orphaned niece and mending his broken heart.

ROCKY MOUNTAIN DREAMS
by Danica Favorite

When Joseph Stone becomes guardian to his newly discovered little sister and inherits his late father's silver mine, he seeks help from the minister's beautiful daughter, who soon claims his love for her own.
